# Sanibel Treasures

A Shellseeker Beach Novel
Book Two

# HOPE HOLLOWAY

Hope Holloway

Shellseeker Beach Book 2

Sanibel Treasures

Copyright © 2022 Hope Holloway

Cover designed by Sarah Brown (http://www.sarahdesigns.co/)

# Introduction To Shellseeker Beach

Come to Shellseeker Beach and fall in love with a cast of unforgettable characters who face life's challenges with humor, heart, and hope. For lovers of riveting and inspirational sagas about sisters, secrets, romance, mothers, and daughters...and the moments that make life worth living.

For release dates, excerpts, news, and more, sign up to receive Hope Holloway's newsletter! Or visit www.hopeholloway.com and follow Hope on Facebook and BookBub!

# Chapter One

## *Olivia*

"Welcome to Sanibel Treasures!" Olivia Whitney called out her standard greeting when she heard the bell announcing the arrival of a customer to the seaside souvenir shop. "I'll be right out!"

"I'd like to see the manager, please," a woman's voice responded. "And tell her I love her."

Laughing, Olivia turned left and right in the back office, searching for a surface to safely place her armload of seashell-covered lampshades. She opted for the not-so-sturdy metal shelves she'd attempted to build herself, dumping everything so she could go out to the sales floor and greet her mother.

"The manager takes all manner of love as payment," Olivia assured her, arms outstretched. "Want a shell-encrusted bookend? That'll cost you a hug." She gestured to one side of the store. "How about a canvas with your name written in clam shells? A kiss." Then she pointed around the corner, where they housed the jewel in the store's crown. "Want to see a Teddy Roosevelt-signed message in a bottle? You better have some fresh-brewed hibiscus iced tea in that travel cup."

Mom offered her the cup and a warm embrace. "Tea,

hugs, and kisses for the current proprietress. Manager? Store staff? Whatever you're called."

"Shop girl?" Olivia suggested. "Or is that too politically incorrect and innocent sounding?"

"Works for me." Mom inched back, her smile so bright it lifted Olivia's heart. The Florida sun had given her mother a peppering of new freckles, making her look young and fresh, and her formerly auburn hair had lightened to a sassy strawberry-blond that totally suited the Sanibel Island version of Eliza Whitney.

There were so many times during the past year that Olivia wondered if she'd ever hear her mother's beautiful laugh, or her gorgeous voice belting out a show tune. These days? She heard both frequently.

In fact, Mom was a different woman from the one who'd buried her husband in California a little over five months ago. She'd struggled with bone-deep grief—they all had—but had made tremendous progress since coming to Shellseeker Beach.

What was supposed to be an overnight visit to meet Theodora Blessing, the woman who'd lived with Mom's estranged father, had turned into so much more. No, things hadn't been drama free, but six weeks on Sanibel Island had been good for Olivia's mother. And getting to know Teddy Blessing, who ran the small resort on Shellseeker Beach, had been even better for her.

Eliza and Teddy had become fast friends and partners, of a sort, although the ownership of Shellseeker Cottages and Sanibel Treasures was totally up in the air right now.

While it was being sorted out in the courts, Mom had decided to stay for a while. Olivia, upon learning that the regular managers of the shell shop had to leave town for a few months, had taken a sabbatical from her job in Seattle and moved into one of the cottages for the summer.

"Livvie Bug, look at this place!" Her mother turned and drank it all in, then settled her loving silvery-blue gaze on Olivia. "You are in your element running this store. It's like when you used to turn my closet into a clothing boutique when you were a little girl and made me buy clothes I already owned with real dollar bills."

"Of course I did, because it's a *business*, Mom." Olivia laughed. "I also used to reorganize your shelves and move the pile of sweaters to your dresser, remember?"

"You said my closet needed white space, whatever that means."

"It means room to breathe and shop, and I'm doing the same thing all over again." She gestured toward a recently pared-down display of souvenirs. "This place is in desperate need of decluttering, which is what I'm doing right now."

"You really are good at this, Liv," her mother said, beaming with maternal pride.

"Thanks. It's what we in the merchandising biz call floor work, and it's aptly named. Working the floor is rung number one on the retail ladder, but I don't hate it. It's kind of liberating to be in the trenches, instead of, you know..."

"A corporate superstar at Promenade Department Stores," Mom supplied.

"Yeah, that." After getting her MBA and spending six years on that very ladder working her tush off at Promenade's corporate headquarters, Olivia had made it to senior buyer and been well on her way to a merchandising VP position.

But then a new boss had knocked her down a rung or three, and the promotion went to someone else. It made perfect sense for Olivia to lick her professional wounds on this enchanting island, finally living that childhood dream of owning a small shop. No, she didn't own this one—that dream was pretty far out of reach—but this summer, she felt like she did.

"I'm honestly having a blast," Olivia said, "and enjoying the break from that relentless corporate climbing I did every day."

Mom's eyes narrowed as she peered at Olivia. "Does this mean you were listening to Teddy and me last night?"

Olivia looked skyward at the thought of Teddy Blessing and her New Age crystals and deep conversations. The seventy-something yogi amused her to no end, but Olivia couldn't deny the woman had some freakishly accurate insights and brewed a mean cup of emotionally charged lavender tea. Lavender grown in her own garden right here in Shellseeker Beach to boot.

"I listened," Olivia said. "It's not the first time you've reminded me that I'm a hopeless workaholic who places success above all else."

"I don't think I ever used the word *hopeless*," Mom chided. "I might have suggested that you have linked your personal success quite closely to your business accomplishments."

"Euphemisms, Elizabeth Mary. What you said is that without my title, office, and salary, I don't know who I am." And, yes, she'd heard it, because the truth of the statement had kept her tossing and turning all night. Or maybe that was the tea. Or thoughts of a certain Shellseeker Beach resident who'd returned after two days away with absolutely no explanation of where he'd been.

*Something* made for a sleepless night.

"I also said you are thriving away from that stifling, backstabbing corporate atmosphere," her mother added. "I like to see you let go of Olivia Whitney, business superstar, and just be...Livvie. Oh!" Mom plucked at some shells in a basket, squinting to see the price without her reading glasses. "Three dollars for *one* of these? I think I just saw this seashell on the beach this morning."

"Right? That price was set before I got here and, whoa, talk about profit margin." Olivia jumped on the subject, because shop talk always beat an existential self-examination. "Look at how many there are." She nodded toward the aisle with ten baskets on either side, each brimming with seashells separated by type and color, all in perfect condition and priced up to ten dollars apiece, depending on their rarity.

"*Seashells*, Mom. Those things are literally free on the ground fifty feet from the door, but people buy them."

"Easier than breaking your back finding one that isn't chipped or broken, I guess."

Olivia pointed at the wall of shelves featuring T-shirts and beach towels and coverups, all bearing slogans like "Sanibel Island Fever" and "I Got the Sanibel Stoop" and "The Seashell Capital of the World!"

"They buy that stuff, too, but it doesn't have the same profit margin."

Mom tilted her head, studying the display with a discerning eye. "Does that section look different than it used to?"

"I hope so. I just cleaned out some junk—er, inventory—and I'm praying that Roz and George don't blow back into town and freak out because I made too many changes while they're gone."

"First of all," Mom said, "they aren't leaving Columbus until Asia has given birth to their grandchild, and that could be a few more weeks. Second, there's so much stuff in here, I don't think anyone, even Roz, would notice if it were moved around. And lastly, Teddy looked at the numbers and Sanibel Treasures is making more money in this week than it did in the same week last year."

Olivia's eyes widened. "SSG comps are up month to month?"

"Whatever that means," Mom said with a laugh.

"Same-store growth, and it means revenue, baby. The bread and butter of retail." She leaned on the counter and looked around the store, thinking—as she always did—of how she could change the visual layout and draw customers to the most profitable items.

"But I didn't come to share the sales numbers," Mom said, her tone serious enough to pull Olivia's attention away from the store. "Teddy just got some big news. Camille and Claire are coming back *tonight*."

"Really?" Olivia's eyes widened. "That must mean something is up."

"What's up is that my sister is an amazing attorney," Mom said, then sighed into a smile. "My *sister*. I know, half-sister technically, but I still can't get used to saying those words. Can you believe I have a sister, Liv?"

"It's still my favorite shocker on Shellshocker Beach," she teased, knowing her mother was absolutely enamored with the idea, but for Olivia? The jury was out...literally. "What does this mean about your father's will?"

"It means Claire worked a legal miracle and convinced the courts to move the hearing to contest the two wills to right here in Lee County, because it was his last permanent address and the property up for grabs is located here."

"Up for grabs?" Olivia snorted. "That's one way of putting it. A legal dumpster fire would also work."

"No kidding. But at least this means the end is near, and we'll finally have an answer as to who will own all this property."

Almost a month before, they'd been under the assumption that Dutch Vanderveen, Mom's father and the legal owner of Shellseeker Beach, had left everything to his only daughter as his "sole living heir" when he died. That in and of itself had been a stunner, because Mom had had a cool and distant relationship with Dutch. He'd also spent his last two years living with Teddy Blessing, close enough that they called each other husband and wife, even though they never married legally.

But after he died, Teddy couldn't locate Dutch's will, leaving the property in probate limbo. Making the situation even worse, Shellseeker Beach's seven cottages, extensive gardens, and this shell shop had all been built by Teddy's family, and she was deeply connected to the land and its colorful history.

It had been months since Teddy had contacted Olivia's mother seeking help. After some deep-dive investigating, they learned that Dutch—a womanizer with a capital W and an airline pilot who didn't have to account too carefully for his long absences—had more than one will.

And more than one wife.

One document named Camille Durant as his heir. The French-born beauty had been Dutch's mistress, and then wife, for many years. Together, they had a daughter, the miracle-working lawyer, Claire.

When the two women blew into Shellseeker Beach a little over a month ago, they revealed that Camille was Dutch's legal heir and living spouse. But Camille assured everyone that she and Dutch had an agreement to give the property to Teddy. Awesome. Problem solved.

Except she wasn't his *only* living spouse.

A private investigator had unearthed Roberta "Birdie" Vanderveen, who Dutch "married" while still wed to Camille. Illegal? So totally. Yet, Birdie claimed to have a legitimate will. And unlike the beautiful and vibrant Camille, Wife Number Three had no intention of giving up the waterfront property worth multiple millions. Birdie was mean as a snake and raring for a fight.

A fight, it seemed, that was about to take place in the Lee County Courthouse on the mainland.

"So what exactly happens at this hearing?" Olivia asked. "Are you certain we'll get that answer."

"I'm not sure, but both sides present their arguments for why their will is more legitimate," Mom said.

"Will Birdie show?" None of them had met the Alabama woman, but Olivia was wildly curious about this lady who refused Dutch a divorce on the grounds of her religion, insisting she had no idea he was a bigamist.

It was the least of his many sins, in Olivia's opinion, and left all of them anxious to know how the ownership of the resort would legally shake out.

"Birdie doesn't need to be there, nor does Teddy, or me," her mother said. "The land hasn't been in Teddy's family for decades, and I'm not named in any will, even though I'm Dutch's eldest daughter. But obviously we're rooting for Camille because she is returning the land to Teddy, where it truly belongs."

"Unless she changes her mind," Olivia said dryly.

Mom shuttered her eyes. "Don't even think that. I know she was only here for one day, but during that time, Camille didn't say or do anything to indicate she wouldn't go through with the deal she made with Dutch.

And Claire seemed ready and willing to help make that happen."

"Some deal." Olivia rolled her eyes. "Not written down anywhere, or known by anyone."

"You heard Camille when she was here. If Dutch had filed anything legally, it could have triggered a flag that he was married to two women. But Camille said he wanted her to inherit it and give it to Teddy for a dollar. And she will." Her mother made a face. "Don't look at me like I'm naïve, Liv."

"Sorry, Mom, but we don't know this French woman or her daughter—"

"Who is my sister—"

"And essentially a stranger," Olivia finished. "I simply don't trust Camille's *je ne sais quoi* attitude." She flicked her hands to underscore the bad French accent. "Why isn't she ticked at Dutch for marrying another woman while they were already married? What woman is *that* understanding? I'd have cut his...hair off."

Her mother didn't smile at that. "Claire says it's the French in her, that Camille is very...loose."

"Come on, there's loose, and there's a doormat. And that woman we met? So not a doormat. She knows what this place is worth to the hotel chains circling like sharks."

Her mother sighed. "We don't really have a choice but to trust her, Liv. Neither Teddy nor I have any actual claim on this property."

"Well, I for one am furious at Dutch," Olivia ground out. "Yeah, I get that my grandfather was some devil-may-care pilot who lived on the hairy edge and apparently was catnip to the ladies. But he left a hot mess with a lot of money and emotions on the line. I still can't understand why he'd do that, especially knowing he was dying of an inoperable tumor." She shook her head, unable to keep the disgust from her voice. "Who does a thing like that? Why?"

"No one really knows what made my father tick."

*Not even the multitudes of women and wives he left behind*, Olivia thought. Then she gave her mother a harder look. "Aren't you mad at him?"

"I spent my life mad at him."

"And Camille," she added. "I mean, she's the very woman who broke up your parents' marriage. I don't think I'd be so lovey-dovey if I met someone who'd been sleeping with Dad while he was married to you."

"Livvie, please. As if Dad would cheat."

"But Dutch did, and with Camille. You're cool with her?"

She thought about it for a few seconds. "I got a sister out of the deal," she finally said. "And you know I'm more than cool with that. Plus, my mother found her way in life after Dutch. She married my stepfather, and maybe she wasn't ever floating on a cloud of bliss, but she found a man who was faithful to her. I guess Camille did her a favor."

"You're a better man than I am, Gunga Din. I know. I'm a cynic. But Dutch left half a mile of beachfront property on one of the most desirable barrier islands in Florida! And two 'wives' vying for ownership, with one claiming she'll give it to his late-in-life lover? Jeez. It's soap opera stuff."

"It's...complicated," Mom agreed. "But Camille has the stronger claim, and she insists she's selling the property to Teddy and the whole thing will be done."

Olivia would believe it when she saw signed legal agreements. "All it would take to change that is for some hotel exec to sidle up to Camille and whisper *beaucoup* moolah in her ear. I'm telling you, people can't be trusted when millions are on the line."

"I don't see it that way, Livvie. Or maybe I just hope you're wrong, because the more time I spend here and the closer I get to Teddy, the more I like it."

Olivia smiled. She was slowly getting used to the fact that when this all shook out, her mother might just stay in Shellseeker Beach.

"And, you know," Mom added, "I didn't get to spend a lot of time with Claire when they were here, but she and Camille are staying longer this time. I'd really like to get to know my sister." She reached for Olivia's hand. "And I hope you will, too. She's your aunt."

Olivia conceded that with a tip of her head. "I'll be nice to her."

"And Camille?"

"*Oui, oui.* Keep your enemies close and all that."

"She is not the enemy," Mom insisted. "Birdie is."

They both could be, but for her mother's sake, and Teddy's, Olivia hoped her opinion was wrong.

"Anyway, Teddy's hosting a little dinner tonight, and I want you to come. And be on your best behavior."

Olivia snorted. "Yes to one, no promises to the other."

"Livvie!" Mom poked her arm. "Have some faith in man—Well, womankind."

"I have faith in the fact that when people smell *that* much money, they usually want to keep inhaling."

The bell over the door dinged as a customer walked in. The man gave Olivia a quick nod when she glanced at him.

Wait...she knew that guy. She squinted, trying to remember the conversation she'd had with him the last time he was here. He'd made an impression, but only because a man in his late-thirties wasn't the average Sanibel Treasures shopper.

"Oh, and before I let you get back to work," her mother said, "I was supposed to tell you that Deeley's back and he can finish the shelves you said were a struggle to build."

"Great." Olivia dug deep into her well of corporate non-expressions. "Maybe this time he'll say where he's been."

"He won't tell you?"

Olivia shrugged. "I don't actually ask, because it doesn't seem like my business. But it's not the first time he sort of disappears for a day or two, sometimes three, with absolutely no explanation of where he's been." And he returns as a complete grump every time, but she didn't add that. "Anyway, yes on the shelves. I did a terrible job and am not strong enough to move them out of the middle of the office and against the wall. Oh, and one of the floorboards is lifting, and I can't get the bathroom window to close all the way. Deeley is more than welcome to come and fix anything in this dilapidated former boathouse."

Mom gave Olivia a *way* too meaningful look.

"Mother. Chill. Fix the building, not the woman currently working in it."

"Honey, Deeley's so nice and clearly he likes you. And you like him."

"How do you know that?" Olivia challenged, praying it wasn't because her ever-growing crush on Connor Deeley was so obvious the world could see it.

"Because you let him call you Livvie," Mom said in a teasing voice. "Only people you really like get that privilege...Livvie."

"Well, sorry. I hate to break the news to you, but the man hasn't had a haircut in two years and is covered in ink."

"His hair is gorgeous, and you know it, and he doesn't have that many tattoos. He was a Navy SEAL, Liv. They all get tattoos."

"Do they all kayak to and from their job in a thatch-roofed beach hut?"

"His job happens to be owning and running a successful business. There's practically a line out the door of that cabana every day to rent paddleboards, umbrellas, and kayaks."

Olivia rolled her eyes and tried to think of other things that were wrong with Connor Deeley. Okay, nothing. "Mom, how many times do I have to tell you that a surfer dude who goes by his last name is not my type?"

"About six hundred since we got here," Mom dead-panned. "Teddy says there's more to him than meets the eye. Although what meets the eye is not awful, is it?"

"It isn't going to happen, Mom. He's not the kind of guy I want. Is he a smokefest of muscles and...more muscles? Yeah, yeah. And maybe if I had as little ambition as he does and wanted to bum around the beach for the rest of my life, I'd be all over him, but that's not at all what I envision."

"You want a husband."

"What I want is a stable professional with a great job and the same values and lifestyle and work ethic as I have. I want someone...like Dad."

That last word ended any and all arguments from Eliza Whitney. "Every woman wants a man like your father," she said sadly.

So sadly that Olivia grimaced with regret for using that particular weapon in this fight. She never wanted to hurt her mother. "I'm sorry, Mom. But Deeley's not what I'm looking for."

"I get that. But you've worked so hard, never stopping since the day you finished business school. I just want you to have fun, honey."

Fun? Oh, Deeley was that, for sure. Olivia blew out a breath. Could anything be *more* fun than making out with that hunk on the beach under the moonlight? She was *so* tempted to find out.

"You *know* what would happen," Olivia said, shifting to the right to check on the guy who was studying the conch shell door wreaths.

"You'd have a good time?"

"I don't care about a good time, Mom. It's never been a driver for me."

"You'd extend your stay and put your job in jeopardy?" she guessed.

If only that were the worst of it. "I'd fall flat on my face in love," she confessed on a ragged whisper.

"And what would be so wrong with that, Livvie Bug?"

Olivia closed her eyes, not even able to imagine the loss of control caused by falling for a guy as elusive and enigmatic and exquisite as Deeley. "Everything."

Her mother just sighed and blew her a kiss as she headed out, and Olivia looked around for the guy, but he'd slipped away without buying anything. *Dang you, Deeley.* Just talking about him cost her too much. Anything else was just...unthinkable.

But that didn't stop her from thinking about him anyway.

# Chapter Two

## *Claire*

W alking through the Southwest Florida International Airport in Fort Myers, Claire Sutherland swore she could smell her mother's perfume before she actually saw her. Of course, they frequently both wore Chanel, so it was probably her own fragrance haunting her as she dragged her rolling bag and squinted at the flow of people deplaning from Atlanta.

Then she spotted the sleek dark hair that had been meticulously dyed since the first gray strand appeared twenty years ago, heard the distinctive laugh made deep and throaty from too many Gauloises before she found out smoking was linked to wrinkles, and braced herself for the onslaught of...Camille.

Claire, like everyone who ever met the woman, thought of her mother by the one distinctive name that seemed to capture her colorful, capricious, and impossibly French personality.

Thinking of her by her first name wasn't due to a lack of respect, or love. Claire called her *Maman* whenever they were together. After all, for so many years, it had been the two of them against the world, with intermittent visits from Dutch Vanderveen, her *Papa*, a larger-than-life figure who alternately terrified and fascinated Claire.

Camille didn't terrify, but she frequently baffled, amused, frustrated, shocked, infuriated, and, yes, fascinated Claire. And there she was, dragging two bags because, of course, her years as an airline employee taught her how to bend the rules so she could have *multiple* carry-on bags. No doubt she had two more waiting in baggage claim. Because...clothes. Camille and her wardrobe were rarely separated, even for a trip to the beach.

"Claire! There you are, *cherie!*" Camille called, waving as she threaded her way through the crowd and nearly mowed down a man. He turned, scowling, then his whole face softened.

"Oh, Camille! Great to talk to you on the plane. Good luck with everything!"

Of course she'd made friends and told him her story. Knowing Camille, she probably had a date with the guy for drinks, despite the fact that he looked to be about Claire's age of forty-five and her mother was seventy-one. Not that Camille would ever admit to that number, nor did she look it.

"*Maman.*"

"My sweet, sweet girl!"

She accepted her mother's hug, which was equal parts dramatic embrace and a cry for everyone's attention. Claire, a privacy-seeking New Yorker to the very bone, flinched at the knowledge that they drew interest, but that was the price one paid to be with Camille.

Her mother went through life in a spotlight, turning her French accent on and off as it suited her or was needed to get the attention she craved. Camille Durant was a little too loud, a little too bright, way too beautiful for her own good, and ridiculously skilled at soaking up all the air in any room she entered.

The strange thing was, Claire's father, Dutch Vanderveen, had been very much the same. The two of them were...too much.

Mother and daughter pulled back and smiled at each other, taking a moment to drink in the reunion they'd planned when they discovered that their flights arrived within the same hour. It hadn't been long since they'd last seen each other—they'd said goodbye at this very gate after spending one day and night on Sanibel Island—but it was always nice to reunite. Well, maybe *nice* wasn't the word.

It was...not boring. Ever.

"This has to be all your bags, right?" Claire asked, taking the handle of one of Camille's carry-ons in her free hand. "Because if you recall, the dress code in Shellseeker Beach is shorts, tees, and coverups."

Camille rolled her eyes high and hard. "I have two more bags, *cherie*. And there is not a short, tee, or coverup in either one. How was your flight from New York?"

"It was—"

"Because mine was wretched, absolutely wretched, starting with the airport in Montreal." She pronounced the Canadian city in her perfect Parisian French, brought out only for special occasions. "An absolute zoo. The flight was unnecessarily turbulent. It was like that pilot *wanted* us to spill our drinks. And the stewardesses?"

"*Maman*," Claire scolded gently. "No one, French or English, uses that term anymore."

She flicked her fingers. "Pffft. It's what I was, loud and proud to wear my wings. But fine." She smiled at a man who glanced at her as they walked past. "The *flight attendants* were terrible! No warmth. No care. No special attention, even in First Class. We'd have been fired, I tell you. I don't know who's training them, and do not start me on the shapeless, drab rags they call uniforms for these poor girls."

"Women," she corrected. "And plenty of men."

"Women? How about *grandmothers*? In my day, you wrinkled, you retired." She patted her cheek, which was remarkably smooth, thanks to gallons of water and probably just as much Juvéderm. "But I'm here now! And it's our big week to win for Dutch. Are you ready?"

"I'm as ready as anyone can be for a situation like this," Claire said as they reached the luggage carousel.

"Courtroom drama! Not really your thing, is it, Claire?"

"Not at all." She was a happy "big law" attorney who spent most of her days reading and writing briefs and torts. She'd made partner by billing mountains of hours and letting the attention-seekers grab the spotlight with major trials. "And I'm not the attorney, *Maman*, just the executor."

"But you must know if we're going to win."

"All I know is that we're on the side of the angels and

the law," she told her mother, although, sadly, sometimes those things didn't matter in court. "You were married to Aloysius Vanderveen first and legally, with a child and a home and a life before he even met Birdie."

She felt her mother's whole body bristle at the name, her bone-deep hatred for Dutch's "worst mistake" palpable.

"That's one of mine." Camille pointed to a brown bag rolling by on the carousel.

Instantly, a man Claire had barely noticed lunged for the bag and retrieved it, rolling it to Camille with a warm smile. He couldn't have been thirty-five, but that didn't matter. She was a magnet, and men from eight to eighty loved her.

A matching bag was shortly behind, and Claire got it, then spotted her simple black suitcase. Soon they were through the car rental line and climbing into a sedan to make the drive to Sanibel Island.

Eliza had offered to pick them up, but Claire begged off, knowing her mother would need downtime after her flight and a chance to regroup and change clothes for the evening ahead. Eliza had been extremely understanding, even promising that they could check into their cottage quietly and without a reunion or fanfare.

Eliza. Her sister. Claire's heart lifted at the very word.

"What has you so happy, *cherie*?" Camille asked as she slipped into the front passenger seat and pulled on her seatbelt.

"I'm going to see my sister," she said without a

second's hesitation. "And the very idea of it makes me grin like a fool."

"Have you talked to her since the last time we were here?"

"We've texted a few times, chatted some on the phone." Not enough to really deepen their relationship, so Claire hoped this visit would give the half-sisters a chance to get closer after a lifetime of separation. "I'm looking forward to spending lots of time with her."

Camille shifted in her seat, quiet. "I don't know how long I'm staying," she finally said.

"A few months, based on your luggage."

She brushed off the comment with a flip of her French-tipped fingers, gem-studded rings sparkling in the light. "Who knows what I'll need? Or what will happen? I'm ready for any contingency, including a quick getaway."

The comment made Claire glance at her mother, somewhat surprised. "I thought you loved the beach. They're giving us the two-bedroom cottage again and the views are spectacular. Not to mention the sunsets. And Teddy's tea! Goodness, why wouldn't you stay longer?"

Camille stared straight ahead, uncharacteristically quiet.

"*Maman?*" she urged.

"I'll stay until...I want to leave. You know me."

Yes, she did. And she knew that whatever she expected, Camille would most likely do something else. Which meant...

"You haven't changed your mind, have you?" Claire

asked, unwilling to dance around the topic or the truth. "About giving the property to Teddy?"

"No," she said simply. "I made a promise to Dutch, and he was dying when he asked. You don't break a deathbed promise, *cherie,* even if it was over the phone and he was not actually on his literal deathbed. It would surely haunt me for the rest of this life and into the next."

Camille dropped the subject and chatted more about her disappointment in travel in general and the airlines in particular until they reached the causeway that arched over a wide blue bay to the lush island of Sanibel.

Claire didn't push the subject back to the contested will, because she was a little afraid of what she might hear.

A broken promise—deathbed or not—would not only hurt Teddy, it might wreck any chance of Claire and Eliza ever being close. That relationship meant so much to Claire, she couldn't breathe at the thought of losing it.

She hoped her mother understood and respected that.

SITTING on the cozy wooden deck of the bright yellow cottage named for the rare Junonia seashell, Claire breathed a sigh of relief when she heard Camille inside humming as she popped open the cork on a bottle of wine that had been waiting, chilled, when they arrived.

They'd unpacked, walked the beach, showered, and

changed for dinner, and through it all, her mother's mood had improved.

Maybe it was because she had a chance to settle in, Claire mused as she looked out at the endless blue of the Gulf of Mexico. Teddy had been out with Eliza, shopping for the dinner they planned to host, so they'd been greeted by the resort housekeeper, the sweet young girl named Katie. No fanfare, as Eliza promised.

But Camille's improved mood didn't completely erase Claire's concerns that her mother might suddenly flip and not give the inherited land to Teddy. Her mother seemed quite comfortable with the idea the last time they were here, and rather pleased with the magnitude of her generosity.

Teddy and Eliza had been dealing with the shocking revelation that Birdie had a legal right to the property when Claire and Camille swooped in with the promise of a brighter future.

Even though the property had been owned by outsiders like Dutch since the 1980s or so, Teddy had worked here her entire life, and surely hoped to spend the rest of her days right here on land that went back in her family two generations. But that wouldn't happen if whoever won the prized land sold it to a big hotel chain.

She sighed and closed her eyes, hoping this all worked out. That would—

"Hello, gorgeous."

Claire turned, blinking into the setting sun to make out the figure of a woman coming closer. Speaking of her only sister—

"Eliza!" She was up on her feet in a moment, unable to wipe the smile from her face, arms extended for a hug she'd been anticipating since they said goodbye.

"Hey, you." They slid into an easy embrace, adding a squeeze before they separated.

And then they stared at each other for a beat, still getting used to the fact they were truly sisters.

Was Eliza, like Claire, looking for some trait they shared? Because there wasn't one, at least not on the surface. Eliza had red hair with stunning gold highlights and Dutch's distinctive gray-blue eyes, while Claire had inherited Camille's darker coloring.

Eliza was taller by an inch or so, and Claire was only a hair over five-four. Life in New York and long lawyers' hours meant Claire rarely saw the sun, so she didn't have Eliza's golden glow. Yes, they had similar builds, but Claire liked subdued colors and simple styles, while Eliza was stunning in a brightly patterned sundress.

But they were...

"My half-sister," Eliza whispered, making Claire certain that no matter how different they were on the outside, their thoughts aligned.

"Can we drop the half?" Claire asked. "It's so unnecessary."

"And begs so many questions," Eliza agreed.

"And, whoa, the answers are messy."

They both laughed at that and hugged again.

Eliza glanced at the open sliding glass doors of the cottage. "Is Camille comfortable? Found her wine?"

"She is, she did, and thank you, and Teddy, for

understanding her many quirks and giving us some downtime. And for giving us the nicest of the cottages again. I know it's the only two-bedroom on the property."

"Oh, please. We're so happy you're back."

"Come and sit." Claire tugged her toward the Adirondack chairs. "We have time, right? Dinner isn't for a little while."

"Plenty of time."

They sat down, both unable to stop smiling at the other.

"So..." They said it at the same time, then laughed.

"I know, I know," Claire said. "This is weird."

"And wonderful," Eliza added, searching Claire's face like she wanted to memorize it.

"You know, from the moment my mother told me about you, I wanted to meet you, Eliza."

Eliza looked a little surprised, maybe confused, at the confession. "Why didn't you find me? There was no reason not to."

Claire looked skyward and sighed with frustration. "I should have," she said. "But I had it burned into my brain that you and your mother hated my father and would never, ever be nice to me. You were off-limits."

"You never even considered reaching out to me?" Eliza asked, the hurt in her voice telling Claire that she'd been wrestling with the question for the last month.

"I looked you up and saw that you were married and had kids and a great job as a talent agent in Los Angeles, and..." Claire closed her eyes because the admission hurt. She *should* have contacted Eliza, but the whole situation with her parents' on again-off again, highly unconventional marriage made Claire uncomfortable. "My mother asked me not to. She was the reason your parents' marriage broke up, and I guess, as their love child, I was, too."

Eliza looked down for a second, then reached over and took Claire's hand.

"I don't care how weird or wonderful this is," she said. "I don't care how unusual our parents are or were—all of them. You're what matters to me, Claire. I couldn't wait for you to come back. I hope this whole hearing business is easy and painless and not the center of your stay here. I want to talk and have fun and make up for all the years we've missed."

"Yes." Claire squeezed her hand. "I want the very same thing. We don't even need to mention that hearing. It's next week, so from now until then, it's just sisters at the beach."

"Awesome. We can go paddleboarding, kayaking, and boating. I'll take you to the Ding Darling Wildlife Refuge and to the lighthouse and all over. But mostly I just want to do what we're doing right this minute—get to know each other."

"Without wine?" Camille stepped outside holding two glasses filled with chardonnay, making Claire wonder how long she'd been there. *"Bonjour, cherie!"* She leaned over and planted a light kiss on Eliza's head. "Do not get up, just take this drink and toast to sisters getting to know each other."

How long? *Long enough to eavesdrop,* Claire thought.

"Hello, Camille," Eliza said warmly, standing anyway to add a quick hug to her greeting and take the wine. "How thoughtful of you."

"The wine was from Teddy, so she is the thoughtful one," the older woman replied, turning to Claire with the other wineglass.

"Oh, let me get a chair from inside," Eliza said.

"No, don't do that, I'm not staying," Camille replied. "I'm going to help Teddy set up the dinner."

Eliza frowned. "Really? Everything's ready, and anyway, wouldn't that be *my* job, since I'm living in her house and co-hosting? You're the guests of honor."

Camille shook her head. "Teddy left a handwritten note in my room, which is too quaint for words." She slipped a folded piece of paper out of the pocket of her silky wide-legged trousers. "She said I should come down early and have a nice one-on-one with her, so I shall. And you two enjoy this time together."

She blew them a kiss and walked down the one step to the path, remarkably stable on something few people wore in Shellseeker Beach—high heels.

"Have fun!" Claire called, getting a wave over her mother's shoulder in response.

"She's quite a character," Eliza mused, watching the older woman leave.

"She is that." Claire gestured to the other chair. "Now we can relax, drink this wine, and talk."

"Yes." Eliza sat and held out her glass for a toast. "You know what I'm going to say, right?'"

"To sisters," Claire replied, tapping the rims. "And no pesky half."

"Who wants to do things by halves?" Eliza asked on a laugh before she sipped.

"Not Dutch Vanderveen's daughters." Claire took a quick drink and set the glass down on the small table between them, more interested in Eliza than the wine. "You didn't know him that well, did you?"

"Well enough," Eliza said, her voice a little taut. "I have...mixed emotions about him."

"And no doubt about my mother."

She conceded with a tip of her head. "I forgive your mother for any role in breaking up my parents' marriage, because it gave me you."

"Thank you," Claire said, happy to have that question answered. "Let's make a deal, Eliza. Right now, on this beach, as we start our real relationship."

Eliza's brows lifted, intrigued. "A deal?"

"Total honesty."

Eliza nodded. "Of course."

"No, I mean *total*," Claire insisted. "The kind we would have had if we'd grown up in the same house, sharing a room, maybe even a bed."

Eliza's eyes flickered and grew sad. "I wanted that," she said softly.

"A shared bed or total honesty?" Claire asked.

"Both. So, I'll start the honesty here. I was a dreadfully lonely child. I mean, wow." Eliza shook her head and laughed. "My mother, Mary Ann, remarried after she and

Dutch divorced and even though I had stepsiblings, they were much older and never felt anything like real siblings. More like an aunt and uncle. Before that was ten years of being an only child, and you know what that's like."

"Do I ever."

"It was the worst at night," Eliza mused. "I just longed for a sister all the time. Someone in the next bed or bunk, someone to whisper to in the night, someone to share clothes with or argue with over who stole a hairbrush or talk about boys and school or how to wear eyeshadow."

"Eliza." She could barely say the word as she reached over to clasp hands again. "I wanted that same thing so badly." In truth, she still kind of did, but she'd never be *that* honest. Living alone, *being* alone, was like breathing to Claire now. She really didn't know any other kind of life.

"This is a very roundabout way of answering your question about Dutch," Eliza said. "I don't understand that man, and honestly? I don't think any of us do. Maybe your mother."

"Even she was frequently confounded by the great and powerful Captain Vanderveen," Claire admitted.

"But I don't want to be fifty-three and carting around Daddy issues. I have enough on my heart mourning my husband, the greatest guy who ever lived."

Claire gave a soft grunt. "I'm so sorry for you, Eliza. Is it six months yet since you lost him?"

"Five months. Two weeks. Four days." She smiled.

"With a glance at the time, I could tell you how many hours."

"Oh." Claire pressed her hand to her chest, imagining the pain of having love, then losing it. In some ways, she didn't have to imagine, though her losses were different from Eliza's. "I'm so sorry."

"It's getting better every day," Eliza assured her. "Teddy has helped enormously."

"I'm glad. And now I want to help, so please—" She smiled as she leaned closer. "Tell me everything about him. What you loved most, the best memories and moments from your life, what he was like and how you met and..." She searched Eliza's face, realizing the impact her words were having. "I'm sorry. I didn't mean to make you tear up. Forget that, we can just—"

"No, no. I don't want to forget that. I want to have that conversation. Most people think I don't want to talk about Ben, when, in fact, he's *all* I want to talk about."

"That's first, then," she said. "Ben. How did you meet?"

"Now?" Eliza asked on a laugh.

"Trust me, once we get to that dinner, it will be The Camille Show and no one else will say a word."

"The Camille Show?" Eliza rolled her eyes. "She's quite an enigma, isn't she?"

Claire nodded. "She is, but you don't have to worry, Eliza. Everything is going to proceed exactly as planned on our last visit, assuming the judge rules in our favor at the hearing. She has not indicated that it will be any different, or that there will be any more surprises."

"No one can ask for more than that."

Claire took a sip of wine, and leaned in. "Now, tell me about Ben. How did you meet him, and did you know instantly he was The One?"

As Eliza told a sweet story about an encounter in Central Park, Claire barely heard the words as she studied the woman speaking them. She had a lovely, warm, bright, delightful sister, a woman she knew she could love, and she couldn't remember being any happier than she was right now.

# Chapter Three

*Teddy*

Whatever she wore, Teddy already knew she would pale in comparison to Camille. Still, she did her best to not slip on a drapey top over capri-length leggings, her usual outfit that worked for yoga and gardening. She chose a white cotton maxi, and hoped it didn't look bridal or like she was trying hard to impress a woman who was probably not easily impressed by a dress purchased at the outlets in Fort Myers.

She ran her fingers through curls the very same color as her dress, picked some matching sandals, and headed to her jewelry box.

There, she plucked out a favorite quartz crystal pendant and simple silver hoop earrings, snapping them into place just as she heard footsteps and a tap on the sliding glass doors of her beach house.

Heading downstairs, she rubbed the stone around her neck. Not for luck—she believed in a lot of "out there" things, but luck wasn't one of them. She touched her stone for strength. For dignity. For patience if she needed it, and power if she wanted it. And, of course, that her always strong empathy would allow her to understand, accept, and care about Camille.

Because the woman held Teddy's whole future in her hands and Teddy had yet to be able to get a good read on her. The last time she'd been here, Teddy had done her best to use her empathic skills to sense what Camille was thinking or feeling. Camille was that rare bird who eluded Teddy's touch, and didn't give off any readable energy.

Too bad Camille was a wine drinker. Teddy would love to ply that woman with some glorious jasmine pearl green tea, which would soften her edges and maybe open up her spirit.

But Teddy doubted she'd have any luck with that.

Smiling at the dark-haired beauty who stood on her deck in a cream-colored top and palazzo pants and heels —seriously, *heels*—Teddy slid the heavy glass door open to let in the warm Gulf breeze, heavy mid-summer humidity, and a woman who slightly terrified her.

"Camille!" Teddy called, reaching her arms out. "*Bienvenue!*"

Camille smiled. "You don't have to speak French for me, *cherie*. I don't even think in that language anymore."

They air kissed on both cheeks, making Teddy feel terribly European. And fake. She never air kissed. She hugged, which was how she got an instant read on the person in front of her. By touching someone, she could pick up the vibes of whatever emotion was rolling through that person.

But once again, Teddy felt nothing. No tension humming through the slender woman, no anger, no doubt, no...nothing.

It was even more unnerving than if Camille were giving off something dark or nefarious.

If anything, she felt...cold. Who on earth felt cold, inside or out, after a stroll in Florida's summer heat?

"Are you all right?" Teddy whispered, still holding Camille's narrow shoulders.

"Of course I am," she said, easing out of Teddy's touch. "I am thrilled to see you."

"Thank you for coming over early," Teddy said. "I thought it would be fun to have a little time alone. Would you like some wine or champagne?"

"Champagne! Only if you'll join me."

"Of course." Although she rarely drank, Teddy would make an exception if it would relax her guest.

She guided Camille toward the comfortable living area, then went to the small bar to pop the bubbly while Camille cooed about her pretty coastal home. A home that was all part of this property...and one that Camille could very likely own before long.

Teddy shoved the thought away, determined to focus on this moment, not give in to worry about a murky future. Holding that in her heart, she returned with two flutes and offered one to Camille.

"To Dutch?" Camille suggested as a toast when Teddy sat down on the sofa near her. "Or has he left us too much of a mess to cheer about him?"

Teddy looked at the sparkling liquid before meeting Camille's penetrating gaze. "I'd rather drink to us, Camille. That we can be friends." She tapped Camille's glass without giving her a chance to disagree. "And that we'll figure out the mess."

Camille exhaled, her beautifully made-up eyelids shuttering. "You're right. And Dutch isn't the object of our fury. Roberta Vanderveen is the one we should hate."

Teddy shifted on the sofa, a strong reaction to a word she, well, hated. "You know, I don't 'do' hate, as they say. I find it saps my energy and joy."

Camille just gave her a look and took another deep drink, eyes closed. When she opened them, her expression seemed hard.

"I have no problem with hate, especially when the subject is Birdie." She practically spat the woman's nickname. "I need her to be annihilated at next week's hearing."

Annihilated? The violent word sent another shiver through Teddy. "I don't think anyone needs to be destroyed."

"Birdie does."

"I'm sure she was devastated enough when she learned her husband was not legally hers at all," Teddy said. "That had to be quite a blow."

"I hope she writhed in pain."

Teddy reached for the rose quartz crystal at the center of the coffee table, one of dozens of crystals around her home. Handing it to Camille, she said, "Hold this. Think about her. Then let go of your hate."

Camille put the stone right back down as if it burned her. "She is a bad, bad woman, Teddy. She kept Dutch in chains."

Teddy frowned. "As I understand the history, Dutch made a conscious decision to be in those chains. For one thing, he married her fully knowing he was legally married to you. And for another, he didn't tell her the truth even when he wanted a divorce. The chains were of his own making."

Camille straightened and subtly narrowed her eyes. "You know why he did that," she said defensively. "If Birdie had known while he was alive, she would have ruined him, wrecked his reputation, and destroyed his life's work. She'd have managed to get all his money and then he'd have never been able to buy this property and wouldn't have met you."

Teddy shifted again, inching back as she finally felt Camille's missing energy...and it was dark.

"You know that, don't you?" Camille insisted.

"I do," Teddy said, "but to be honest, it confuses me."

"Dutch could be confusing," she said lightly. "God knows he confounded me for, what? Forty-five years of a very complicated and unorthodox marriage."

"He confounded me, too," Teddy admitted, almost smiling at the understatement. "I thought I knew the man, having lived with him for the better part of two years. But he didn't tell me about you or Claire, and he certainly didn't tell me about Birdie. Only Eliza's mother, and he rarely mentioned her."

Camille lifted a shoulder. "And yet here I am."

"And I have to trust you," Teddy whispered, the source of all her angst over this woman surfacing no matter how much she wanted to keep it hidden.

Camille sighed gently and added a smile that certainly seemed genuine. "You can trust me," she said. "I have no beef with you, Teddy. My anger has always been directed at that woman who..." She swallowed and then let out a light laugh. "She took my man, and even though it wasn't legal and I got him back and then I didn't really want him anymore, it still hurts, all these years later. My revenge is directed toward her, not you."

Putting a hand on Camille's arm, she felt more tension emanating from her. Revenge. Yes. That was a good word for what was vibrating off this beautiful woman.

Teddy had healed a lot of people in her day, including Dutch, who she'd given two extra years of life using nothing but her touch and tea, and a few well-placed crystals.

She could help this woman. And maybe that was the answer to this whole conundrum. If she could take away that hatred and bitterness and resentment, Camille would surely do the right thing with her inheritance. Maybe. She hoped.

"We both know that Dutch made many questionable decisions in his life," Teddy said carefully. "And we also know that there was something magnetic and irresistible about him, so we forgave him those decisions."

Camille put her hand over Teddy's. "You know, he told me the last few times we talked that you were like this."

Teddy tried not to react to the fact that Dutch was communicating with Camille while he was living here in this house, with her. Was it when she'd make a comment about his "plans for the estate" and then he'd disappear for the day? Had he gone to call his *wife*?

"Told you I was like what?" she asked, covering her tight voice with a sip of champagne.

"Good. Kind. 'She's like a balm,' he said." Camille reached for her champagne, but stopped, her fingers inching toward the quartz. "Does it really do all those things you said?"

"The crystal? Of course. Pick it up. You'll see."

Her hand hovered over the pink stone as if she was afraid of it. "I don't believe in things like that."

"You don't have to," Teddy said. "Dutch didn't think crystals were anything but shiny rocks when he got here, but then he wore one like this." She lifted the quartz pendant on the silver chain around her neck. "I gave him a big one when he first got here, and he called that one his fake magic diamond."

"Was it magic?"

"Of course not, but it gave him seven hundred and four more days than the doctors said he had when they discovered that tumor."

Camille gave a quick laugh. "You don't really expect me to believe that nonsense."

"A crystal interacts with the body's energy field," Teddy explained. "The healing properties create balance and alignment. They can invoke feelings of grounding, of strength, of hope, even. Sometimes, that's enough to keep even the hardiest brain tumor from growing."

"Oooh." She held her hands up, away from the crystal. "Too...what's the term? New Age. No, thank you. Keep that thing away from me."

Teddy nodded. "No one will force you to hold it, Camille. Although..." She couldn't help smiling. "It might make you feel better when you have to face Birdie Vanderveen."

She grunted. "I can't even think about it. She ruined us. Emotionally, I mean."

And she could ruin Teddy financially. But Dutch's "marriage" to Birdie hadn't been the end of his relationship with Camille. "He came back to you," she said.

"But it was never the same. I couldn't really trust him because he hadn't just cheated, he'd *married* her."

Teddy flinched at the thought, her natural instincts to feel so bad for Camille, and yet she found herself wondering about Dutch. For the millionth time in a month, Teddy wrestled with the reality that she, an empath who read people like others read newspapers, didn't know the man she thought she loved.

"He should have told Birdie the truth," Teddy said. "Yes, it could have carried a high price for him, but now all the cleanup has to be done after he's gone."

"Which was what he wanted," Camille said dryly. "Now, Teddy. Tell me all about Shellseeker Beach. I understand you have quite a history. Your grandfather discovered it?"

She knew all this, didn't she? Maybe she hadn't been listening to the history of Shellseeker Beach when they met a month ago, or maybe she just wanted to change the subject. Teddy took the hint.

"My grandfather, John Blessing, homesteaded the property. The Calusa Indians, who lived around here for thousands of years, actually discovered it."

"And you've lived here your whole life?"

"Every single day."

She sighed. "Remarkable. Just remarkable. No wonder you want the property back in your name. And no wonder Dutch asked me to make sure that happens."

"Yes," she said softly, putting her hand on Camille's arm, aching to get some idea of what the other woman was thinking and feeling. "And I'm so grateful for that."

Camille just sighed, and Teddy felt...nothing. What on earth was going on inside this woman? It wasn't going to be easy, but Teddy wanted to find out.

❧

"How DO you think it's going?" Teddy whispered to Eliza a few hours later while they worked side by side to get the cookies and fruit on a dessert tray.

"Great," Eliza said, glancing out to the living area where Claire, Olivia, and Camille had moved for tea and dessert. "We're all sort of dancing around the heavy stuff, and Camille's a bit much, but oh my gosh, I adore Claire. Don't you?"

"She's lovely. So different from her mother. She's..." Teddy couldn't think of the word. "Honorable, I think. And genuine."

Eliza looked at Teddy with understanding and concern. "Trust the process, Theodora," she whispered.

"I don't exactly have a choice." Teddy glanced toward the living room before adding, "I'm truly scared that she's such a wild card that when all is said and done, if she does win, she'll just keep the place. Sell it to a hotel. And I'll be..."

"Hush." Eliza put a gentle hand on Teddy's arm. "Maybe we need more one-on-one time with them, instead of this group gabfest. Let's make plans to divide and conquer."

"Not sure I follow," Teddy said.

"Tomorrow is Saturday. Let me have Claire. You take Camille. Let's do something with them that gives us both personal time." Eliza dipped her head and looked into Teddy's eyes. "Are you okay with that?"

"I am, and it's a good idea. But she's...a lot. She sucks the energy right out of me."

Eliza nodded. "You want me to take her and you can spend time with Claire?"

"No. You need to be with your sister, and I'm determined to solve the puzzle of Camille. I need to find common ground and connect with her," Teddy said as the three women in the living room let out a burst of laughter. "We'd better get back out there. Take this tray of desserts and I'll brew some comforting lemon balm and chamomile tea."

When Teddy finished that and carried the tea tray to the table in the living room, she caught a snippet of Olivia and Claire's conversation.

"Work *is* my life," Olivia admitted on a laugh. "And it sounds like you can relate."

Claire pushed back her thick chocolate-colored locks and pinned her gold-flecked gaze on Olivia. "I've got, what? Fifteen years on you? Are you thirty?"

"About to be."

She gave a slow and sage nod. "Be sure that's what you want in life, my friend. It's a high while it's happening, and then you wake up and..."

"And what?" Olivia asked.

Claire looked at her mother, who, along with Eliza, had paused to listen to the more interesting conversation happening across from them.

"She's going to tell you that you wake up and your eggs are gone," Camille interjected. "Correct, *cherie?*"

Claire smiled and gave a shrug that was almost as French as her mother, but somehow more genuine. "It's a risk you take. A big risk."

"I guess, but I kind of would like a husband first," Olivia added on a laugh.

"Pffft!" Camille let out her standard response to anything she disagreed with, always accompanied by a riffle of her fingers. "Just have a baby if you want one."

"Roz and George's daughter is," Teddy chimed in. "They run Sanibel Treasures, our shell and souvenir shop. Asia is thirty-four? Five? I can't remember. But she decided to have a baby. Little Miss Independent, Roz calls her."

"And Asia also has pre-eclampsia," Eliza added. "So it would be nice for her *not* to be so independent right now. It's why Roz wanted to go up there." She smiled at

Olivia. "I'm in the husband-first camp, Liv, you know that."

"The right husband, Mom," she said, narrowing her eyes and making them all laugh. "Someone who matches my ambition and dedication to work."

"Careful with that," Claire warned. "That was exactly what broke up my short marriage to Jeffrey Sutherland. He decided that the track to a partnership was more important than showing up in our marriage, and we divorced in less than three years."

"Oh, Jeffrey," Camille said on a sigh. "He wasn't your wisest decision."

Claire rolled her eyes. "Take it from someone who has a history of falling for men who love work more than life, Olivia. They're not always the best choice."

"Men?" Camille asked pointedly. "I can't remember anyone except Jeffrey...oh, yes. That Italian boy you met at Fordham. He went off to be an architect, right? In California?"

Instantly, Teddy could feel a bubble of emotion rolling off Claire and knew Camille must have hit her daughter's weak spot.

"Yes, he did," Claire said, adding a tight smile as she turned to Olivia. "I guess what I'm saying is, balance is important."

"I do remember you quite liked him," Camille continued, still stuck on this ex of Claire's. "Handsome devil, if you go for that dark and swarthy type. No name, just initials, if I recall correctly. JD or BJ or..."

"He went by DJ." Claire's voice was cool, but Teddy

picked up powerful sensations of discomfort. So it was no surprise when she turned from her mother to change the subject. "Maybe we should use this time to talk about next week's hearing."

"Yes, we should." Teddy jumped in, the healer in her wanting to help poor Claire. "Tell us what we need to know, Claire."

"I hope the process will be fast and simple," Claire said, leaning forward, clearly more at ease with court talk than dwelling on a man from her past. "There will be a very small and private meeting, in a conference room, I imagine, not a courtroom. The attorney representing our side is Michael Ortega, from my firm's Miami office. He's a probate expert. I can't speak about Roberta's attorney."

"Wait a second," Eliza interjected. "He's in Alabama. The private investigator we used who found her has already met with him. How can he practice in Florida?"

"It's something called *pro hac vice,*" Claire explained. "Essentially, it's a temporary way for an attorney to argue one case in a state even though he's never passed its bar exam. I'd represent our side if I could, but Dutch named me executor of the will, so it's a conflict. But Michael's awesome and we'll be in good hands in that room."

"What exactly will happen?" Eliza asked. "Are there witnesses? Do people take oaths?"

"It's a little more like mediation than a trial, at least at this point. Each side presents their documents, which the judge will have already seen and read. He'll allow us to make our arguments, present our cases, and explain why we think our wills are valid. Michael will do all of that for us. The judge might ask direct questions, but he might not. It depends."

"Who do you think has the better case?" Teddy asked.

Claire considered that, tilting her head. "Birdie's will is older, which doesn't help her at all, and Camille's marriage was first and last, which is in our favor. Never a slam-dunk, but I think we are well-positioned to win."

Teddy leaned back with a sigh of relief, but she noticed that Eliza was frowning as she looked at Claire.

"Are you planning to reveal Camille's agreement with Dutch?" Eliza asked. "Will you tell the judge that the entire property will be returned to..." She swallowed and put a hand on Teddy's arm. "The original owner?"

"That's a game-time decision," Claire replied. "Michael knows, but has to decide if it will work for us or against us. Since we can't prove those were Dutch's desires..." She spoke slowly, choosing her words with care. "It might not be the best thing for us if we reveal that the inheritance will be immediately transferred to someone not mentioned in either will."

Olivia turned to Camille. "You don't have anything that confirms you had this arrangement with Dutch? A text message? A letter? Anything?"

She shook her head. "We talked on the phone about it, but that's it."

There was a beat of silence in the room while everyone let that sink in. None more than Teddy, who felt her heart tumble to the floor.

"Anyway, there is a chance that the judge will want

witnesses and a more official trial later," Claire continued. "We won't know that, or who he'd want to talk to, until after the hearing. Until then, there's not that much to do."

"Except something fun, I hope," Camille interjected. "What shall we all do this weekend?"

"I'll be working tomorrow," Olivia said. "But if you want to go out on the water, we can arrange paddleboards or kayaks."

Camille looked at her like she'd lost her mind. "Fun to me is shopping, not...kayaking."

Claire laughed. "I can't say I'd do that well in a kayak myself. Any other options?"

"Sightseeing," Eliza said. "Sanibel and Captiva are beautiful, and we have a shell museum and history center. Lots to see."

"I'd do an island tour," Claire said, looking at her mother. "Will you join us?"

Teddy was scouring her brain to think of something she could say to get Camille to stay with her to implement Eliza's "divide and conquer" idea, but it was much too hot to garden. Then she had a thought.

"Take me shopping, Camille," she said.

"Now you're speaking my language. What's on your shopping list?"

"I'd just love your advice on fashion." Teddy didn't dare look at Eliza, who surely knew that fashion was the last thing on Teddy's mind. "You're always such a vision in whatever you wear. And I'm..." She plucked at the white dress. "I have no sense of it."

For the first time, Camille truly lit up. "Oh, I'd love that! You'd look so good in something bold and jewel-toned. And fitted, to show off your slender physique. Yes, let's shop!"

"Just the two of us," Teddy added. "Let the girls sightsee."

Camille definitely seemed to like the idea, which made Teddy feel better. She'd crack that wall and find those feelings and, if Camille would let her, maybe Teddy could help her.

Then they could be...friends. And Camille wouldn't pull the rug out from under her friend. Would she?

# Chapter Four

## Eliza

After they finished a hot but spectacular tour of the J.N. "Ding" Darling Wildlife Refuge, Eliza climbed behind the wheel of the black Honda coupe that once belonged to Dutch Vanderveen. Not for the first time since she and Claire had started their sightseeing tour of Sanibel, Eliza wondered if Dutch ever dreamed that *both* his daughters might someday be cruising in the car that Teddy said he loved.

She hadn't mentioned the fact that Teddy had offered her Dutch's car to drive so she could give up her pricey rental. It felt like that would take their conversation back to Dutch, and they seemed to easily avoid the subject of their father. Not that they needed to, but the whole day, the driving, the refuge, the stop at the lighthouse had all been so stress-free and uplifting, she didn't want to change any of that.

"Ding Darling was fantastic!" Claire exclaimed as they pulled out of the parking lot. "I've never seen anything quite like it."

"I got a lot more out of this visit than the last," Eliza said. "Teddy and I took a bunch of four-year-olds on a field trip."

"Four-year-olds?"

"You met Katie Bettencourt, the housekeeper at Shellseeker Cottages? We chaperoned a field trip with her daughter's class."

"She's a mom?"

"A young and single one," Eliza told her.

"Really." Claire sounded more intrigued than surprised. "That must be a challenge for her."

"Youth and energy," Eliza said on a laugh. "Teddy and I were so wiped out after that day we had to break into Dutch's secret stash of Chivas when it was over."

"The one he kept next to his bed?" Claire asked a soft snort. "Some things never change. What a guy, huh?" She waved her hand like she didn't want to talk about him, either. "Where to next? I'm up for anything that includes air conditioning, food, and something cold to drink. And by cold, I mean a beer on tap."

"Yes!" Eliza let out a soft hoot at how on the money that suggestion was. "I know just the place."

The Seaside Saloon met every one of Claire's criteria, and this late in the afternoon in the middle of summer, it was cool and quiet as they settled down at a table that looked out over the water.

After they got IPAs and ordered appetizers, they toasted the fun day. Then Claire propped her chin on her knuckles and looked right into Eliza's eyes.

"We're, what, eight or almost nine years apart?" she asked. "I wonder how our lives would have been different if we'd known about each other all along."

"I have no clue," Eliza admitted. "But you know, even

after I married Ben and moved to L.A., I was frequently in New York for client business and to see my mother, who lived on Long Island until she died. I wonder if we walked right by each other sometime."

"Bizarre to imagine, huh?"

"Yes," Eliza agreed. "Do you love living there?"

"It's all I know, really. I spent most of my childhood in Quebec City, having left Paris when I was practically still a toddler. Then my mother moved us to Montreal while I was in high school. So I've always lived in a big city. I don't know any other life. It's a grind, for sure, but I have a great job and a gorgeous apartment on the Upper East Side." She added a smile. "A lonely grind for a single woman in her forties."

"Single by choice, I'm sure."

"You heard all about my shortcomings in the romance department last night."

Eliza had heard, and later, when everyone had left, Teddy shared that she'd felt deep emotions from Claire during the conversation, especially when Camille zeroed in on one man in particular. And that just made Eliza so curious about him.

"I know about your marriage and why it fell apart, but what's the deal with the guy who went to California? The man with the initials? Was he important?"

A soft flush in her cheeks gave the answer. "Not really," she said quickly. "But at least he didn't come back and break promises like my—er, our—father did."

Eliza nodded knowingly. "I learned not to expect anything from Dutch."

Claire just let her eyes close for a moment, lost in thought. "'I'll be back, Coco,' he used to say. That was his nickname for me, Coco."

"I was Boo Boo," Eliza said. "I hear from everyone that he had a nickname for them."

"He couldn't remember names, that's why," Claire said with a humorless laugh. "It took too much energy to remember someone else's name when his mind was always focused on Dutch, on his next adventure or flight or...woman."

The words eerily echoed something Teddy had told Eliza not too long ago. "Teddy told me that just moments before he died, he said something very much like that. He admitted he'd been a—I actually think 'bastard' was the word he used. And he said the same things about himself."

"So maybe he did repent at the end," Claire said. "Although I doubt it."

Eliza studied her sister, realizing that she honestly didn't know Claire's intense feelings toward their father ran *that* deep.

The server came with shrimp and round crab cakes, which they both tasted and adored, forgetting their past while they enjoyed the moment together. But before long, they were chatting about more serious things again.

"Can I ask you something and get your honest thoughts?" Eliza asked.

"Always," Claire said. "I've made you a promise that I'll be honest and that's another thing I learned from bad examples. Keep a promise. Neither of my parents are very good at it."

"Your mother, too?" The last bite of shrimp caught in Eliza's throat as the thought landed. "Like, she breaks promises?"

Claire looked at her. "Not as much as Dutch, but she is capricious. And by that, I mean the only thing predictable about her is that she will be unpredictable. Just when you think you know what Camille will do, wham! She pivots and does the opposite."

Dang. Eliza felt her shoulders drop.

"Stop worrying, Eliza," Claire said with a reassuring look. "I've already drawn up the agreement. You saw it the last time we were here. She'd have no reason to renege on that."

"Um, money?"

Claire shook her head. "She has enough, and despite her weakness for couture, her needs are few."

Olivia's many warnings about how people change when millions are in the mix echoed in her head. "We all know, although no one is saying it, that the property is worth quite a bit of money. There are numerous hotel chains that would pay millions in a heartbeat to get their hands on a property like that. The only way they can get a piece of the lucrative Sanibel tourism market is to buy something like Shellseeker Cottages and run it without putting the hotel name anywhere too obvious. They don't care about the name or sign. They want the income."

She nodded. "I've done the research. I know that."

"Then you know what Dutch's will is worth to your

mother, and, I assume, to you."

She lowered her fork, not taking the bite of crab on the end. "I am not motivated by money, Eliza, and neither is my mother."

"What is she motivated by?"

She thought for a second, then smiled. "Fashion." At Eliza's look of disbelief, Claire laughed. "Maybe it's more than that. She likes looking good to others. Yes, that's shallow, but it isn't just how she appears on the outside. She also wants to look good on the inside, not because she is, but because she cares what people think about her."

"People might be impressed with a woman who has a lot of money," Eliza mused.

"Really, she does have money. Like Dutch, she had stock options from Pan Am, and invested wisely. But she does love *beauty* the way some people love *money*. Does that make sense?"

"A little."

Claire put her hand on Eliza's. "I want to tell you to rest easy, so I will. That's not to say my mother doesn't occasionally shock the stuffing out of me, but I have had no hints that's what she's going to do this time."

Eliza sighed. "Okay. So I should relax, but not too much."

"That'll work."

"And what about you?" Eliza asked.

"Me?" Claire picked up the beer glass. "I'm relaxed."

"No. You said what motivates your mother. What motivates you? Work? Travel?"

"Ah, good question." She took a sip and thought

about it. "I guess I'm motivated to stay as busy as humanly possible, without giving myself any time to sit and be...alone." Claire's whole face softened, even her eyes seemed to moisten a little bit. "I have no husband, no child, no siblings, no cousins in this country, and a mother who is...flighty at best."

Eliza's heart cracked thinking of Claire having a lonely childhood and an even lonelier adulthood.

"Well, now you have a sister," she said softly. "And wherever I am, you are welcome. Anytime at all."

Claire blinked and a tear escaped the corner of her eye. "Thank you."

"And my daughter is your niece," Eliza said, putting her fingertips over Claire's knuckles as she rested her hand on the table. "So you officially have family. Oh, and my son, Dane, in Silicon Valley. More family!"

For a long moment, Claire didn't speak. Couldn't speak, Eliza guessed, as they just looked at each other. Then Eliza heard her phone softly ring with the familiar refrain from *Somewhere*.

"That's Teddy," she said, fishing for the cell in her purse.

"Who has probably purchased a mountain of Chanel by now," Claire said dryly.

Smiling at that, she tapped the phone and put it to her ear. "How's the shopping going, Teddy?"

"Not. Good. At. All." She ground out the words, making Eliza gasp.

"What's wrong?"

"Just please come and help me." The words were

barely a whisper and sent an alarming chill through her.

"Of course." She looked across the table at Claire, who inched closer, concern in her eyes and she was only hearing half the conversation. "Where are you?"

"Just get to Beachside Boutique as fast as you can and rescue me!"

"What's—"

"Off the phone, Theo!" Camille's distinctive throaty voice could be heard in the background. "I've found more dresses!"

"Now!" Teddy added with breathy desperation as the call disconnected.

Frowning, Eliza lowered the phone and looked at Claire. "That was weird. Teddy asked me to come to a local store and rescue her."

Claire gave her a knowing groan. "She's doing a makeover. It's never easy for the poor victim." She grabbed the check with one hand and drained her beer with the other. "Let's go save Teddy before she's spent every dime on a wardrobe she doesn't want but *Maman* thinks will change her life."

Sarah Beth, the sweet sixty-something owner of the upscale boutique in a strip shopping center on Periwinkle, greeted them at the door, her usual calm demeanor looking...frazzled.

"Teddy will be glad to see you," Sarah Beth whispered to Eliza when they walked in. "That French lady knows her fashion, for sure, but she doesn't take no for an answer. She's a bulldozer over customer objections. She should work here, and I'll make a fortune."

Eliza smiled and gestured to Claire. "This is Claire Sutherland, her daughter."

"Oh!" Sarah Beth put a finger over her lips. "I'm sorry, I—"

Claire laughed it off. "It's fine, and she *is* a bulldozer. Oh, God, look at those chairs."

Eliza looked past Sarah Beth to the sight of a mountain of clothes covering the grouping of guest chairs outside the private dressing rooms. Claire strode right through the boutique toward the sound of her mother's voice, which was a bit louder and more frustrated than her usual *laissez-faire* tone.

"Oh, Teddy," Claire said. "Look at you."

Just as Eliza reached them, Teddy turned from a full-length mirror outside one of the draped dressing rooms. She wore bright red skinny trousers, three-inch heels, and an off-the-shoulder lace top that looked like it belonged on a fifteen-year-old. Or a window.

"What are you wearing?" Eliza exclaimed, a hand to her mouth.

"I think it's stunning!" Camille said, more clothes the color of a carnival in her arms.

"Yes, it's a jaw-dropper all right." At Camille's very unhappy look, Eliza held up her hands in mock apology. "But she can't wear those shoes and not fall flat on her face."

"She needs height!" Camille shot back. "She's only

about five foot two!"

"Five three and a half," Teddy said. "And my feet are screaming in pain."

"You'll get used to it," Camille said, her own heels tapping on the hardwood floor. "Okay, not that top. But keep the slacks and try it with this. Very Jackie O, don't you think?"

Eliza caught Teddy's expression of sheer horror in the mirror.

"Let me help you out of that zipper in the back," she said, darting closer. Without waiting for anyone to argue, she guided Teddy back into the dressing room, sliding the curtain closed for some measure of privacy.

"Oh, *Maman!* Come and see these fabulous earrings," Claire called, moving her mother to another part of the store like they'd choreographed the save.

"Teddy!" Eliza said in a hushed tone. "What is going on?"

"That woman," she breathed back. "She's either crazy or blind or she just hates me. Look at this, Eliza."

Eliza's gaze dropped over the outfit, which was actually quite fetching, but not on Teddy. "It's not you."

"No kidding! But she's an absolute tornado. I can't stop her. Sarah Beth just gave up trying. And she's determined to put me in...oh!" She kicked off one of the heels so hard it smacked the wall.

"Shhh." Eliza ran a soothing hand over her friend's bare shoulder. "Let's get you out of this top and those pants. Red pants? I can't believe Sarah Beth even carries them."

"She doesn't! Camille went digging through the storeroom for older inventory."

"For a sale price?" Eliza guessed, wanting to give Camille the benefit of the doubt.

"For something different!"

"Well, she found it."

With trembling hands, Teddy stepped out of the pants. Standing in her underwear, she looked thin and old and helpless, unlike the strong, yoga-practicing healer Eliza knew her to be.

Impulsively, she wrapped her arms around Teddy and squeezed. "Well, I'm here now and I won't let you buy anything but the leggings and tunics that you love."

"Why does she want to change me?" Teddy asked in an uncharacteristically weak whisper, even though they could hear Claire and Camille's voices and knew they were far enough away not to hear this conversation.

"Claire says she loves a makeover, but doesn't like her ideas to get pushed back." Eliza found Teddy's black leggings on a hook and handed them to her. "Here, get dressed. You can buy one thing to shut her up and—"

"She wants me to get a haircut!" Teddy ground out. "She said something like Jamie Lee Curtis and showed me a picture of a woman whose hair is one inch long. Maybe."

"Well, you are not touching your magnificent silver curls," Eliza promised, giving the soft hair a fluff as Teddy pulled up the leggings.

"I can't fight her on anything."

"I can," Eliza said.

"But I shouldn't," Teddy hissed. "I don't want her to get mad or not like me or...change her mind."

Eliza nodded, following the logic. Not liking it one bit, but following it.

"Theodora Blessing." She put her hands on Teddy's shoulders. "You are a powerful, bright, beloved, and beautiful woman. You are grounded by meditation and love and tea and me."

That made Teddy smile, so Eliza powered on. "You will not let yourself be pushed around by Hurricane Camille and you will not let fear dictate your behavior." Eliza snagged the crystal pendant that was hanging on another hook and slid it over Teddy's gorgeous hair that no one would cut. "Let this channel all your awesome energy and inner strength. She has no power here."

Teddy smiled. "You sound like the Good Witch on the *Wizard of Oz* that I watched while babysitting Harper the other night."

"I am the Good Witch. And that one"—she notched her thumb toward the sound of Camille's laughter—"is not going to make over someone who is already perfect."

"I found the earrings I'm buying you!" Camille called, her voice much too close to the dressing room for them to continue. "They will look *magnifique* with that haircut. Sarah Beth says the best hair stylist in Sanibel—"

Eliza whipped the curtain open just as Teddy straightened the cotton tunic over her leggings.

"Teddy's not cutting her hair, Camille," she said as sweetly as she could.

Camille blinked, almost as if she was completely

unused to anyone derailing her plans. Behind her, Claire stood with her arms crossed, watching the exchange.

"Nonsense, Eliza. Her hair is as old as those shoes she's wearing." She glanced at Teddy's beloved Birkenstocks, worn only when she had to be on her feet for a long time. "And just about as unattrac—"

"Camille." Teddy took a step forward in front of Eliza, her narrow shoulders squared, her chin up. "I have loved shopping with you, and I am definitely going to buy that turquoise blouse because—"

"Oh no, it's hideous."

"Because I like it," she finished, undeterred. "But nothing else. And my hair may be as out of style as my clothes, but I love it."

Camille stared at her, the fight slowly, very slowly, fading from her dark eyes. "Suit yourself, Teddy. A woman has the right to choose comfort over style."

Claire stepped forward and put a light hand on Teddy's shoulder. "I love my Birkenstocks," she whispered. "The day my mother saw me wearing them, she decided I must have been switched at birth."

They all laughed at the light moment, and Eliza beamed at Claire, grateful for the support and her very quiet but effective style.

"I hope you weren't," Eliza said, wrapping an arm around Claire's waist. "Because then you wouldn't be the sister I've longed for my whole life."

All three of them smiled at Camille, who was smart enough to know when she was outnumbered.

# Chapter Five

*Olivia*

He was back.

Olivia looked across Sanibel Treasures at the tall, dark-haired man who walked into her store for the, what? Third time in about five days? He'd definitely been here yesterday while she was talking to her mother, but left without talking or buying.

He either really wanted a shell-covered Christmas wreath or...something else. Her gut said it was something else, and the way he smiled at her, she kind of suspected what it was.

And of course, instantaneously without even thinking about it, she started finding flaws. He wasn't unattractive, but he was...cookie-cutter. Short brown hair receding enough that she'd put him closer to forty than thirty, a forgettable face, and an ill-fitting Polo shirt that hung over shoulders that probably hadn't seen the inside of a gym recently.

*Stop it, Olivia. Do you want to be forty-five and alone like your aunt?*

She tamped down her inner voice and dug up her brightest smile.

"Can I help you find anything?" Olivia asked before

even giving him time to leave if she talked to another customer. "I seem to recall you liked the shell artwork last time."

He smiled, angling his head as he studied her. "You remember me?"

"I don't get a lot of men alone in here. Did you want to look at that piece again?"

"Maybe." He held her gaze for a second, then looked away quickly. Darn. She didn't like shy men, but she powered on, walking closer.

"Are you looking for a gift or something for yourself?"

"A gift."

*Well, good*, she thought. At least he didn't buy shell art for himself. "A special lady?" she guessed.

"You could say that. My mother."

"Oh." *Don't think "Mama's Boy," Livvie. Think "nice guy who is thoughtful."* "That's sweet. What kind of things does she like? Art? Or maybe jewelry?"

"Um, she likes..." He looked around and settled on the holiday section she longed to get rid of but couldn't, since Roz had told her that ornaments and wreaths were top-selling souvenirs year-round. "The holidays."

"Then let's focus on that," she said.

He smiled and nodded, quiet in the face of her inner-longing for a snappy retort that made her laugh. Nope. Nada.

"We have a great selection for Christmas or any holi-day, really. The manager has assured me that Christmas items sell well all year long. Apparently ornaments make great souvenirs and gifts."

Finally, something sparked in his eyes. She couldn't read what it was, but it was the first time his eyes—which were honestly the color of mud—showed true interest.

"You're not the manager? Or the owner? I got the impression you called the shots around here."

Just how many sneak peeks of her had he taken? "I'm working here for the summer."

The front door opened, chiming the bell as two older women came in, chatting animatedly and reeking of sunscreen under their beach coverups.

"Welcome to Sanibel Treasures," Olivia greeted them with a smile.

"Do you have flipflops?" one asked, sounding a tad desperate as she held up a broken sandal. "Mine just bit the dust, or sand, as the case may be."

"Oh, I do," Olivia answered with a laugh, then glanced at the man, who, it had to be noted, hadn't even smiled. "'Scuse me."

"Take your time."

"Don't run out without getting this gift," she said, keeping her voice light, maybe even flirtatious, because she didn't want to dismiss him like every other man who showed any interest in her.

His brows flickered ever so slightly, as if he liked that, and he nodded. "I'll wait for you."

*Please don't, because I'm a bad bet for a nice, bland guy like you.*

But she walked toward the women who'd already found Roz's overcrowded section of T-shirts, coverups, and flipflops.

"All right, ladies. We have plastic flipflops, and more plastic flipflops. For a few extra dollars, you can have them decorated with seashells."

As they cooed and laughed, she stole a glance at the man, who was actually looking at his phone, or texting. Oh, no—wait. He was taking a picture of the seasonal display.

No doubt sending a few options to his mother, because he didn't know her well enough or didn't trust his own judgment or was—

"I love these, Madeleine! How much are these shoes, miss?"

Olivia shoved all her negative thoughts away and turned to the women, focusing on the shoe purchase. With ease, she was able to upsell them each new coverups, and close the sale with one puka shell necklace for Madeleine and a large pink conch shell that Olivia assured the other woman would look beautiful next to her bathtub back home in South Carolina.

That done, she turned back to her mystery man, who had worked his way to the back of the store and seemed more interested in what was around the corner than in any of her inventory.

"You are nearing sacred ground," she teased as she came back, seeing that light flash in his eyes again for just a second.

"I am? This area is sacred?"

"It kind of is," she told him, guiding him into the only section of the store she hadn't really touched. George's "history department" was, well, George's. In it, he sold much more than books and maps and old photographs of a wooden bridge. This was the section that housed the message-in-a-bottle collection, including one signed by Theodore Roosevelt himself.

"This is the historical department of the store, run by one of our managers, who is a Sanibel history buff. I'm not really qualified to sell it as he does. But you'll find books on the island, some old maps, quite a few lithographs and original art painted by local artists over the years." She ushered him closer to the back wall, since he clearly seemed interested in it. "There's a shelf with replicas of tools handmade by the Calusa Indians, believed to have lived here for thousands of—"

"What are the bottles?"

She slid into a genuine smile for the first time since they'd started talking. "That, my friend, is the pride and joy of George Turner and, some might say, all of Sanibel Island. The one in the display case?"

He leaned closer, squinting at the small plaque, then pulled out a pair of reading glasses to get a better look. Yup, *definitely* closer to forty. Maybe past it.

*Which just might make him ready to settle down and get serious*, a little voice inside her head said. A voice that sounded way too much like Eliza Whitney.

"Theodore Roosevelt wrote that message?" he asked, clearly fascinated by this news.

"He did indeed. He lived on a houseboat here on Sanibel back in—" She should know the year, but didn't. "His day," she finished. "And the man who built this store —it used to be a boathouse—was the son of the man who found a message in a bottle that President Roosevelt had written and thrown into Pine Island Sound, I think it was."

She'd heard the story exactly twice before taking over the store, so she didn't feel too bad about not knowing the details. Without George here to promote the whole concept, she didn't expect to drive much revenue from this section. Still, a sale was a sale, and her guest seemed truly interested.

At least he liked history more than holiday wreaths, which was a point in his favor.

"So you see that row of bottles with messages up there?" she asked, pointing to the shelf. "We sell the bottles and paper, and customers are encouraged to leave a message in a bottle, then toss it into the Gulf." At his look, she added, "The bottles and paper are completely biodegradable. But if you find one and return it to this store—this is all written on the back of the paper—then Sanibel Treasures makes a sizeable donation to the Historical Society."

"And that is the row of returned bottles?" he guessed.

"Yes. Isn't it a brilliant idea?"

He nodded, then returned his attention to the Teddy Roosevelt display, studying the historic object.

"I don't suppose your mother might want a message in a bottle in her name?" she suggested. "Or you?" she added when he didn't answer.

"No, I think she'll want one of those wreaths. Old ladies love shells."

She drew back, a finger to her lips. "Shhh. Don't alienate my target market."

Finally, he laughed. Okay, there might be a sense of humor under all that forgettableness.

"So, are you a local?" he asked, the sudden change in topic surprising her.

"Nope, I live in—"

"Miss? Excuse me, miss?" The call from a customer she hadn't even heard come in startled her. It wasn't like her to not hear the bell—and the man in the Polo shirt wasn't exactly mesmerizing—but she'd definitely been caught off-guard. "Can I pay for this, miss?"

"One more minute," she said quickly to the man, stepping back into the main section of the store to head to the cash register, where a woman waited. "Did you find everything, ma'am?"

"Just these frames."

"Great for vacation memories," Olivia said, using the line she trotted out every time someone bought a picture frame. Normally, she'd upsell some shells, but she stole another look in the direction of the history section, her unfinished response to his question still echoing in her head.

*No, I live in Seattle. I'm a senior buyer for a major department store chain. I'm the best at my job but some boneheaded new guy handed my promotion to a Harvard MBA and I took my toys and left the sandbox for the summer.*

Maybe *that* was the problem. Maybe it wasn't her

deep—or, in this case, shallow—dive to find flaws. Maybe *she* was the one who needed to change.

What if she didn't open with a résumé? What if, for once, she was Livvie the local shop girl and not Olivia the corporate spreadsheet slayer? Just to see how that played out with a guy who was, okay, bland. But not *offensive*. She had to start somewhere, and he'd be good practice. He was probably a tourist who'd be gone in a day or two. He sure didn't strike her as a local, who would already know all about the Teddy Roosevelt stuff.

As she walked back, she saw him slide his phone back in his pocket, making her guess he'd been taking more pictures, which George said lots of people did here.

"Sorry," she said.

"No problem. You were saying where you live," he reminded her.

"Locally," she said, purposefully vague. "How about you?"

"Chicago. How long have you worked here?"

Oh, Chicago. Good. Definitely a tourist. "Just a week."

"Oh." He seemed surprised. "You're so good at your job."

"You think?" She smiled at him, not sure where he got that, since she'd let him slip out twice without making a sale. "Well, I like it."

"What do you like about it?"

The question felt a tad more like a job interview than a dance for a date, but it was okay. The approach kind of reminded her of the men all over Seattle.

"What do I like?" She gave a shrug, not sure how to answer the direct question. "I guess the world can never have too many shell flower arrangements, right?"

He smiled at that, and she had a sense she might be breaking down a wall and maybe, behind it, he was more interesting. Maybe.

She couldn't wait to tell her mother that she'd actually given a guy a real chance today.

"What's your name?" he asked.

"Livvie," she said, purposely using the nickname as she extended her hand. "And you are?"

"Scott." He shook her hand, and she couldn't help noticing his palm and fingers were smooth. But then, the only man's hand she'd held recently—completely by accident—was callused from hauling kayaks from the water to the sand.

Deeley's hands were rough and big and masculine. Scott's were none of those things.

"How long are you visiting Sanibel?" she asked, not because she really cared, but because she suddenly wondered how long she'd have to keep up her new Shop Girl persona.

"Just a few weeks."

Weeks? "Extended vacation?"

"Actually, I'm...yeah. Sort of working remotely, and hanging out."

Okay, he was as vague as she was. A couple of alarm bells rang in her head. One sounded like "weird" and another was "married."

"Alone?" she asked, giving a glance over her shoulder

to make sure she hadn't missed the arrival of another customer.

"Yes, alone," he said. "You can go watch the shop. I'll come with you."

She smiled at the offer, which was thoughtful. A point in the woefully short "pro" column. "What brought you here alone?"

"I really needed a break from the rat race," he said as they crossed the store floor.

Oh, a rat race. That had potential, she thought with a secret smile. "What race do you run in, Scott?"

"Just investment stuff. Nothing as interesting as...seashells."

She looked at him, ready to find the glimmer of humor she so wanted to see, but, dang. He was serious. Or maybe that was deadpan done so well she missed it.

"What did you do before you worked here?" he asked, keeping that job interview banter alive.

"Just retail, mostly." Which wasn't a lie.

"Retail like this?"

She flipped both hands out with a shrug. "Is there anything quite like this?" she joked.

"No, this is definitely..." He tapped the shell wreath as they passed the display. "Unique."

Another joke? She couldn't tell.

"I notice how close it is to those little bungalows," he said. "Is this gift shop part of the same business? And that tea house place at the other end?" He pointed toward the beach where Teddy's little hut and luscious gardens were. "All one company?"

"It is," she told him.

"So, one owner? That's kind of an interesting conglomerate, right?"

"Oh, you have no idea," she said with a wry chuckle. As tempting as it was to add that the ownership of the place was currently under dispute by three women who had all been married to, or lived with, the same dead guy, she resisted.

He turned as another customer came in, this one with two really noisy kids. "I better let you get to work, Livvie."

"It's fine," she said, eyeing the new arrivals as one of the kids zoomed down an aisle. "Unless they break the merchandise."

The mom looked like she needed help at the conch bookends, so Olivia stepped away to talk to her. The explanation of what a conch was took a minute, then the customer wanted to look at Sanibel mugs and that was on the other side of the store.

When Olivia finally returned to the front desk, Scott was making a show of studying all the jewelry under the glass countertop. She'd had enough of the less-than-stimulating conversation and hoped it was time for him to leave or at least drop some cash.

"Interested in some shell earrings for your mom?"

He smiled, looking up. "Interested in you."

Or it was time for *that*. She felt her brows rise at the straightforward response.

"Well, Scott, I'm not for sale," she countered with a light laugh.

He looked genuinely disappointed. "I see. Already spoken for?"

The archaic phrase made her smile, and she didn't want to answer it with a lie by telling him she was. Yes, she'd been slightly massaging the truth this whole conversation by pretending to be Livvie the Shop Girl and not Olivia the World Beater, but she didn't want to flat-out lie and tell him she was spoken for.

No one was currently speaking for her. Just ask her mother.

"Not exactly," she said. "But I, uh, work a lot." Again, not a lie. An understatement, in fact.

"Then I know where to find you. Right here at Sanibel Treasures." He tipped his head. "Mind if I stop in tomorrow?"

It was quaint and cute and not as pushy as asking for her number. And she had to give somebody a real chance sometime. He was in investing, so that was the kind of guy she thought she wanted. And he wasn't obnoxious or full of himself, which was nice. So what if he was dull as tarnished silver. She could find some Brasso and make him shine, right?

*Right?*

"You're staring at me like I just proposed," he said, and that made her laugh.

"Yes, I'll be here," she promised. "You're always welcome."

"I'll be thinking about..." When his voice faded out, she actually felt herself hold her breath. "What to write on my message in a bottle."

"Oh, but you didn't buy one."

"I will. I needed an excuse to come back tomorrow."

"You don't need an excuse, Scott."

*There. Take that, Mommy Dearest. I can give a guy a chance.*

Just then, she noticed someone outside the shop, a tall man with a broad silhouette and golden hair and some distracting ink and...oh, crap. *Now, Deeley?*

"Do you get a lunch break, Livvie?" Scott asked.

If she did, she'd go down to the beach and hang with a former Navy SEAL who did really stupid things to her heart and gave her way too many goosebumps and always had the perfect comeback and laughed at her jokes and had big, rough hands and shoulders for *days*.

"Um, I don't take breaks, but things are slow mid-day," she said with a smile, hoping her cheeks didn't flush when Connor Deeley pulled the glass front door open, shaking back his sun-kissed hair so it brushed those stupid, stupid shoulders.

The bell dinged and Scott turned, then looked back at Olivia. "That sounds great, Livvie. See you tomorrow." With a smile that was still pretty bland, he turned and walked out, nodding silently at Deeley on his way out.

"Livvie?" Deeley asked as he came closer, a teasing light in his whiskey-gold eyes. "I thought that was only for people you liked."

She lifted her chin and met his gaze, refusing to let him know that way down in her sneakers, her toes were curling. "And customers eyeing almost-seventy-dollar wreaths. I really hope you're here to work on my shelves. My inventory overfloweth."

"Along with your conversations with customers." He threw a look in the direction of the door. "Customers who don't buy a thing, I notice, even after, what? An hour in this store?"

A billion chills blossomed all over her. "Were you watching?"

"I was eating my lunch on the bench outside when he walked in. I coulda had a six-course meal in the time he was in here."

Wait. Was he *jealous?*

"He was interested in the, um, inventory."

Deeley lifted a brow. "Which could also be known as casing the joint, my naïve friend."

"Casing the—" She choked softly. "You think he's going to rob Sanibel Treasures?"

He lifted one of those impossible shoulders.

"Deeley, he was..." *Had* Scott been in the store for some nefarious reason? And she'd been so distracted she didn't notice that he was just a little too interested in shell-covered wreaths? Not like her, a seasoned skeptic.

Nah. He just wanted to flirt with her. Deeley knew it and didn't like it. "He was shopping for his mother, if you must know. While he's here taking a break from his investment business."

"Investing in loot he gets from stores like this."

"Deeley!" She blinked at him, a little furious that he thought she was that dumb. Or that she *had* been that dumb. "He was asking me out, for crying out loud."

He grinned. "You think?"

She just stared at him, but he jutted his chin toward the back of the store. "I better fix the shelves. Unless you'd prefer Mr. Investor handles it when he comes to get you for your date."

"There's a loose floorboard back there so maybe you'll trip on it." She all but stuck her tongue out at him.

"So basically, you've missed me and need me. Am I getting this right?"

"Miss and need are big concepts, Connor." She frowned at him, hand on her hip, humming inside enough to just ask what she wanted to. "Where have you been, anyway?"

His smile vanished. "Just...doing stuff."

What kind of stuff? Where? With whom? She narrowed her eyes and swallowed the litany of questions about things that were really none of her business. "Well, go do *stuff* in the back of my store. Those shelves are wobbly, and I want to fill them with inventory."

"I might not have the tools for that today, but I'll look at them, I promise. You just stay out here and—" He winked. "Flirt with the customers."

"I was not—" She bit back the rest and gave his arm a jab, of course hitting a steel muscle. "Go."

She could hear his chuckle when he disappeared into the back, which just infuriated her and...made her wonder if maybe he was jealous. Or maybe she was just hoping he was.

*Oh, Connor Deeley. Why do you drive me nuts?*

# Chapter Six

## *Claire*

For a person who claimed that she "suffered" from loneliness, Claire Sutherland had long ago recognized that she also had a bone-deep need for solitude. That was different from being lonely, she knew. Solitude was for sanity, especially when she spent a little too much time with her mother.

They'd made the most of the rest of the afternoon after Eliza saved poor Teddy from a Camille Makeover, but then they'd parted for a pre-dinner break. Her mother liked to rest in the late afternoon, and Claire used that as an excuse to slip out of the cottage they were sharing and walk along the beach. The day had grown a bit cloudy, and Teddy had warned them that one of the frequent summer showers would be moving across the island, but that it would be gorgeous after that.

Claire didn't wait for "gorgeous" and she didn't worry about a little rain. After her mother settled in for a nap, Claire headed down the long wooden walkway to the beach, inhaling the salty, heavy, humid air.

There weren't many people around, just a few stragglers looking for shells or getting their feet wet in the surf. The sky, which she'd never seen as anything but blinding blue here, was gray with a bank of clouds moving in, the rain inside them practically visible.

She headed down the sand anyway, walking with purpose and a little speed to get some much-needed exercise, her face turned up to the clouds. The first fat drop of rain on her cheek didn't even slow her, but the downpour came shockingly fast, making her laugh at herself for ignoring Teddy's warning.

As the raindrops increased, she glanced left and right, considering if she should run back to the cottage, when her gaze landed on a sweet white gazebo perched on a sandy rise, tucked near a grouping of palm trees. Perfect.

Jogging toward it, she squinted as some rain blurred her vision and slid down her cheeks, but she wasn't entirely drenched when she reached the two steps that led up to the structure. Then she gasped out loud at the sight of a young woman sitting on the floor, curled into a ball.

When the woman looked up, Claire recognized her as the Shellseeker Cottages housekeeper, Katie, and was stunned to see she had more rivulets of moisture on her face than Claire did. But hers was not caused by the rain.

"Oh!" they both exclaimed in unison.

"I'm so sorry," Claire added, sensing she'd just stepped into a very private moment. "It started raining and—"

"It's fine," Katie said, waving her into the dry interior of the gazebo and giving her a sad smile. "I was just..."

"Getting some alone time. I understand," Claire said, glancing over her shoulder to gauge how soaked she'd be if she made a run for it to the cottage. "I don't want to intrude."

"No, please. Intrude. I..." Katie wiped her cheeks and gave a self-conscious laugh. "I don't own the gazebo. Teddy does. Or..." She smiled. "Somebody does. I guess we don't know who yet."

"Soon," Claire assured her as she took a step to get under the covering. "You know all that?"

"Teddy tells me everything. I'm not like the standard employee. Here." She tapped the bench behind her. "You can sit and not get too wet."

"Or..." Claire eased herself to the slatted wood floor next to Katie, where it was completely dry. "I can park myself right here and find out why you're crying. Want to talk?"

"Sure, I'll tell my tale of woe." Katie's mouth slid into a real smile, which made her youthful features even prettier. She couldn't be twenty-five, with glorious skin and pretty blue eyes. She had an air of, not sophistication, but a worldliness that didn't fit with a girl who cleaned cottages on the beach.

Not a girl, really, as she remembered what Eliza had said. A young, energetic single mother. "Tale of woe? I haven't heard that expression in a while."

"Well, I read a lot of old historical romances when my baby goes to bed."

"My favorite kind. But..." Claire frowned. "A baby? I thought Eliza said you had a four-year-old."

"She's right, but Harper's always going to be a baby to me. I guess all mothers think that, huh?"

An old pain pinched Claire's chest. "I guess," she said vaguely, only realizing now how very young Katie must have been when she had her baby. She had to have been a teenager.

The pain ratcheted up from a pinch to a punch.

"Teddy tells you everything, you say?" she asked, reaching for small talk in a somewhat awkward situation. "You must be close to her."

"She rescued me," Katie said simply. "I left my family, who did not approve of a single teen mom, and met Teddy and here I am."

Her heart shifted in her chest. "Oh, that's...amazing. Tell me about this four-year-old. Harper, did you say? A girl? All I know is that she recently went on a trip to the local wildlife refuge."

"And she's still talking about it," Katie said with a cute roll of her eyes. "She's kind of shy unless she's singing, which she loves to do. She also loves to color, wear sparkly shoes, and bake, but we're both famously bad at that."

Claire closed her eyes for a second, blocking out the drumbeat of the rain on the roof to imagine a shy, singing child in pink shoes and an apron. "Oh, she's the one who likes to sing show tunes!" she exclaimed. "Eliza told me about that, too."

"Just *State Fair* until Aunt Eliza came along and introduced her to the rest of Broadway."

"Aunt Eliza?" Claire frowned. "She's Harper's aunt?"

"Oh, no. Not technically. No more than 'Aunt

Teddy' is," Katie said. "It's just a term of endearment for the people who love her."

"It's sweet," Claire said, wondering if she could qualify for that term. She liked it. "Is everything okay with her? You're not crying because you have a problem with Harper, are you?"

She shook her head. "She's great. It's just..." She swallowed. "You know, life."

"Kind of vague," Claire said on a soft chuckle. "Is work getting you down? Family problems? Money? Health? Or...I honestly can't think of anything too awful when you're as young and pretty as you are."

Her face crumbled a little bit. "Am I?" she asked on the softest sob.

Is that what this was? A crisis of confidence? "Um, got a mirror handy?"

"I don't feel young or pretty. I feel like my twenties are slipping away and I can never get them back and I shouldn't care because I have Harper and that was my decision that I made at great personal cost but it's Saturday night and I just realized I don't have that many Saturday nights as a twenty-something left and..." She finally ran out of air and words with a noisy sob. "I guess I have PMS or something."

"Oh, honey!" Claire wrapped her arms around the younger woman and squeezed. "You *are* having a moment out here in the rain."

She sniffed. "The gazebo is good for moments. Teddy says there's magic out here because this was built on an old Indian shell mound and there's always honesty out here."

"Honesty?" She glanced around at the quaint, open structure decorated with corbels and laced white wood.

"Truth-telling," Katie explained. "Teddy found a hundred arrowheads around here when she was little, so her father built this gazebo. Her mother said a Calusa king liked to stand on the mound and..." She smiled, shaking her head. "It's a bunch of folklore, but it does seem that anytime I'm in here, the truth comes out." She swiped under sad blue eyes. "Or tears."

Everything in her wanted to just hug the kid and tell her not to cry, but she resisted the urge, rooting around for the right words to say. "It can't be easy being a single mom. I bet people tried to talk you out of it."

She nodded vehemently. "Like nobody's business. In fact, I don't even talk to my family, and they've never met Harper."

Claire grunted at the thought, not surprised as emotion welled up inside her. "I think that's an incredible journey that only a very strong woman could make."

"That's what Teddy says." She sniffed again. "And usually I believe her, but..."

"You should talk to her more, then."

"I can't right now," Katie said. "She's up to her eyeballs in personal stuff. What's going to happen to the resort, what will become of her if that Birdie person gets it. And now you and your mother are here, which is a reminder that she didn't really know Dutch as much as she thought she did." She huffed out a breath, surprising

Claire by how nuanced her understanding of the situation really was. "And I'm just vomiting words to a complete stranger. I'm sorry."

"Do not apologize," Claire said, keeping a comforting hand on Katie's back. "This is a big issue that affects a lot of lives."

"You have no idea." Katie's whole body seemed to shrink with the words. "I don't know where I'll go or what I'll do. I mean, I have an apartment and could stay on Sanibel, but without Teddy? She's all Harper and I have now. She's really like our family. And I'd never find a job like this where half the time I can bring my child to work and she just wanders around singing and being adorable. I can't lose this job!"

Claire stroked her back. "You won't." She hoped. "And you're very good at that job, you know. I can tell you make every one of these cottages like a home for guests, and to think you do it with a little girl in tow? That's remarkable."

Katie looked like she didn't think anything she did was so remarkable.

"But you're feeling a little trapped?" Claire guessed, easily stepping into this girl's shoes and imagining her thoughts.

"I guess that's the word. But 'trapped' sounds so negative."

"These aren't positive tears, Katie."

"I'm just...panicked. Not like anxiety panic that I can't breathe, but sometimes I look at the years ahead and they aren't what these years should be. I'll be twenty-five this year. And I don't do anything but work and be a mom."

"I'm sure there's no shortage of sitters around here."

"Please." She rolled her eyes again. "Teddy begs me to go out and I do, once in a while. I'm in a book club and I sometimes shop with my girlfriend, but she really wants to go, you know, clubbing. I can't do that with a four-year-old at home."

"Do you want to?"

She shrugged. "I don't know. Why? To meet a guy? Who wants a girl my age with a kid?"

"I think you might be surprised."

She made a face. "I don't want to blame Harper, because I love her to death, but I honestly don't think a single mom is what most guys want."

"Maybe not, but..." She took a deep breath, knowing she had some powerful words of wisdom for Katie, but they'd be hard to say. "Some people might think you're very lucky to have a child because you will always have a family and a friend."

"Not when she grows up, and I'll be a hundred by then."

Claire chuckled at the exaggeration, which probably felt quite true at twenty-four. "You'll be about my age and..." Her throat tightened. "I'd love to have a grown child right now."

Katie looked at her. "Your life would be different."

"Very much so," Claire agreed. "I might not have gone to law school. I wouldn't have worked my rear end off as a junior associate or billed astronomical hours in my thirties. But I'd have a...a..." She couldn't even finish. Still. After all these years. "And I would love that."

"I guess..." Katie searched her face as if she sensed there was more to this than a pep talk.

"No guessing," Claire insisted. "I'd have a child, a friend, and a forever family. Someone who will care for me when I'm old, who'd share their dreams and worries with me."

She had to close her eyes to fight utterly unexpected emotion that left her weak and raw, and then tried to cover it with a self-conscious laugh. "Not sure why I confessed all that."

"Told you," Katie said on a smile. "It's the gazebo. Teddy Blessing's Honesty House."

Claire managed a smile. "There must be something to that, huh?"

Katie looked at her for a long time, her tears gone like the rain outside the gazebo. "You're Eliza's sister," she said. "You know what that means?"

"That I'm very lucky?"

"Yes, and that Harper will call you Aunt Claire. Is that okay?"

"Oh, my, yes," she said with a sigh. "I would love that."

Katie leaned forward, looking so much stronger and happier than when Claire arrived. "And speaking of, I'm late to get her. On Saturday afternoons, she takes a little art class at the museum and I only work a half day."

"I bet she brings you a beautiful picture."

"Yep, she will. And we practice baking on Saturday

nights, and I promised we'd tackle our first pie tonight. I guarantee you, it's going to be a mess." She tilted her head and smiled. "Some wild Saturday night, huh?"

"Sounds kind of dreamy to me. I love to bake."

"Really? Maybe you can teach us. We're atrocious, but everyone is too nice to say so."

Claire laughed. "I'd love to. I promised Eliza and Teddy dinner with them tonight, but I'm here for a bit longer, so let's make a plan for me to bake with you and Harper."

"We'd love that." She started to stand, then froze, leaned in, and gave Claire an unexpected hug. "Thanks. I appreciate your, well, honesty."

Claire hugged her back, smiling when Katie stood, blew a kiss and headed out with a light step and a swing of her long blond ponytail.

But Claire didn't follow. Even though the rain had stopped, she stayed right there on the gazebo floor, eyes closed, her heart drifting back many, many years, twisting with an old pain that never really disappeared.

# Chapter Seven

## Teddy

Sunday dawned in shades of peach and teal as Teddy finished her morning meditation on the deck, opening her eyes to greet the endless horizon of Shellseeker Beach. It was a little cooler than yesterday, so she knew exactly how she wanted to spend her morning. In the garden, where she could think and grow and prune and meditate.

A few minutes later, her curls clipped up and sunscreen slathered on, she practically danced down the wooden steps to answer the siren call of the earth she loved so much.

She opened the tea hut and went into the tiny back kitchen to brew some hibiscus tea that she'd no doubt give away to a few early beach stragglers who wandered by. That was fine; she didn't run Shellseeker Tea Garden for profit. She ran it because her mother, known all over Sanibel Island as "Miss Delia," had done the same thing —grown the plants that made the tea, then gave the stuff away.

That business model might not be smart, but it hadn't hurt anyone.

Except in the 1970s, when her parents ran out of

money and sold the whole property so they could survive, and then managed it for the next fifty years.

"Oh, Mama," she whispered after she'd put out plastic glasses and three insulated pitchers on the counter where people were supposed to order and pay. "Maybe if you hadn't set that standard, this property would never have left the Blessing family."

No, she couldn't blame that wholesale change on some free tea.

She went to the back and gathered her gardening tools, then carried the basket to the slightly overgrown herb garden. She settled on her knee pads to work on the lavender and basil, the bright, sweet scents of both filling her nose. The oregano needed some work, as well as the thyme and sage, so before she knew it, she'd filled another basket with clippings and worked up a gloss of perspiration, even though it wasn't even eight in the morning.

While she gardened, she sifted through the conversations she'd had at dinner with Claire and Camille and Eliza last night, turning their words over the same way she worked the soft earth around her plants. Just as she coaxed the nutrients out of the dark soil, she coaxed good thoughts from her memories of the night before.

But with each flip of her trowel, she realized more and more that something was bothering her, deeply. She had to figure out why—

"I thought I might find you out here."

She turned at Eliza's voice, sitting up and smiling from the heart at the sight of her. "Good morning, beautiful!" she called, waving her closer. "Do you want some iced tea?"

"I'll grab a glass." Eliza perched on a stone bench tucked against a queen palm, leaning into the trunk. "I feel like a slacker, just getting up at nine-thirty. Olivia's been at Sanibel Treasures for two hours already and you're out here growing tea leaves."

"The shop isn't open on Sundays," Teddy said, frowning. "I know she's a go-getter and wants to make a profit, but it's a Shellseeker Beach tradition that Sanibel Treasures stays closed on Sundays. Old school, but we can't lose all the traditions around here."

"Oh, she knows, and it's not open. She wanted to use the quiet time in the store to move some inventory and clear out some of the...I think she called them SKUs that don't move." Eliza lifted her brows. "You think Roz will be upset when she gets back?"

"Not when she sees the bottom line," Teddy assured her. "Roz is practical, and she wants Sanibel Treasures to be profitable as much as if she owned, not managed, the place. She's just been flying by the seat of her pants, with none of the retail experience Olivia brings. Roz will be thrilled."

"Good, because Livvie is having a blast. She seems happy, don't you think?"

Teddy leaned back on her heels, pressing her thumb into a tight muscle in her lower back as she regarded Eliza. "You do, too, you know."

"Oh, I know."

"All you do is laugh and gab with Claire."

"We have a lot to laugh and gab about. But everyone laughed last night at the restaurant. It was such fun. I just loved it." She searched Teddy's face, her eyes narrowing. "Didn't you?"

"Oh, I had a marvelous time. I even drank some of that champagne, though not as much as Camille. She must have had three, no four, glasses."

"But who's counting?" Eliza teased.

"I was, because I hoped it would take down some of her French walls and I could finally get a read on her."

"Any luck?"

She shook her head. "From the first time I met her, I tried to feel what was bubbling under the surface. It doesn't usually take me this long to discover fears and motivations and hopes and frustrations."

Eliza let her head fall back against the tree trunk. "You know, when you first shared this unique skill of yours, I thought it was so cool. But I can only imagine that sometimes it's a drain on you."

"It is," Teddy agreed. "But only when I'm getting nothing."

"Does that happen very often?"

"Rarely. Almost never." She swallowed and lowered her trowel to the ground to make her confession. "It happened with Dutch."

Eliza lifted her head and opened her eyes. "Really? For how long?"

"In the beginning, it was really bad," she admitted. "I never knew what he was feeling or thinking. His health? Yes. I could feel when he was waning. I actually knew all night before he died in the morning. I knew it was imminent. But his deepest emotions?" She gave a wry, bittersweet laugh. "No clue. Obviously, since he had two wives, a daughter I didn't know about, and God knows how many other secrets. You know, I've done nothing but question my empathy skills since it all came to light."

"You don't have to question anything, Teddy."

"Oh, but I do. Especially with Camille. I have to know what's ticking in her heart, because what if she's planning to back out of this deal?" Teddy gave a shiver despite the ever-increasing heat.

"Look, Teddy, I know you're good at what you do, but do you really think you'd know that by...by touching her? You can't be so hard on yourself. No one knows what she's thinking, not even her half the time. Claire says the one thing you can predict with Camille is that you can't predict anything."

Teddy made a face, not liking that. "Still, I should feel something, like trepidation or fear, love or trust, or maybe something darker, like anger or resentment or even guilt. Definitely guilt. With that woman? Zilch."

"You can really feel things like that?" Eliza shook her head. "I do not get that."

"I don't expect you to, and it isn't like a screaming voice that only I hear. It's more like an energy, a color, a vibe, if you will."

Eliza smiled at her. "God, you are strange and magnificent and unlike any human I've ever met."

That made Teddy sigh as she leaned over and

returned to her work on the soil. "Nobody doesn't have a color," she murmured. "I just need to figure her out."

"Why don't you bring her over here and teach her to garden?"

Teddy looked up, frowning. "You think?"

"It's therapeutic and this is where you and I got to know each other. There's something about the dirt that gets people to talk. Kind of like your magic gazebo."

Teddy smiled. "I guess I could try that, but I can't imagine anyone who dresses like she does and takes such great pains to have perfect nails would want to dig in the dirt." Then she squinted past Eliza at the sight of Olivia striding toward them, holding a paper cup she must have snagged from the tea hut. "There's Olivia."

Eliza turned. "Oh, she quit awfully early. She said she wanted to work deep into the afternoon."

"Hello!" Olivia called as she got closer. "I thought I'd find you here."

"Hey, Liv." Eliza waved her to the bench, then gave her a kiss on the cheek when she sat. "Morning."

"Am I missing the post-mortem?" Olivia asked in a stage whisper. "Are we mulling over everything they said last night, trying to decide if Camille is real or not?"

Teddy gave up on the herbs, settling on her backside because her knees were starting to hurt and chatting with Eliza and Olivia was so much more fun than gardening.

"You quit early," Eliza said, putting a hand on Olivia's leg. "I hope that means you just want to relax today, maybe go to the beach."

"I left because"—she set the drink down—"I needed an excuse to leave."

Teddy frowned, picking up a strange tone in her voice. "Why?"

"I had company," she said,. "and he wanted to hang out and help me and I didn't want him to."

"Deeley?" Eliza asked with just a little too much hope in her voice. Well, too much for Olivia, based on the look she gave her mother.

"Not Deeley. You remember that guy that came into the store when you were there? I told you he'd been there before."

"Oh, yes. He was kind of good-looking."

"Kind of," Olivia agreed with about zero enthusiasm.

Teddy laughed softly. "Why did you have to run away from him, Olivia?"

"Because he was, I don't know." She groaned a little. "He's nice, I guess. Not the greatest sense of humor. And by that, I mean none."

"Then he's not the one," Teddy said.

"Because Olivia won't give him a chance."

She elbowed her mother. "I have tried so hard. This is the, what? Third or fourth time he's come in. Yesterday we had a long talk while you all were sightseeing and getting makeovers. And then he came back at nine this morning!"

"Didn't he see the 'closed on Sundays' sign on the door?" Eliza asked.

"Right? I don't know. He almost acted like he didn't expect me to be there, but was so happy I was. We talked some more. He does investment stuff—not sure exactly what—and is down here alone, working remotely, and clearing his head. I'd question that, except I'm basically doing the same thing. He's definitely interested in me."

"Did he ask you on a date?" Teddy asked.

She nodded, then curled her lip. "He asked me to go out tonight and I...said yes."

"Really?" Eliza blinked at her. "That's great."

"Is it? Didn't you say you were taking Claire out on Miles's boat for a sunset cruise?"

"You are?" Teddy asked, sitting straighter. "When did you decide to go out on Miles's boat, Eliza?"

"When you were deep in conversation with Camille last night," Eliza said. "He texted, knowing Camille and Claire are here, and invited everyone. But to be honest?" She lifted her brows and leaned in to whisper, "Claire told me that Camille gets seasick, so she won't go, and I think she was kind of glad for the time away from her mother. Will you go, Teddy? I know sometimes you feel seasick, but it's calm today and Miles won't go too fast."

"I might, but I don't want to ditch Camille. Let me see if I can talk her into going."

"And you can bring your new friend on the boat," Eliza said to Olivia. "I'm sure Miles wouldn't mind."

Olivia thought about that for a nanosecond, then shook her head. "No. Not a chance. I agreed to a drink and if it's awful, I'll need an escape."

"What's his name?" Teddy asked.

"Scott. Scott, the investment guy from Chicago with

a slightly receding hairline and mediocre shoulders and a nice smile."

"You're giving him a chance," Teddy said. "And that's a step in the right direction."

Eliza choked out a laugh. "Mediocre shoulders? Doesn't sound like a chance to me."

Olivia shrugged. "I'm too judgey, I know. Where are Camille and Claire?"

"Claire said she was going to do a call with the Miami attorney from her law firm who'll be at the hearing," Eliza said. "Camille might still be getting her beauty sleep."

"I'm going to invite her to come and garden with me," Teddy said, making the sudden decision. "In fact, I'll go down to Junonia right now and take her some muffins and tea and give her a pair of brand-new gardening gloves."

"Do you want me to come with you?" Eliza asked.

Teddy considered that, then shook her head. "If Olivia can step out of her comfort zone and go on a date with a boring, balding investment guy, then I can face my demons with Camille. Off I go!"

"Are you sure?" Eliza asked, true concern in her eyes. "Because I can go with you."

"Nope. But if I crash and burn, as Dutch used to say, I know you have my six." With that, she gave a wave over her shoulder and headed off.

CAMILLE HAD ACCEPTED the gardening invitation to be polite, Teddy could tell. She donned a pair of khaki pants that were a little dressy for a day in the dirt, accepted the gloves with a gracious smile, and went through the motions of learning about herbs, flowers, and tea.

At least she did for the first half hour.

But as the sun got higher and they sought shade, moving to another section of the herb garden, Camille started to get into the process of pruning and picking. She'd never be a gardener, Teddy thought, but she took the time to smell the various scents, and seemed fascinated to hear that Teddy's mother believed that everything grew so wonderfully because they were on ancient Calusa land.

The day took on a relaxed vibe, enough that Teddy took a sip of tea, leaned back on her heels, and studied Camille openly. She had yet to break a sweat and, somehow, her jet-black hair stayed in its perfectly smooth style, sleek and attractive.

"I can't imagine what it would be like to spend your entire life as beautiful as you are," Teddy confessed.

Camille barked a laugh. "It's more work than this garden, trust me."

"How so?"

"No one is beautiful naturally, not at our age. And the older I get, the more work it is."

"Then why do you do it?"

"Why do you work so hard in this garden?" Camille countered.

"Because it's what matters to me, this earth and these

plants. They are...my soul. One of the main reasons I get up every day and sleep well at night."

Camille lifted a shoulder. "Well, then you understand."

No, she didn't. "You feel that way about your looks?" Teddy was sorry her voice rose in mild disbelief, but it did seem a little preposterous once a woman hit and passed seventy.

"I like being beautiful," Camille said. "It has defined me my whole life. It got me the best job in the world, and..." She chuckled. "Okay, I guess he wasn't the best husband, but it certainly was my looks that attracted him and kept Dutch coming back."

Teddy stared at her, digging around in her brain for a better explanation. There had to be more. "But beauty is so fleeting."

On a soft chuckle, Camille fluttered the browned edges of a sage plant. "So is everything in this garden. Nothing will last and you'll plant and prune more. Everything is fleeting, my friend. But we fight it, don't we?"

"I guess." Still, placing that much emphasis on looks was a new one to Teddy. She picked up her pruning shears and returned to the overgrown oregano, not even sure what to say next.

Was that why she couldn't get a read on Camille? Because she was so shallow there was nothing to read? It was possible, she supposed.

"I know what you're thinking," Camille mused.

Teddy hoped not. "Tell me."

"You think I'm flighty."

Hmm. Maybe she did know what Teddy was thinking. "Not exactly, but I do firmly believe that no one can live an entire life and have their looks be the most important thing in the world."

"I didn't say they were the most important thing," she countered. "Claire is, of course."

"And what else?"

"I have friends and I still travel a lot, since I will fly for free for the rest of my life. I've been to every continent, most countries, and speak multiple languages with flawless accents. All of those things matter to me, as does my extensive wardrobe and, yes..." She patted her cheek. "My pretty face."

Teddy chuckled at that, but her smile waned when she realized Camille was utterly serious. "Well, you're very self-aware, then, Camille. I think that's what they call it nowadays."

"Oh, Teddy. You're so grounded." She scooped up some of the soil as if to underscore that point. "You're connected to this very earth. And me? I'm connected to the air." She waved her hand. "That's why I was a flight attendant, or"—she winked—"a stewardess, as I like to say. It sounds so much more attractive, don't you think?"

"I suppose." She stared at the other woman, processing all this information and reaching a new conclusion. "This is why the property doesn't matter to you? You really don't care about it? Or the money it could represent?"

"I don't need more money than I have, and I have plenty," she said, eyeing Teddy. "I wouldn't mind a purpose in life, something I could really dig my teeth into, but..." Her voice trailed off and so did her attention as she stared out at the horizon. Then she swallowed and whispered, "I don't have any idea what that could be."

For the first time, she felt a glimmer of something. Of pain or desire or something pulling at Camille. And, Teddy, being Teddy, wanted to help coax it out, then heal it.

"You could be a personal shopper," Teddy said.

Camille lifted a brow and gave her a "get real" look. "You hated the red pants."

"With the heat of a thousand suns," she agreed, making them both laugh. "But you really have an eye for fashion, so..."

"Maybe." After a moment, Camille put down her pruning shears and slipped off her gloves, checking her nails as if she might have broken one. Then she pushed up to a stand.

"I'm terribly warm," she said. "I think I'll go rest. And please don't take it personally, but I won't be joining you for dinner tonight, or going on that boat. Claire's going to bring me some dinner. Thank you for the gardening lesson, Teddy. I enjoyed it."

With a quick smile, she headed back down the path toward her cottage, and disappeared behind a large oleander hedge.

Teddy just stayed stone still, staring after her, wondering if she could ever unpack the enigma that was Camille Durant. Or if she even wanted to.

# Chapter Eight

## Eliza

With Camille begging off and Olivia meeting her new man for a drink, the outing on Miles Anderson's sport-fishing boat turned out to be a smaller party than expected. Just Claire, Teddy, and Eliza made the drive to the residential section of Sanibel, and on the way, they shared what they knew about their host.

"How many times have you been on Miles's boat?" Claire asked from the backseat where she and Eliza could see each other through the rearview mirror.

"Several times in the last month," Eliza told her. "He loves to go out at this time of day for the sunset and sometimes fishing, though we probably won't do that tonight. But the boat is very comfortable, at least thirty feet, and he always has food and wine. You'll like Miles." Then Eliza laughed. "And Tinkerbell, the dog who loves me."

Few things made Eliza as happy as Miles's totally lovable Frenchie-Boston terrier mix. And Eliza, it was clear, made Tink happy, too.

"And Miles is the investigator who found Birdie, right?" Claire asked.

"He tracked her down, and I still don't know how,"

Eliza said. "Nobody can track a person down like Miles, and he's a former military lawyer."

"Ah, JAG." Claire nodded. "Some of the best attorneys out there." She frowned and leaned forward, thinking. "So, he's a good investigator, huh?"

"Fantastic," Teddy chimed in.

"What's his technique for finding people?" Claire pressed.

"I don't know, but you can ask him tonight," Teddy said. "That is, if he's not utterly consumed with Eliza."

"Teddy, please." Eliza threw her a look, closed her eyes, and shook her head.

"Ohh?" Claire sang the word with a playful voice. "Is there a budding romance I don't know about?"

"I'm six months widowed," Eliza said, pointing at Teddy. "But this one sees things that aren't there." And was usually right, Eliza thought, but didn't add that. "Miles is a friend, and that's all. I'm making lots of them on Sanibel."

"I made a new friend yesterday," Claire said. "I had a long chat with Katie."

"Really?" Teddy looked surprised and pleased. "She's a sweetheart, isn't she?"

"Very much. But she's struggling being a young mother."

Teddy exhaled noisily. "I wish she could have a more normal life for a girl her age, but she puts Harper above all else."

"I admire that," Claire said. "It shows a real level of commitment."

Teddy shared Katie's story, telling Claire how the young girl had left a wealthy family who wanted her to give up the baby, and the next time Eliza looked at Claire's reflection, she almost sucked in a surprised breath.

Claire looked...lost. No, that wasn't the word. *Affected.* Her dark eyes were pained and her brow was furrowed. For a second, it looked like she'd cry.

"You okay?" Eliza asked softly.

"Oh, yes, just..." She fluttered her hand in her face. "Backseat, you know."

"You sure you can handle a boat?" Teddy asked, turning to look at Claire with a concerned expression.

"Absolutely," she promised.

"Well, we're almost there," Eliza said, studying her sister again.

Claire seemed normal when they pulled into Miles's driveway and Tinkerbell came bounding out the front door to Eliza. They shared a moment and made introductions and Miles took them through his ranch house to the dock in the back, where his pride and joy, *Miles Away,* floated in all its glory.

"Eliza called this a fishing boat," Claire said. "It's like a yacht."

"Not even close," Miles replied, standing on the dock to offer his hand to each woman to help them board the boat. "Big enough to take us out for a beautiful cocktail-hour sunset, so welcome aboard."

When he gave his hand to Eliza, Miles added a squeeze and a smile, which almost startled her when she felt it. That was strange, because he'd helped her board this boat a few times before.

Teddy's words echoed in her head.

*That is, if he's not utterly consumed with Eliza.*

If anyone else had made jokes about Miles being attracted to her, she'd have given it no credence. But Teddy knew people, the way few others did. And when she said something, Eliza listened.

They were friends, and even had the occasional lunch together. He knew she was a grieving widow, and surely he didn't think she'd be interested in dating yet. It could be years, if ever.

If she ever were interested, Miles Anderson wouldn't be a bad choice.

He was a good-looking man in his mid- to late fifties, with thick, mostly silver hair, a bit of a goatee, which she didn't usually like but fit him so well, and kind eyes that were green with flecks of brown but always warm. He was in great shape from climbing around that boat, and drank coffee like it must run in his veins.

She knew he was divorced, though he'd never shared any details about that. She also knew he had a daughter in her thirties, Janie, who he obviously adored, and a son, Henry, who was in the military, like Miles had been.

He made anyone and everyone on his boat feel comfortable, and tonight was no different as he opened wine and served appetizers on a table in the bow seating area.

"I almost had Deeley joining us tonight," he said, "but he backed out at the last minute."

"He probably found out Olivia wasn't coming," Teddy said, giving her brows a meaningful flick.

Miles laughed. "So I'm not the only one who picked up on that not-so-subtle chemistry?"

"I keep hearing about this Deeley," Claire said, "but have yet to meet him." She turned to Eliza. "Didn't you say Olivia had a date tonight?"

"She does?" Miles looked surprised. "Well, no wonder Deeley sounded downright surly when he called to tell me he wasn't coming. He really likes her."

"Pretty sure it goes both ways," Eliza said, "but she's nothing if not finicky, stubborn, and determined to find what she thinks is perfection."

"Deeley's pretty perfect," Miles said on a laugh. "And he's a good man. Don't let the long hair and tats fool you."

"They don't fool me," Teddy said. "I think Deeley is a catch."

"He may be, but my daughter makes up her own mind and goes at her own speed." Eliza rubbed Tinker-bell's head, which was, of course, planted firmly on her lap.

"Speaking of speed." Miles stood. "I'm going to keep it slow tonight, because I know you prefer that, Teddy."

"Thank you, Miles." She beamed at him. "I'll let you know if it's too much, but, please, let Claire get the full Sanibel experience."

The women chatted while the boat got underway through the canal and out into the open blue water of the Gulf. They talked less when Miles kicked the engines into a slightly higher speed, making the wind whip their hair and creating a gorgeous white wake behind them. The occasional misty spray blew over them as they held their glasses and drank in the beauty of a summer night on the water.

Once he found a spot he liked, Miles gave Eliza a questioning look. "Look good here?" he asked.

"This is perfect. Want me to get the anchor?" She pushed up toward the anchor locker, but he turned off the engines and came around to help her, their hands brushing as they both reached for the rope.

*Oh, dear.* Was that a chill that just danced up her spine?

Eliza inched back to let him take the lead, sucking in a breath to center herself. Instantly, Tinkerbell came to her, and she used the dog as an excuse to cover her unexpected reaction.

She forced herself to concentrate on the conversation, and the questions Claire was peppering Miles with about his business. How did he go about finding people? What were his specialties?

But Eliza had her own questions, like...could Teddy be right about him?

Worse, could she be feeling...something? No. Impossible. Too soon.

She tamped down the voice in her head with a deep drink of chardonnay and another head scratch for Tinkerbell, who looked at her with unabashed adoration. She was mixing up the man and his dog, she told herself.

"That's so interesting, don't you think, Eliza?" Claire asked.

Oh, boy. She'd missed the whole conversation. "He's very good at his job," she said smoothly.

"No, I mean what he said about Birdie. When he met her."

Damn. She was as bad as Olivia was with Deeley. What had he—

"I, for one, have had enough Birdie talk," Teddy interjected, leaning in with a save. That might have been by chance, or because she could feel Eliza's moment of discomfort. Either way, Eliza was grateful to have the conversation steered to other things.

But before long, it was back on Birdie anyway, or at least the upcoming hearing as they chatted about what would happen.

"Well, you're in Lee County probate," Miles said, "so at least you have a great judge in Jonathan Macgregor."

"Oh, do you know him?" Claire asked.

"Quite well," Miles said. "He's balanced, smart, and knows the law inside and out. Is there an arbitration clause in either will?"

While they chatted about the legal details, Eliza let her gaze shift to Miles again, the memory of that instant of their connection playing at the edges of her mind. He was a good-looking man, no doubt, but there was something else about him that appealed to her. He seemed grounded and good-hearted and—*Holy heck, she had to stop.*

She looked for her wine glass and, in the process, caught Teddy's gaze directly on her. And that knowing look in her blue eyes almost made Eliza laugh. Almost. She would have, if this were funny, which it wasn't.

"There's no codicil," Claire was saying. "And Dutch's will clearly states that it is the legal and binding will and no others can present a challenge."

"So this is open and shut, right?" Teddy asked him. "Doesn't it sound that way to you, I mean, as a former JAG attorney?"

"Most likely," he agreed. "Unless Birdie's attorney is going to claim that the will Camille has was written under duress or he signed it under undue influence. Then he's going to want to bring in witnesses."

"I hope not," Claire said quietly. "I really don't want to put my mother through the agony of facing Birdie Vanderveen in person. And our attorney in Miami doesn't think she'll be present this week, just her counsel."

"I don't know," Miles said. "But I can recommend you relax and enjoy that sunset." He smiled at Eliza. "I think the legalese is boring one of my guests."

"Not at all," Eliza said quickly. "I'm enjoying the view."

They all turned and took it in, snapping a few pictures, and letting the conversation lighten up again.

By the time they'd packed up and Miles got them underway to head back home, she'd almost forgotten about the "electricity moment," as she thought of it.

Almost.

It was dark when Claire finally got up to leave Teddy's house, where the three of them had been chatting after returning from the boat ride.

"I'll walk out with you," Eliza said. "I want to peek at Olivia's cottage to see if she's home from her date yet."

"Has she texted for a save?" Teddy asked with a laugh. "I'm sure you two have some kind of secret code so you will know to call her and she can escape."

"Actually, we don't, but she hasn't texted to say she's bored to death, either. Let's go look, Claire."

Claire gave Teddy a hug goodnight and she and Eliza walked out into the warm, humid air, both of them looking up at a yellow three-quarters moon.

"Oh, I don't think I could ever get used to the beauty of this place," Claire said, inhaling deeply.

"I know. Doesn't Sanibel just smell like heaven?"

"It does. Come on," she said, putting a hand on Eliza's arm. "Let's go spy on Livvie."

Eliza laughed as they trotted down the wooden stairs and headed to the smallest, closest of the cottages, called Sunray Venus, where Olivia was staying.

"Looks dark," Claire said.

"Maybe she's having the time of her life," Eliza mused, somehow sensing that wasn't true, but she hoped.

"Maybe she's not coming home tonight."

"Ooh. Really?" Eliza laughed. "Not sure how I feel about that. She may be twenty-nine, but she's still my baby. First date? Not like my Livvie."

"You think you know them, but..." Claire teased, elbowing Eliza as they walked.

"Yeah, yeah, yeah. You don't understand, Claire. It's..." Her voice trailed off and she instantly regretted her words. Claire had confessed her loneliness and Eliza should have been more sympathetic, not saying things like, "You don't understand," just because Claire didn't have kids.

"It's fine," Claire said, locking her arm through Eliza's. "You didn't hurt my feelings."

"Oh, I know. I just don't want to make you feel like we can't relate on every level, so I shouldn't—"

"I do."

Eliza slowed her steps, shaking her head a little, because she didn't get what Claire was saying. "You do relate on every level?"

Claire stopped walking in the darkest section of the path, between any lights from the cottages and where a thick live oak blocked the moon. But even in the dim light, Eliza could see that same expression of sadness and loss she'd noticed in the car.

"Eliza," she whispered. "Total honesty, right? And total secrecy."

"Of course." She got closer, sensing the moment was important. "What do you mean, you do? You do what?"

"I do have a child."

"What?" she breathed the word, rubbing a million goosebumps on her arms. "Really?"

"A boy. He's twenty-six and I..." Her eyes filled. "I gave him up for adoption."

"Oh, that's—"

"I want to find him." Her voice cracked. "Do you think I can ask Miles for help?"

Eliza nearly swayed as this news nearly knocked her over. "Claire. You have a son? A twenty-six-year-old son? Then you were—"

"Nineteen," she said, her eyes filling. "Exactly Katie's age when she had her little girl. And after I talked to her, I just couldn't stop thinking about him, and then I met Miles and finding adopted kids is what he does..." She reached for Eliza. "I have to find him," she said on a ragged whisper. "At least, I have to try."

Eliza put her hands over her mouth, letting it sink in. "A boy? Do you know his name? Where he is? Anything at all?"

"Nothing. It was a closed adoption. I last saw him on the day he was born, in a New York City hospital."

"Wait. You said secrecy. Does Camille—"

She shook her head vehemently. "She has no idea. I've never told her."

"And the father?"

She didn't answer, but something in her eyes told Eliza everything.

"Let me guess—an architect in California?"

Claire whimpered and slid Eliza into a loving hug. "My sister knows me already."

As they hugged, Eliza let a thousand emotions roll over her, like gratitude and joy and concern and hope. "Why didn't you tell your mother? She doesn't strike me as someone who'd be that upset."

"I was afraid of what she'd ask me to do."

Eliza wasn't a hundred percent sure what that meant, but she let Claire continue.

"At that time, she was traveling constantly, and I was in college in New York. We rarely saw each other. I hid it for five months, then didn't see her for four, went through with the adoption and..."

"Oh, Claire." She hugged her again, humming with this news. "That couldn't have been easy. Did you ever consider keeping him?"

She shook her head. "I had plans to study law, and I just wanted to be sure I did right by the baby. I never told the father because he...he had big dreams, which I assume he's fulfilled by now. Talk about ambitious! He was four years older, and planning to be the next Frank Lloyd Wright. The last thing DJ needed or wanted as he entered graduate school was a child or, to be perfectly honest, me. I was going to tell him, but he broke up with me before I could. I admit to some deep guilt and grief for not ever telling him, but what's done is done." Her voice cracked. "But maybe...if I find my son...I wouldn't feel so bad."

"Or lonely," Eliza said softly, getting another solid hug from her sister.

When they broke the embrace, Eliza took both of Olivia's hands. "You have my word of honor on our sisterhood that I won't tell a soul. Not Teddy, not Olivia, not anyone. But Miles? Yes, he can help you. I know he'll try."

"What'll I do if he finds him?"

"I guess we'll figure it out when he does."

Claire smiled. "We? When? Those are some supportive and optimistic words."

"Because I am both supportive and optimistic," Eliza assured her.

Claire sighed. "I don't even know his name, and the records were sealed; although a few years ago, there was a change in New York State's adoption records laws and I could find out his name. I just haven't yet."

"Oof," Eliza grunted. "That has to be hard. You must lose a lot of sleep wondering."

"Only recently," she said. "Something about being here, away from the world I've built. I don't know. I've just realized how much I've missed and how much I'd love just to see him, to know if he's happy, to know his name."

She half-groaned, half-cried and Eliza hugged her until they both felt calm and the tears had dried, agreeing to give Claire some time to think about it before talking to Miles.

"I'll walk you to Junonia," Eliza said, keeping her arm around Claire. "You want to be good and centered when you face your mother."

"Thank you, Eliza. Thank you for understanding. Even about her."

"Well, she's...a lot."

"And she's mellowed. But twenty-six years ago? I couldn't bear her then, and didn't want to share this with her."

As they neared Junonia, they could see one light on inside, but the sliding glass doors were closed.

"Think she's still awake?" Eliza whispered.

"I don't know, but I feel better." She turned to Eliza and took both her hands. "I needed you in my life, Eliza. I had no idea how much. I just..." She frowned, looking over Eliza's shoulder toward the beach. "Is that Olivia?"

"Where?" Eliza turned, following Claire's gaze. The moon was bright enough, along with one light in the rental cabana, that she could see the silhouettes of two people standing side by side. "Yes, that is Olivia."

"So her date's ending with a moonlight stroll? I'd say that's good."

"So would I," Eliza gave a very soft laugh. "Except that's Deeley, not the investment guy from Chicago."

Claire's jaw dropped and then she stifled a giggle. "What do you think of that?"

"I don't know, but I can't wait for her to show up for morning coffee so I can find out."

"Keep me posted." Claire planted an impulsive kiss on Eliza's cheek. "Love you, sis."

The words, the kiss, the confession, all of it just gave Eliza the biggest grin. "Love you back."

Eliza wore that smile all the way back to Teddy's house—even while she peered into the darkness looking for her daughter and Deeley, but she couldn't see them again. She was still happy when she went to bed, but she didn't sleep for several hours, thinking about life and kids and sisters and all the changes in the air.

# Chapter Nine

## Olivia

"Why are you down here?" Olivia asked as she squinted at the broad shoulders she really didn't want to see right then. Well, maybe she did. Maybe that's why she'd come for this little starlight stroll after saying goodbye, *sans* kiss, to Scott. She'd made it through the small talk, the awkward moments, and an actual dinner. But a kiss? There she drew the line.

"Um, I work here?" He stabbed both hands into his hair, pulling it back, further exaggerating the size of his biceps.

"At ten-thirty on a Sunday night?"

"I had to do some accounting and I never work at home. There's no better time than this, when I don't have any customers." He got a little closer, his golden-brown eyes narrowing. "What are *you* doing down here? I thought you had a date."

She scowled at him. "How do you know that?"

"I saw you get in his car in front of Treasures."

A weird feeling zinged through her, a mix of fury and...something she didn't like. "Are you stalking me, Connor?"

He laughed. "Only my mother calls me that, Livvie."

"Well, only my mother calls me Livvie."

"And your gentleman investor."

She gasped. "You know what he does?"

"You told me the other day when I came to the store, and by the way, I was not stalking you. I brought the tools to work on the shelves, and as I walked up, I saw him hold the car door for you, like a gentleman."

A boring as hell gentleman who didn't have eyes the same color as a shot of Jack Daniels. Which she could kind of use right now. "Oh. Did you fix the shelves?"

"No. You locked up five minutes before closing time, so I guess you were pretty anxious to go on the date."

"He was early."

"And you're home alone at ten-thirty walking the beach." He waited a beat and leaned closer. "Dud date?"

"It was fine," she said, wanting to turn away, maybe continue her walk, but...she couldn't. His eyes held her like a magnet, riveted. Mesmerized. Crushed.

Oof. This man.

"So, where'd you go?" he asked, almost as if he cared. Or didn't want her to keep walking.

"A place called Papa...somethings."

"Papa Luigi's. You got in? That's impressive. There's usually a mile-long line for that pizza, which is the best in Sanibel, maybe the whole county. Maybe Florida."

"It was amazing, and yes, we got in." She hugged herself, rubbing her arms even though it wasn't the least bit cold. She still had chills.

The move made him chuckle softly. "Livvie. Just

relax, okay? I'm just making small talk, not out to hurt you."

Oh, no. Like he couldn't destroy a woman's heart and laugh all the way home. "I know you're not going to hurt me. I just don't want to talk about my evening."

"Fair enough. Want to go for a kayak ride?"

She drew back and blinked at him. "In the dark?"

"Even better that way."

She considered that, looking out at the black water. "Are there sharks out there?"

"Maybe, but they don't usually bite the kayaks. I'll go with you. I have a two-seater with proper lighting for night kayaking. I'll take care of any sharks."

Why did that sound so, so good?

"C'mon, Liv." He angled his head toward the cabana. "Free ride."

Oh, she doubted that. Nothing was free with this guy. But maybe, out there in the dark, she'd have the nerve to ask him—and demand he answer—just where he disappeared to so frequently.

"Okay. I had to miss a real boat ride tonight."

"Had to?" he asked, turning back to the rental shack. "Or wanted to go on your date more?"

She shrugged, following him as headed into the cabana. "How was the sunset cruise?"

"I didn't go."

"Why not?"

He didn't answer right away, but flipped on a light and walked to the very back of the small space, easily lifting the two-person kayak like it weighed nothing. "Grab those paddles, will you?"

"One or two?"

"One if you want to lean back and enjoy the ride, two if you prefer control."

"As if there's any question that I prefer control." She closed her hand around two paddles, smiling as he snorted at her answer.

He hauled the kayak out to the sand and glanced at the shorts and T-shirt she wore, the clothes she'd changed into after she'd gotten home from her date. "Okay to get that wet?"

"Will I?"

"Not likely. It's pretty hard to capsize a tandem. It's wide and stable."

"Plus, you *were* a Navy SEAL."

Even in the dark, she saw him roll his eyes, reminding her of how he never talked about what he did in the military, and when it came up, he acted like it was no big deal. The humility about a job she imagined few were humble about was one of the many—too many—things she found attractive about him.

He dragged the kayak to the water's edge, settled it in the sand, then reached for the paddles.

"You climb in the front. I'll hold it steady and get us going."

She did, easing into the low seat in the front, then taking one of the oars—but he called them paddles—he handed to her.

"Hang on," he said with a tease in his voice, giving

the craft a hard shove right before the next wave crested. On the break between waves, he easily climbed into the back, steadying them with his paddle.

Suddenly she felt the warmth of his body near her back and his arm came around her.

"What are you doing?" she asked with a gasp of surprise.

"Just reaching for..." He tapped something on a side panel and a thin white beam of light broke the blackness in front of her. "That."

"Oh, good. Yes, that's good."

The warmth disappeared and she sensed he'd leaned back.

"You set the pace, Liv," he said. "I'll follow your paddle speed."

"Just straight?"

"Unless you want to go around in circles." He laughed softly. "I've seen you do that, too."

"What's that supposed to mean?"

"Shhh. Just paddle. The best part of being out at night is the dead quiet. Listen."

Resting on the plastic seat behind her, she slid the paddle into the water, stroking one side, then the other. The movement pulled her arm muscles in a nice, refreshing way...and made her imagine his muscles as he mirrored her movements behind her.

She wished she could watch him, but it made sense that the stronger of the two sat in the back, so she gave in to the rhythm and the sensation, the soft splash of each stroke, and the briny smell that mixed with the warm summer night air.

The kayak seemed to go straight west, cutting over the water with that silver beam leading the way, out to the blackness and the unknown.

Now was the time. The perfect time. *Where do you go every week or so, Deeley?* But the words didn't form. So she stayed silent, enjoying the quiet and, before long, letting her paddle rest on the lip of the kayak while he did all the work.

"Arms sore?" he asked, his low voice near enough to give her a shiver.

"Just letting you have a rare moment of control," she said, throwing a smile over her shoulder. When she did, she caught his huge grin. "What are you smiling about? My giving up control?"

"You coming home early from your dumb date."

"That makes you smile?"

"Apparently."

"Well, hate to wipe your grin away, but he wasn't dumb. Dude might be a lot of other things, but he is no dummy." Although he hadn't gone into the specifics of his job, they'd talked business in general, investments in particular, and even some aggressive trading strategies.

"Okay, not dumb. So what is he?"

*Not you,* she thought with a shudder. Then, she stole another look at him and asked a more interesting question. "Why do you care, Deeley?"

His smile might have waned, but her gaze got snagged on his biceps as he made a wide semicircle with the paddle, easing them around. She felt a small thud of disappointment that the unexpected ride was ending so quickly, but she could see by the distant light of the rental cabana that they'd gone quite a bit offshore.

If they were turning around, she should ask her question.

"I'm curious, is all," he finally answered. "Intrigued as to why you'd pick him."

She took a slow breath and considered her answer. "My mother is breathing down my neck to give more men a chance."

He snorted. "Your mother? I thought you'd say, you know, his sense of humor—"

"Didn't have one."

"Or his manly physique."

"You saw the guy."

A laugh, maybe just a little smug, rumbled in his chest. "Maybe his bank account?"

"No, that's not what I'm looking for."

He was quiet for a long time, and she braced for it.

"What are you looking for, Livvie?"

Yep, she knew that was coming.

And she wasn't going to lie. They were flirting with each other enough that he should know what she wanted.

"I want someone stable and secure," she told him. "A forever guy who values family and stability and, yes, work. Someone stable."

"Three times," he murmured.

"Excuse me?"

"If you say stable one more time, I'm gonna guess you're looking for a guy with horses."

She laughed. "You know what I mean."

"You mean not this." He rocked the boat on purpose, making her gasp and jab her paddle into the water to steady them.

"Yeah, not like that."

Still chuckling, he started to paddle them back to shore.

"So your mother must have a lot of influence over you," he mused, obviously still hung up on her answer about her mother.

"Sometimes. I mean, I chose to spend my first real time off in seven years with her."

"I get that. Eliza's a good lady. You're lucky."

"I know." She frowned, hearing something in his voice that didn't sound quite normal for him.

They were nearly at the end of the spontaneous trip and time was running out. Mustering up her nerve, she turned a little, snagging his gaze. "All these questions, Connor Deeley. Don't I get a few?"

"I didn't go on a date tonight."

"But the other day you were gone, and a few days before that. And last week for three days." She squeezed the oar, waiting for his answer.

But there was none.

Even in the moonlight, she could see his skin grow pale and his eyes narrow as he looked past her to the thin white light that led them.

"Deeley?" she asked when just too many seconds

went by. "Why won't you tell me?"

"Why? Because you don't need to know."

She frowned. "Is this some military thing? Like only on a need-to-know basis? Can't you tell me that much?"

Finally, he shifted his gaze to lock on her. "No," he said simply.

With that, he started to row, a little harder, a little faster.

She stuck her paddle in to help him along, effectively silenced, and sad. When they reached the shore, he hopped out and pulled the kayak up, with her in it, to secure it on the sand.

"Thanks for the ride, Deeley," she said as she stuck her paddle in the sand to use it as a brace for climbing out.

"And now I'm Deeley." He angled his head. "You're welcome, Olivia."

"Oh." A soft groan escaped.

"What? I thought you hate when I call you Livvie."

She searched his face, standing on her own without reaching for him, no matter how much she wanted to. "I don't hate it. In fact, I kind of like it." She waited a beat, then added, "Connor."

He looked down at her—almost a head taller and so much broader—quiet for a few seconds; the only sound the splash of the surf and a breeze in the palm trees.

"I like it, too," he said softly.

And another few seconds passed, like a pause in a dance, before...the next move. But neither of them made it.

"Well, thanks again," she said, taking a step back. "You saved a pretty crappy night."

"I knew you didn't like that guy."

"He's okay," she said honestly. "He's very..." What could she call dull Scott without throwing a nice guy under the bus?

"Stable?" he suggested.

"Yeah, he qualifies."

"Isn't that exactly what you want?"

*Not right this very minute*, she thought, looking up at him and wondering—as any woman with a beating heart would—what it would feel like to kiss him.

"He had his moments," she said, realizing she'd drawn the line at a kiss with Scott but was standing here literally aching for one from Deeley.

"Name one," he challenged. "One moment that made your night memorable."

She let out a sigh. They both knew damn well *this* was the moment she'd remember. So she just shrugged and grabbed the obvious. "He answered all my questions."

He tipped his head in concession. "If that's important to you, Liv, then you should hang with him more often."

In other words, he wouldn't answer her questions. Ever.

"I might," she said. "Night, Connor."

"Night, Liv."

She turned and headed back toward the cottages feeling utterly and completely...unstable.

# Chapter Ten

*Eliza*

Eliza brought some of Teddy's best morning tea to Sunray Venus, ready for post-date girl talk that she hoped would explain why Olivia had been with Deeley on the beach. But she found the tiny cottage locked tight, no Olivia in sight.

But the store didn't open for well over an hour.

She couldn't have...

Well, yes, she could have. Livvie was almost thirty years old and a healthy, normal woman and Deeley was catnip. Eliza couldn't actually blame her if she'd spent the night with the guy, although it would be quite the turnaround. And probably not how Scott expected the night to end.

With curiosity buzzing in her head, Eliza took the tea right down to the path, walking nearly three-quarters of a mile on the beach to Sanibel Treasures, a mother on a mission to find out if her daughter was at work or in the arms of a handsome man.

The front door was locked, with no sign of Livvie anywhere on the store floor when she peered through the windows. Eliza almost gave up, but something deep inside made her really doubt her daughter slept with Deeley last night. It would be so out of character.

Holding that thought, she went around to the back where an employees-only door led to the office.

As she came down the side, she realized a car was parked in the small lot that once housed boats, leading to a canal now blocked by mangroves and pepper trees.

She frowned as she neared the back of the building, aware of a man's voice having a one-sided conversation.

"I'm doing my best to crack this woman's shell, but Olivia Whitney is a puzzle wrapped in an enigma, and just not that interested in me," the man said, bringing Eliza to a full stop, still hidden by a corner of the old boathouse.

That had to be Scott. Seeking advice for how to crack Livvie's shell? He should talk to Eliza, she thought with a smile. *Play hard to get, Scott, and have patience.*

"Yes, yes, I took her to some epic pizza place last night, and greased the hostess with a hundred so we didn't have to wait two hours for a table."

Whoa. Impressive. Eliza leaned in to hear more.

"Sure. We talked a lot. Not about anything, you know, specific or hopeful, but, man. I wish she liked me more, plain and simple."

Oh. Eliza felt her lip come out, imagining her son calling a friend when a beautiful woman was keeping him at arm's length. Dane was not what girls would call "hot" or "sexy," but a man with a good heart and a great brain. And, in Dane's case, the soul of a musician when he sat down at the piano. Why couldn't young women recognize the important qualities in a man?

She pushed thoughts of her son away and closed her eyes to listen even more closely, not caring that she was essentially eavesdropping on a stranger's phone call. The stranger was talking about her girl, so she had a Mom Pass.

"But I'm telling you, she's the one. She is *the one*."

Oh, wow! A man thought she was his soulmate and Livvie wouldn't even give him a chance? Unless it was just stalkery. She inched closer, trying to determine if he was a fool in love or a creep on a mission.

"Oh, she's gorgeous. Smart. Knows how to run this business, and is making it profitable. A little shell shop. I can't imagine what she's truly capable of if given the chance."

And he saw more than just her pretty face. That was sweet.

Pressing her whole body against the clapboard building, she fought the urge to peek out. She really wanted to get another look at him and maybe see what was so *wrong* with him. She leaned forward, poking around the corner of the store. If he saw her, she'd just march forward as if she were heading toward the back door, not eavesdropping on her daughter's new man.

She finally stole a glimpse, but he was sitting in the front seat of a car, window down, phone to his ear, facing the other direction.

"I'm not going to give up," he said. "I'm leaving her flowers right now and if I can get one more date, I'm telling her everything." He listened for a minute, then said, "Okay, you're right. Timing is important and that could scare her off. I'll take my time, but she's not here forever and I don't want to miss this opportunity. I'll never find someone else I can connect with like this."

Really? What could she say to make Livvie see the absolute appeal of a man who didn't want to give up when he sensed the connection was real? That was rare, and she shouldn't let a receding hairline or less than stellar shoulders make her blind to things that meant more in a man.

She stood perfectly still at the sound of his car door closing, then chanced one more sneak peek.

He was carrying a huge bouquet of roses, looking down at the flowers like they were his last hope. He wasn't bad looking! Yes, his hair was thinning, but he wasn't bald and who cared anyway? A man who talked about a woman, thought about her, considered her *the one*? That was worth more than all the hair in the world. All the hair...that Deeley had.

She watched him carefully place the bouquet on the step and look at the door like he might knock. Then he apparently changed his mind, stepped down backwards, and pivoted to his car.

"Come on, Olivia Whitney," he muttered as he walked. "Change my life."

Eliza leaned against the wall and let out a breath, wishing she'd somehow recorded the incident. Why was Livvie holding this man to some kind of false standard?

Ben. Yes, Benjamin Whitney, father and husband

and human extraordinaire, was a high standard. But Ben would be the first to tell his daughter to loosen up and give the guy a chance. He'd know exactly what, when, and how to advise her, and Livvie would listen.

Fighting an unexpected wave of missing her husband on a bone-deep level, Eliza slipped back the way she'd come, glancing into the front windows again. This time, she spotted Olivia moving some of the artwork around, and got her attention with one quick knock.

She came instantly to the door, and when she opened it, Eliza knew something wasn't right.

"Are you okay?" Eliza asked, handing her the cup of tea. "Did something happen with Deeley last night?"

"Deeley?" Her frown deepened. "How do you know I was with him?"

Eliza flinched, regretting the question. "I wasn't spying, I swear. I just happened to walk Claire back to her cottage and we saw you talking to him on the beach. Not, you know, the guy you had a date with."

*And not the one who just left you roses,* Eliza thought, biting the words back so they didn't escape. Timing is everything, as Scott had said.

Olivia groaned and took a sip. "This is cold, but good. I have to finish this cleanup before we open. Can you help me?"

"Yes, but are you going to answer me?"

Her eyes shuttered. "I'm seriously confused, Mom. Like...*whoa.*"

"I know, honey."

Putting the cup down on a shelf, Olivia lifted some

picture frames and studied them for a moment, then finally looked at Eliza.

"I should have come over and talked to you this morning," Olivia said. "But I thought I'd do some decluttering instead. It helps me figure things out."

"What's to figure out?"

She blew out a breath. "Why am I tossing and turning and longing for something from a man who makes me feel unstable?"

Deeley. Yep. Eliza wasn't Olivia's age, so the former Navy SEAL didn't have any effect on her, but she could see the man was eye-candy and Olivia was...hungry. Scott was more like a spinach smoothie—good for you, but not so tasty.

"Honey, I think you should be wise and have your eyes wide open to any and all possibilities."

"I assume you mean Scott."

"Well, first of all, I'm curious as to how you ended up on the beach with Deeley when you went out with Scott."

She didn't answer right away, but scooped up another shell-covered frame, angling it from one side to the other. "I took a walk. A simple, innocent, no agenda walk on a hot night with a beautiful moon."

"Sounds romantic," Eliza mused.

"It wasn't supposed to be. I wanted to clear my head and walk off dinner and think, because I ate too much pizza and I didn't really like my date. Well, I didn't hate him, but...but..."

"But Deeley," Eliza supplied.

"Took me on a midnight ride in a tandem kayak."

Eliza bit her lip. "That sounds incredibly romantic."

She finished scooping up the frames and jutted her chin for Eliza to grab the tea and follow her to the back.

"It wasn't incredibly anything, but it was nice." She slowed her step, then came to a stop and turned to Eliza, misery on every inch of her face. "I've got the stupidest crush on the guy, Mom. What am I going to do?"

Her heart turned over at the ache in Olivia's voice. No matter what the subject, when her baby hurt, she hurt.

"First of all, you're only here for the summer, so it's not like you're juggling long-term boyfriends or anything."

"True."

"But..." She put down the cup and took a deep breath. "I happen to have seen something a minute ago that I think you should know about."

"What?"

"Scott was in your parking lot, and he left you something."

"He was?" She frowned toward the back door. "I didn't know that."

"I overheard him telling someone on the phone that you are 'the one' and he thought you could change his life and he really connected with you and thinks you're amazing. I can't remember the exact words, so I'm paraphrasing."

Olivia's jaw dropped.

"I know, it's a lot."

"What's a lot is you...spying on me."

"I wasn't, honey, I—"

"And Deeley knowing I had a date." She shook her head. "I'm starting to understand the 'everyone knows your business' aspect of small-town life."

"I wasn't spying on anyone," Eliza insisted. "I was looking for you and the front door was locked. When I went to the back, I heard him."

"You heard him say all that to who?"

"I don't know. Someone on the phone. A friend. A sister. Maybe his mother. It's obvious the guy has a crush on you, and it might not be stupid at all."

"Mom, please. You don't know that."

"I heard him, Livvie. And I don't want you to have such crazy high standards that you miss a really, really good guy."

"High standards? I just told you I'm falling for the Sanibel Island equivalent of a pool boy. A beach bum. A kayak rental guy. With long hair. And tattoos. And, oh my God, I want to kiss him." She dropped her head in her hands and moaned in misery.

"Poor Scott," Eliza said with a half-laugh. "Boy doesn't stand a chance."

"Should he?" She lifted her head with agony in her eyes.

"If you had heard what he said, Liv..."

"Maybe I could, if you'd teach me these extraordinary eavesdropping skills you've developed." She smiled to take the sting out of the tease, then looked toward the back door. "He left me something?"

"Go look."

She went to the door, unlatching it and slowly opening it as if she were scared of what she might find. She looked down, saw the bouquet, and her shoulders sank.

"Oh, that's sweet. And they're pink, not red. I told him I liked pink."

"He listened."

She bent over and picked up the bouquet, looking out toward the small parking area as if she half expected to see Scott, too. But then she came back in, closing the door behind her.

"I see a card," Eliza said.

Livvie just sighed. "What else did you hear him say?"

"Just that he thinks you're beautiful and smart and talented. That he didn't want to scare you off, but knew he didn't have a lot of time, and thinks you're—"

"The one," Livvie said, eyes shuttering. "I heard." She took a deep inhale of the roses, then pulled out the card. Before she opened it, she looked at Eliza. "He's safe, you know? Steady. Kind. Interested. And..."

"And you *don't* want to kiss him, I take it."

"Maybe. I don't know." She slid the card out and read it, then turned it so Eliza could, too.

*Thank you for an amazing evening. Hope there can be more. Scott.*

"That's sweet," Eliza said.

"Yeah, it's..." She sighed again. "Unoriginal. Am I awful for saying that?"

"Kind of, but it's straightforward, and I imagine he is,

too. And all I can tell you is that certain things do wane over time in a marriage, but not honesty. Not stability."

She dropped her head back and whimpered at the word. "I know, Mom. I know. You're right. And guys like this have come into my life and I just want to push them away because it's too easy and dull. That's really dumb, isn't it? It's why I'm pushing thirty and all alone, right?"

"I think you're answering your own questions, honey. I'm not saying settle, nor am I saying you can fall for someone without chemistry." Eliza reached for her hand. "I'm just saying don't ignore the chemistry if it's subtle. That's all."

She nodded, and gestured Eliza back toward the front of the store. "Come on. I have to unlock and open up. Let's talk about something else. How was the sunset cruise?"

"It was fun, although I missed you. Camille didn't go."

"She didn't?" Olivia threw her a surprised look as she walked to the front door to unlock it and switch the open/closed sign.

"She needed to rest."

Olivia snagged her "Rise and Slay" mug of now cold coffee that she'd left by the cash register earlier, lifting the gift her mother had given her to prove she loved it, and also underscore her point. "That woman is high maintenance."

Eliza laughed. "But I got even closer to Claire, and I love that." She thought about her sister's secret, and the promise she'd made to keep it—even from Olivia. "We had a lovely time and maybe even a little lovelier because Camille wasn't there to dominate everything."

"How was Miles?" Olivia asked as she came back to the cash register after putting the mug in the back sink.

"Fine."

"Fine?" She lifted a meaningful brow. "Just fine?"

"What's that supposed to mean?"

"I mean, did you talk with him? Have a private moment with him? Let him whisper sweet boating phrases in your ear?"

"Livvie!"

"What? He looks at you with the same puppy dog eyes that Tinkerbell does." She stuck out her tongue. "Two can play this game, Elizabeth Mary."

Eliza felt a rush of warmth to her cheeks, remembering that moment of electricity on the boat she kind of wanted to forget...but hadn't. "Honey, I'm not interested in a man. Your father hasn't been gone six months and I'm just not ready to think about dating."

"Okay, fair enough. I'll back off." She added a saucy grin. "Maybe you can take some lessons in that."

Eliza laughed and held up her hand. "Got it. I won't say another word about the man who left you roses and is standing on his head trying to get a smidgeon of your attention."

"I'll give him a smidgeon," she said. "Will that shut you up for a while?"

"A little while," Eliza said with a smug laugh.

"I'll take it." She looked up when two women came in, chattering and laughing.

"Welcome to Sanibel Treasures, ladies," Olivia called out. "Can I help you find anything?"

"Seashell-covered picture frames!" one of them said.

"Yes. We want to remember our girls' weekend on Sanibel forever!"

Livvie slid a surreptitious look to Eliza, then smiled. "I have a few right there, and plenty more in the back."

"I'll let you get to work."

"Bye, Mom. Go use your eavesdropping skills for good and listen to Camille."

"Why?"

"Because the hearing is tomorrow," Olivia reminded her. "And we still don't know what she's going to do. Not for sure, anyway."

"True. I guess I have bigger things to worry about than..."

"The Scott sitch," Olivia joked.

Laughing, Eliza blew her a kiss. "See you later, Livvie Bug."

But on her walk back to Teddy's house, she didn't think about the *Scott sitch*, or the hearing tomorrow. She surprised herself by thinking about Miles, which would never, ever admit to anyone. Maybe not even to herself.

# Chapter Eleven

## *Claire*

**M**iles had been right about two things when he'd helped Claire prepare for today's hearing. One, the Honorable Jonathan Macgregor was an eminently fair judge; a good listener with a wonderful blend of humor and gravitas. In her nearly twenty years as an attorney, Claire had learned that judges who could balance those two things could also weigh the law with just a hint of common sense. And she hoped that prevailed today.

The other thing Miles had been correct about? Birdie Vanderveen's lawyer was good. The Alabama attorney had an accent that made him sound like he was trolling for catfish, not a win in the Lee County Courthouse. In his sixties, Lenny Buckells was a good ol' boy who dropped cute Southern phrase bombs that were endearing...and meant to make the opposing legal team relax a little too much.

Not to worry. Michael Ortega, a senior counsel from Wills, Sears, and Killian's Miami office, was not relaxed. Her Florida colleague was supremely well-prepared, intelligent, and well-spoken, but he also had that underlying buzz that "grinders" had—the need to dominate and emerge victorious. She'd despised that type at Cornell Law, but had long ago accepted these case-crushers as part of a lawyer's life. Today, she not only accepted it, she appreciated the focus and drive.

When both sides finished their opening statements and rebuttals regarding contesting the wills, it was clear Judge Macgregor had done his homework.

He sighed deeply after a moment of quiet in the room, shifting one piece of paper in front of him.

"I've read Roberta Vanderveen's affidavit stating that she was entirely unaware that Aloysius Vanderveen had been married when they took their vows. I realize she acknowledged that she refused a divorce. Do you know why, Mr. Buckells?"

"My client is a devout Catholic and does not acknowledge the dissolution of a marriage due to her profound religious beliefs."

"There are legal ways around that," the judge said. "A civil divorce, for example. An annulment." He turned to Michael. "Mr. Ortega, why weren't those options pursued?"

"Your Honor, Captain Vanderveen knew he had committed bigamy and he knew that if he pursued a divorce, that fact would become glaringly obvious. He would have lost his job with Pan Am Airways, his pension, his stock, and his reputation. Right or wrong, none of that affects his will."

The judge managed not to even give in to the slightest smile, but Claire could read the wry sarcasm in his dark eyes. Dutch's reputation? The man married two women at the same time. He didn't deserve a reputation. And, it could be argued, that very much affected his will.

"The other sticking point is the timing," the judge said, flipping a page of court docs. "He was married to Ms. Camille Durant before he exchanged illegal vows with Ms. Roberta Milton. But his will naming Ms. Milton-Vanderveen as his heir is dated earlier than the one naming Ms. Durant, making everything quite complicated."

No kidding. Claire felt the faintest smile pull at her lips as she looked up at the man on the bench, catching his dark eyes for just one split second. It was enough time to communicate exactly what they were both thinking. Enough time to give her some hope this would go their way.

Lenny Buckells leaned forward. "He gave his estate to Birdie first, Your Honor."

"Knowing that his marriage was not legitimate," Ortega interjected.

"Apparently Dutch didn't give two hoots about the law, then, did he, son?" Buckells shot back.

"Strike that," the judge instructed the court reporter at the end of the table.

"'Scuse me, Your Honor," Buckells apologized. "But the second will is an afterthought. We have no idea if that statement there that reads 'of sound mind and body' was true at the time at all now, do we?"

The judge said nothing, looking down at the legal papers in front of him. "Can you prove that Ms. Durant's version of Mr. Vanderveen's will was not signed under duress?" he asked Michael.

"This document is witnessed by two individuals, signed, notarized, and filed, naming his only legal wife as the heir of his estate," Michael said in response. "Statements from those witnesses are included in our paperwork, Your Honor, and neither indicated that it was written, signed, or witnessed under any pressure at all."

"And, Ms. Sutherland." He pinned Claire with a direct gaze. "As executor, can you provide proof that this will was not written under any pressure from an outside party?"

"I'm Aloysius Vanderveen's daughter, Your Honor," she said, "and I can certainly speak for the relationship my parents had. It was...unusual, certainly. But it was also deep, strong, and abiding." *Also sometimes ridiculous*, she thought, but merely held the judge's gaze. "My father was a flawed and, as you noted, complicated man, but this will is not."

He nodded and looked down again, making her wonder what he was thinking, since his expression didn't give away any clues.

*Your father was a bigamist. He spent more time away from your mother than with her. You lose. Case closed.*

Or it could go the other way.

*A newer will supersedes the older one. He was never really married to Birdie. They haven't seen each other in thirty years. Case closed.*

Her heart thumped more than it did when she was the working attorney in the room.

"I want to continue this," he finally said, directing the comments to the attorneys. "I'd like testimony from pertinent witnesses."

Claire stifled a sigh of defeat. Not that it was a loss, but...Camille. She'd hate having to be in the same room as Birdie. And even if she could stomach it, her mother could be an out-of-control witness who said way too much. If she revealed her plans to sell the property for a dollar to Teddy? That could blow up in their faces.

Michael agreed to the judge's request, but Birdie's lawyer did not look happy.

"Your Honor, my client has been through a very difficult time since she learned her husband of thirty-one years committed bigamy when he married her. She's deeply emotional and wronged."

"All the more reason to move this to a courtroom and do some questioning of all parties. We can work that testimony into my calendar and reach a reasonable and timely conclusion. Without it, I'm not making a ruling."

"Anyone else to question and cross, Your Honor, besides the will's beneficiaries?" Michael asked, no doubt wanting to know if Buckells could call Claire to testify.

"Anyone who will help make this a clear case, Mr. Ortega." The judge put his hand on the table like he held a gavel. "The court will contact you with a date shortly." With that, he stood, and they all did, too, waiting while he left the room.

When he was gone, Buckells turned to Michael. "Would your client be open to a discussion?"

"A settlement?" Michael inched back and glanced at

Claire. "As far as I'm concerned, there's no room for a division of assets as that is not what either will states. But you are the executor, Claire. What's your reaction to that?"

She thought about it for a moment, knowing it could get sticky and ugly, and no one would be completely happy in the end. But a settlement could solve the problem.

She'd learned something else from Miles, who had met Birdie Vanderveen. The woman didn't want a piece of Shellseeker Beach; she wanted cash. And that could work in their favor if the judge dug that deeply in his questioning.

"Mr. Buckells, do you know what your client intends to do with the property in question?" she asked.

"I don't see how that matters one bit."

"It matters very much," Claire said. "Is she planning to sell it to developers or a hotel management company?"

"That has no bearing on this case."

Claire knew it had a great deal of bearing. The woman didn't want a resort on the beach in Florida. She wanted millions of dollars. Dutch didn't leave money—he left *property*.

"Then no settlement," she said. "We'll let Judge Macgregor decide."

With a quick shake of hands, they parted, and Claire walked to the parking lot with Michael.

"A settlement might not be the worst idea in the world," Michael said as they stepped out into blazing sunshine. "Give her a piece of the land, let her do what she wants with it, and you keep the rest."

She gave him a professional smile. "I don't think that's what anyone involved wants, but I'll present the idea to my mother." Who would flutter her French-tipped fingers and drop a French-tipped curse to go with it.

He paused when they reached their cars and shook her hand. "I'll be back for the hearing when it's scheduled. If you change your mind or want to discuss all the options, including drafting a compromise we can present to Judge Macgregor, just call me, Claire."

"I will. Thank you. Great job in there."

She climbed into the rental car and sat in the oppressive heat for a long, long time. This wasn't a slam-dunk. This wasn't going to be easy. And, oh God, her mother was not going to want to face off against Roberta Vanderveen in court.

But she had to deliver the bad news anyway.

CLAIRE DIDN'T TELL anyone anything, except to say there wasn't a resolution yet, until she had gathered her mother, Eliza, and Teddy together. Once they were all at Teddy's house, she explained what the judge wanted to do next.

And her mother looked stricken.

"*Non, non. Je ne peux pas faire ça.*" She slipped right into rare French, which she sometimes whipped out during emotional turmoil. "I can*not* do that," she self-translated as she stood. "No. I...*non*."

She rubbed her hands, then crossed her arms, then looked like if there was a random Gauloise nearby, she'd smoke the living daylights out of it.

"*Maman*," Claire said calmly, looking up at her. "We will prepare you for every possible question the judge could ask."

"I won't do it."

"Then we'll lose!" Teddy exclaimed.

"You'll lose," Camille fired back, her eyes flashing. "I might lose, I might not."

"Much worse, *Maman*." Claire stood and put a hand on her mother's shoulder. "If you don't go, Birdie will win by default. You don't want that."

She looked even more horrified at the thought of that possibility.

"So, you will do it," Claire added.

"Will they make me? Will she?"

"You can be subpoenaed to appear by the opposing counsel, but he likely will not do that," Claire said. "He knows that if you don't appear, the decision goes in Birdie's favor."

"Oh, *mon Dieu*." She groaned and fell back on the sofa next to Teddy, closing her eyes. "I don't know what to say to her."

"You don't have to say anything to her, Camille," Eliza said. "Does she?"

"You'll merely answer the questions put forth by her attorney," Claire said.

"What kind of questions?" Camille asked. "Like... about my relationship with Dutch?"

"Possibly. We'll get you ready to answer in non-personal but clear ways. I do think he might ask you about what your plans are for the property."

She looked at Claire, then blinked. "What difference does that make?"

"To this judge? I don't know. But you can't lie under oath, Camille. You have to tell him you are planning to transfer ownership to Teddy, and make the compelling argument that Shellseeker Cottages, Sanibel Treasures, and the tea hut and garden have all been in her family for a hundred years. Birdie will have to be honest about her plans to sell to a hotel chain, too. It could very much work in our favor."

"It's a powerful argument," Teddy agreed softly, putting a hand on Camille's arm. "And anyone from this area is going to appreciate—"

Camille's eyes flashed as she yanked her arm away. "I cannot do this," she ground out in misery. "I never wanted to see her, and I'm sure she doesn't want to see me. Is there any other way?"

"Birdie's attorney asked if we were open to discussing a settlement," Claire said.

And then everyone stared at her, but no one looked quite as shocked by that as Teddy.

"A settlement?" Eliza asked. "Like sharing the property or paying her off? What would that kind of compromise entail?"

"It could go many ways," Claire said. "You could pay

her a substantial sum of money and call it a deal. You could give her a portion of the property. You could—"

"No!" Teddy whispered.

Camille stood again, the current conversation lost on her as stress played out over her features. "I can't be held responsible for what I say or do to that woman. I cannot be controlled and I will not!"

Eliza sighed, clearly over Camille's theatrics. "You forget she didn't know he was married," she said. "She shouldn't be the object of your wrath. *He* should be."

"Whose side are you on?" Camille whipped around and practically spat the question at Eliza, and they all sat in stunned silence for a beat.

"I'm on the side that makes Teddy happy," she answered softly. "The side of the angels. The side that is right. For the record, that is not Birdie."

For a long moment, Camille stared at Eliza, her color rising but her tongue uncharacteristically quiet. Finally, she held up one hand as if to say goodbye. "I'm going back to the cottage. I can't discuss this now."

Stunning them all, she swept out of the room with no arguments, her high heels clicking on the wood as she disappeared.

Teddy looked up at Claire, who blew out a noisy breath and said, "I'd better go talk to her."

"No." Teddy reached to the table and picked up one of the shiny crystals that decorated so many surfaces of the room. "Let me do it. I think I can help her." Without waiting for an argument, Teddy left, still carrying the fist-sized stone.

"How can she help her?" Claire asked, rubbing her bare arms at an unexpected chill dancing over her skin.

"She can heal her," Eliza said, standing up and offering a hug. "Did anyone ever tell you what an amazing sister you are?"

Claire melted into the embrace, shocked at how much she needed it. "No, but feel free to elaborate."

Eliza laughed, then inched back. "What do you think of the settlement or compromise idea?"

"I don't think Birdie will go for it, and I think it's very dangerous, and it will probably blow up in Teddy's face because half this property will be owned by a hotel. Oh, unless you and Teddy can scare up a couple of million to make her go away."

Eliza didn't answer, as if she were actually thinking about that.

"You really love her, don't you?" Claire asked.

"Teddy? I guess I do."

Claire grinned at her. "Did anyone ever tell you what an amazing sister you are?"

"No, but feel free to elaborate."

"Get the wine," Claire said on a laugh, "and we can *both* elaborate."

# Chapter Twelve

## *Teddy*

There was no sign of Camille at Junonia, so Teddy walked down to the beach, scanning the sand left and right for her. There were a few tourists, some shellers, a dozen or so families with kids in and out of the surf.

But she didn't see Camille's jet-black hair or the bright green designer sheath she'd been wearing.

Teddy almost went back home, but something made her walk a little further, toward the opposite end of Shellseeker Beach, to the gazebo.

And there she was, sitting alone on one of the benches, leaning against the white wood and staring out to the horizon.

Teddy gripped the crystal tighter, letting one of the jagged edges stab her palm. Even from thirty feet away, she could feel Camille's pain wafting over the sand. She ached. It was the strongest energy she'd ever received from Camille.

And when Teddy felt that kind of agony from anyone —*anyone at all*—her chest burned with the need to help and heal.

Even when someone didn't want that help, like Camille, she simply had to try.

"I thought I'd find you here," Teddy said as she approached.

"You did? I didn't even know this thing was out here."

"This thing?" Teddy laughed softly, stepping up to join her inside. "It's called a gazebo."

"Ah, yes. That's the word. In French, it's *belvédère*. I keep wanting to say...pagoda? Pergola?"

"They're all similar, but a gazebo has all these open windows and it's always round or octagonal."

Camille nodded, obviously disinterested in the architecture lesson, her feet bare and relieved of the high-heeled shoes that rested at odd angles on the wooden floor.

"My father built this," Teddy told her. "It was a gift to my mother."

"That's nice." Still didn't care.

"Notice how much higher it is than everything else?"

"I noticed it's on a hill," she said flatly, her tone all but screaming *please leave me alone*, matching her crossed arms and unwelcoming body language. But the one thing Teddy knew about people who needed to be healed? They didn't start out wanting help. Camille was no different.

"Not a hill at all. I mean, look around, Camille." Teddy sat on the bench a few feet away from her. "There are no hills in Florida."

Finally, a flicker of interest. "Then what is this?"

"A shell mound," Teddy told her.

"Of course."

"But one that's very special. Sacred ground for the Calusa Indians, a tribe that lived here for thousands of years, until around 1600. They were here when Ponce de Leon came to this coast."

Camille finally turned her attention to Teddy, her dark eyes dubious. "Really? That's what you came out to tell me?"

"No. You asked why I thought I'd find you here. The answer is that the gazebo draws people. Well, the land it's on does. The mounds had lots of purposes. Some were temples, some were burial grounds, and some were formed just to gain the advantage of height over any incoming enemies."

Camille's eyes narrowed as if Teddy qualified as just that—an incoming enemy.

Undaunted, she continued. "This one, my mother believed, was built for the king, what they called the Calusa Paramount, and he was known to have supernatural ties to the heavens."

"Teddy, *please.*"

"I know, I know, you don't believe that. But you can tell by the skies. For one thing, you have a direct view of the sunset from these benches, although you have to move to a new bench every month or two as the Earth travels around the sun. My father built it that way, but guess what? When he did, he discovered that you can also track the stars. This turned out to be the perfect spot for viewing the moon, too, and the stars. That's why my mother believed the Paramount would come to this mound to commune with the heavens and whoever he believed was in them. Which is wonderful, because it works no matter what your faith."

"Fascinating," Camille said dryly. "But can't you see I need to be alone out here?"

"That's just the thing. You can't be alone here because..." Teddy lifted her arms, flattened her hands toward the sky in a classic worship pose. "There are spirits here."

Camille just groaned.

"And do you know what they do? They fill your heart with the truth. My mother used to say that when you want to know the truth, or face it, or understand it, or even go to war with it, come out here to the gazebo. It's an Honesty House."

"Teddy, I—"

She placed the crystal on the bench between them. "I always add the energy of a good crystal, too."

She looked at Teddy like she wanted to clock her with that crystal. "I don't need energy or spirits or truth or honesty or *company*," she ground out. "Let me sit out here and be alone with..."

"Fear," Teddy supplied.

"I'm not—"

"And anger," she added.

"You don't—"

"And hatred."

She swallowed. No contradiction.

"You don't need to feel any of those things, Camille,"

Teddy said softly. "You can replace them with courage and hope and love."

"Oh, for crying out loud, Teddy! You don't have to face a woman who your husband loved and married while he was married to you. I do!"

Teddy laughed softly. "You're looking at a woman your husband loved and married while he was married to you. Why am I any different than Birdie?"

"Because he met you long after we were done. He met Birdie when we were having a silly, stupid, meaningless argument."

"I should have every right to be hurt, too," Teddy said. "Dutch might not have legally married me, but we stood in this very gazebo and had a unification ceremony in front of friends. So, in my heart, he *was* my husband. And you are a woman he not only loved before me, he spoke with you behind my back, and conspired with you...long after we had that ceremony."

Camille blinked at her as that sank in. "Conspired about helping you," she said softly. "He would never have contacted me if he didn't want my help giving you this property. He didn't care that I knew if he was dying or not. He just wanted to help you."

Was that true? Oh, how Teddy wanted to believe that. Sadly, she didn't.

"The fact is, Camille, I'm struggling, too, with the memory of Dutch, of who he really was and why he lied or kept things from me. I refuse to let that struggle turn into hate, anger, or fear."

Camille huffed out a breath. "It's not him I hate. Not

him I'm mad at. And not him I'm afraid of. It's...her." Her whole body shuddered. "I cannot look at her. I will not. I simply cannot face her and know...what she did to me."

Teddy put her hand on the crystal, drawing in some of its energy, then she closed her eyes and dropped her head back. While they sat in silence, she dug for an answer, for the truth that she'd grown to expect to find when she stepped into this gazebo.

"But it's him you resent," Teddy finally whispered. "Because of what he did to you."

She didn't answer, but sat with her gaze fixed straight ahead.

"And resentment makes you bitter and crisp and..." Teddy swallowed. "Unattractive."

Camille's eyes flashed. "Going straight for the jugular, are you, Theodora?"

"Maybe a little." She laughed with the admission. "But it's true. The negativity that's brewing in you isn't pretty, inside or out. I know that matters to you."

"It'll only get worse if I have to look at her," Camille said.

"But your beef isn't with her," Teddy insisted. "It's with Dutch."

"So what if it is? I still don't want to see her. I can't."

"You keep saying you can't, but why not? You're strong, you're beautiful, you're here because you're a good woman who wants to honor a dying man's wish and thank the woman who nursed him to the end." With each word, she very slowly and soundlessly inched the crystal closer and closer to Camille. "You are the woman with power in that room, the one he stayed connected to for multiple decades and the one who bore his child."

Camille sighed and dropped her hands, her right one landing on the crystal. She snapped it up and turned to look at what she'd hit, then lifted her gaze to meet Teddy's. There was just a flash of amusement in her eyes, enough for Teddy to know one wall—maybe just one brick—had just come down.

"What are you doing, Teddy?"

"Offering you some help. Pick that up, hold it in your hands, and close your eyes again."

She didn't move, but, after a few seconds, she followed Teddy's instructions and sat very still with the crystal in her hands on her lap. Teddy slid a little closer.

"Now tell me one thing about Dutch. Just one thing. Anything at all, whatever comes to mind."

"He couldn't resist a cigar."

"Ain't that the truth," Teddy agreed with a snort. "Okay, tell me one thing that most people don't know about him."

"He rubbed his feet against each other when he slept," she said, without a nanosecond of hesitation.

Teddy smiled, remembering that she went through two sets of sheets during their time together since he actually wore a hole in them. "Now tell me something that no one but you could possibly know about him. Not me, not Claire or Eliza, and not Birdie."

She thought about that, her fingers moving over the crystal as if even she couldn't resist the energy coming off it.

"He killed a man in Vietnam when his gun went off, an enemy soldier he was supposed to bring in as a prisoner of war. And he left him to die in a swamp. It haunted him."

A chill traveled over Teddy's body, and somehow she managed not to react, but Camille looked at her and raised one brow.

"You didn't know that, did you?"

"No, but he told you that, Camille. Doesn't that tell you something about how much he trusted and loved you? I'd bet my bottom dollar he never told that to Birdie."

The warmth in Camille's eyes deepened and a smile lifted her lips. "You *are* betting your bottom dollar on me, Teddy, aren't you?"

"In some ways."

"Is that why you're out here trying to help me out of this abyss?"

"Not the only reason," Teddy said. "I heal people, Camille. That's what I do. I'm an empath, and I can feel your pain. When I feel pain, I want to take it away." She closed most of the space between them, putting her hand over Camille's so they were both holding the crystal.

"You have nothing to fear from Birdie," she whispered.

"Except that she is a reminder of my greatest failure," she said softly. "That's why I can't see her. It's a glaring light on my darkest moment."

Teddy frowned, not following. "When you and

Dutch split up, and he met her? That's your greatest failure?"

Silent, Camille stared straight ahead.

"I don't know what happened, Camille," Teddy said. "I have no idea what caused your issues with Dutch that sent him off to marry a virtual stranger more than twenty years his junior when he was already married and had a child."

She let out a little whimper and blinked back a tear. "You don't have to know."

"You're right, I don't. But you do. And whatever it is, the pain of that memory is eating at you from the inside out."

Camille swallowed noisily, fighting tears. "Stop this, Teddy," she whispered. "Please."

Should she? With a few more minutes and a few more sentences, she could get that last wall down and let the waters rush free. Camille could be healed. She had to try.

"Camille, if you—"

"Stop it!" She leaped to her bare feet and let the crystal fall with a thud to the wooden floor. "Just stop it right now." Her eyes were brimming with tears and fire. "I don't want this. I don't want your truth or silly rocks or your...your...*intrusion* in my history."

Teddy looked up at her, gut-punched by the words. "I'm not trying to intrude."

"Well, you are. And I don't like it. I don't like any of this."

"Sometimes it hurts to heal," Teddy said.

"I'm fine! He's the one who died, not me. I'm fine. I don't need this...garbage." She spat out the last word and strode out. "I'm done. Completely and utterly done."

With that, she practically leaped onto the sand and ran off barefoot, leaving Teddy alone with the crystal and the high heels and a deep ache of failure.

Her mother used to say, "There is such a thing as too much healing. It sends the hurt right back in place." Teddy was pretty sure she'd just learned that lesson firsthand.

* * *

MUCH LATER THAT NIGHT, Teddy sipped tea in Olivia's cottage, not surprised by the comfort she got from two women she'd grown to depend on. Eliza and Olivia had listened to as much as Teddy was comfortable sharing about her conversation in the gazebo—not including the story about Dutch in Vietnam—but they had different reactions.

Eliza, with the perspective of her own mother who spent an enormous amount of time despising Dutch for his many sins, was deeply sympathetic with Camille. But she repeatedly praised Teddy for trying to heal the broken woman who held their fate in her hands.

Olivia, on the other hand, was wildly pragmatic and saw the situation as a huge red flag that could bring their plans to a halt.

"Yes, Mom," Olivia said. "Teddy is an absolute angel for trying to help Camille. And she's right in saying that

Camille's issue isn't with Birdie, it's with Dutch. But that just worries me more. She could easily back out, change her mind, or refuse to sign that document giving Teddy the property."

Teddy turned her cup in her palms, staring at the burnished gold liquid, but seeing all the dark, dark emotions on Camille's face. "She could," she agreed quietly.

"So you don't trust her?" Eliza asked, her voice sounding a little pained.

"I don't know. Do you?"

"I trust Claire," Eliza said. "And I think she has a lot of influence over her mother."

"Not that much," Olivia chimed in. "I really feel like Camille calls the shots and Claire puts up with it as much as she has to. But this decision isn't going to be Claire's, Mom. It's Camille's."

They were all quiet, thinking about that.

"We need something else," Eliza mused. "Something that would put her over the edge."

"Like proof that Dutch wanted Teddy to have this place?" Olivia asked.

"Maybe, but Teddy says that doesn't exist."

"I've looked through all his things, over and over. He was quite good at documenting his life as a pilot. But as a husband or my partner? He didn't document much."

Olivia groaned. "You know, even if she does win this case and does turn over the property to Teddy? Birdie could come back for another legal fight and it could get ugly. All we have to go on is alleged phone calls between a crazy lady and a dead man."

"Alleged?" Eliza asked.

"Crazy?" Teddy chimed in right over her.

"No one's questioning dead, I see," Olivia said dryly. "Look, sorry, I'm a realist. And a cynic. And pragmatic. And...what else, Mom?"

"The voice of reason," Eliza said on a sigh. "And I don't hate that."

Olivia smiled at her, then shifted her attention to Teddy. "All I'm saying is maybe Camille is saying that she had this 'promise' with Dutch for another reason. Maybe she has some kind of ulterior motive. I don't know."

"What could it be?" Teddy asked. "Nothing motivates her but her *looks*." She scoffed at the word. "Is anyone really that shallow?"

"No," Eliza said. "There has to be more than that."

"Well, she's fueled by hate and resentment toward Birdie," Teddy said.

"And Dutch," Olivia added.

"But not you." Eliza pointed to Teddy. "Why does she hate Birdie so much, but not you, who came after she did and carried him to his final resting place?"

"Maybe she *does* resent you," Olivia said, leaning forward. "And this whole thing is a ruse to break you..." She caught herself, probably because Teddy could feel the blood drain from her face. "Or not," Olivia said quickly. "We're just speculating, and it's based on nothing."

But Teddy stood, fighting the emotion whirling in her chest. "Maybe this *is* her act of revenge against me. Set me up for joy, only for me to fall and lose everything... twice." Her voice cracked and Eliza was up in a flash, arms around her.

"No, no, Teddy. Don't think that."

"But why can't I...*feel* her? I mean, I get the flash of emotions from her, anger and hate, but mostly, she's kind of...blank. I don't get a sense she's lying or trying to hurt me, but I don't get a sense that she is aching to help, either."

"She's a self-centered woman," Eliza said. "She's so internally focused that she doesn't send vibes out to the world, to you. She just concentrates on herself."

Teddy returned the hug, awash with gratitude. "Oh, Eliza. It would have been so much easier if he'd just left it to you."

"Then we'd be digging into a nice little summer renovation and working side by side."

The very thought of that made her hurt more. "I do wish you'd move in and stay here. Forever." She drew back, smiling through tears. "I'm one big fat dreamer of ideas that will never come true."

"We don't know that yet," Eliza said softly. "Dreams do come true. Remember the one I had before I got here? Walking on the beach with a woman who was family? I think that was Claire. Or you. Or both."

"Oh, Eliza." Teddy almost crumbled with her next thought. "If I believed you were going to stay and then didn't get the property? I don't think I could stand that disappointment."

"We're getting ahead of ourselves, Teddy. We just don't know how this is going to shake out."

On a sigh, Teddy sat back down on the sofa and picked up her now cool tea. "We don't," she agreed. But she was very, very worried anyway.

# Chapter Thirteen

## Claire

"Knock-knock!" Claire tapped on the door of Apartment 2B in the small complex off Sanibel's main drag.

"Who's there?" a childish voice called from the other side.

"Claire!"

"Claire who?"

The lock flipped and the door opened to Katie Bettencourt wearing a huge smile and a small child wrapped around her legs. "You better have a punchline to that knock-knock joke or you're toast," Katie said.

Claire glanced down at the little girl, recognizing the sweet but super shy kid she'd seen around Shellseeker Beach but had never spoken to. "Claire..."

Oh, boy. She had no idea how to turn that into a knock-knock joke. "Claire-ly you want some baking lessons!" She held up her shopping bag, full of supplies and ingredients for the afternoon she and Katie had planned.

"Really?" Harper inched her blond little head out from behind her mother's legs.

"Miss Claire came to—" She gave her head a shake.

"*Aunt* Claire. You can call her Aunt Claire because she is Aunt Eliza's sister, and she's come to give us baking lessons so Uncle Deeley doesn't call us the Bad Baking Sisters."

"Cause we're not sisters," Harper said softly.

"And not *that* bad," Katie added, laughing. "We just need some help."

The words all sounded so good, every syllable stuffed with family and love, that Claire beamed at both of them.

"And here I am to give you that help." She gave the child a pat on the head as Katie ushered her into a bright, cozy apartment.

"Come in and teach, Aunt Claire!" Katie said, taking her to a small kitchen.

After some chatter and elaborate unbagging of the ingredients, it didn't take long for Harper's shyness to ease. She really loosened up when Claire let her experiment with filling the measuring cups and scraping the top with a knife to make everything exact.

"Eesh, we do a lot of estimating on flour and stuff," Katie admitted from her seat at the kitchen counter. She'd let Harper stand on a small stool next to Claire, to enjoy watching her daughter soak up everything Claire said. "Maybe that's why we're the Bad Baking Sisters."

"No estimating, no guessing, no eyeballing." Claire leaned close to Harper and circled her finger around the little girl's eyes, making her giggle. "You never guess on an amount of anything, because baking is science, but cooking is art."

Harper looked up at her, fascinated and confused.

"Too much flour?" She tapped the tiny nose with a little All-Purpose, making the tip white. "The cake will be too dry. Too much baking soda?" She lifted the container and gave it a shake. "You'll have a bitter mess on your hands."

"Too much chocolate?" Harper asked.

"Hmm." Claire narrowed her eyes playfully, using a kitchen towel to wipe the flour off Harper's nose. "Is there such a thing as too much chocolate?"

Harper giggled and reached for some of the ingredients Claire had brought to make simple cake from scratch —including icing and colorful sprinkles.

"When can we put decorations on the cake?" she asked.

"Uh, first we have to make it," Claire said with a laugh. "Step one? Preparing the pan."

Harper was a willing student with a surprisingly long attention span, but it was Katie who asked the most questions. She knew so little about the basics, but that wasn't surprising, considering her privileged upbringing.

By the time they got the cake in the oven and it was time to make the icing, Claire sensed they'd lost Harper, at least for a while. Katie gave her break with some free time with toys in her room, and offered Claire a cold drink and a chance to sit for a while.

"So, do you think there's hope for the Bad Baking Sisters?" Katie asked on a laugh. "I'd love to prove Deeley wrong with that handle he hung on us."

"You will prove him all wrong, I have no doubt," Claire said. "And can I just add that my little helper?"

She glanced toward the bedroom where Harper had gone. "What an absolute treasure she is, Katie. You're doing an amazing job with her."

"Thank you." She flushed a little, but smiled broadly at the compliment. "It's not always easy, but I get a lot of help from the people at Shellseeker Beach."

"I'm sure you do, but you're the one teaching her manners and kindness and listening and...all the things that I guess are difficult to teach."

She sighed as she brought two glasses of iced tea to the small kitchen table. "I'd offer you a cookie, but I only have store-bought."

"I'm good." Claire smiled at her, struck once again by the fact that this young lady had done the most courageous thing by defying her family and having her baby.

"I'm grateful to hear someone who just met her say all those nice things, Claire. Thank you."

"Actually, I should thank you." Without giving it much thought, she reached out and put a hand on Katie's arm. "I've really enjoyed this. You and Harper and...this."

For a moment, the two near-strangers looked at each other and Claire could just feel a connection forming. Intangible, indescribable, but she genuinely liked this girl, and felt a kinship she couldn't—or wouldn't—explain. As she'd told Eliza, Katie was not only the same age as Claire had been when she'd gotten pregnant, she was now about the same age, maybe a year or two younger, than the child Claire had given up.

"Well, while we're exchanging gratitudes," Katie said, "I want you to know that you helped me so much that day I saw you in the gazebo. It was like a shot of much-needed adrenaline and hope and reality all mixed into one."

"I'm glad. You need to go easier on yourself, you know?"

"I know. And it helped to get another person's perspective. I live in a weird kind of isolation, with my life at the Cottages or with a four-year-old. You just sounded like you understood and saw it in a different light." Katie lifted her glass of iced tea. "I do appreciate that."

As they toasted, Claire looked at her and mulled over the obvious dilemma. Should she tell her? Would it help either or both of them to talk about it? Was it safe to confide her secret to someone other than Eliza?

"So, tell me about your life, Claire," Katie said. "You're an attorney in New York and...single? No one special in your life?"

"I was married briefly almost twenty years ago, but that ended. I work a lot." She made a face. "I guess I could do something about that, but..."

"You should take your own advice and get out there," Katie said on a laugh, pushing up when the oven timer went off.

Claire smiled and watched Katie walk away, letting her brain slip back into her earlier thoughts. This girl was brave—so much more so than Claire had been.

Katie pulled out two pans of springy yellow cake. "Look at these! Now we know how to make our own cake! Ta-da! Is it icing time?"

Claire laughed. "You're as bad as Harper with the sprinkles. Let them cool first or we'll tear the cakes."

"Icing?" Harper came zooming down the hall and launched toward the kitchen. "And sprinkles!"

Laughing at her exuberance, Claire stood and nearly lost her balance. She felt so *good*. And a little regretful. *This* is what life would have been like, she thought. And she probably would have loved it.

Instead, she'd let fear steal her life and paralyze her, and deny her the chance to be a mother and know...her son. Taking a deep breath, she reached for her phone, impulsive for a change.

"I just have to send one quick text," she said, tapping on Eliza's name in the contacts.

*Can we go see Miles tomorrow? I'm ready.*

She hit Send before she could chicken out.

LATER THAT WEEK, with an hour to kill before the meeting they'd scheduled with Miles, Eliza and Claire sat under an umbrella breathing the incredible Sanibel air and sipping lattes at a local coffee shop.

Claire was more than a little nervous about taking the next step to unlock her past, but Eliza had such a wonderful way of putting her at ease. She hadn't asked any probing questions, but let Claire set the tone of small talk between sisters, not big talk of adopted babies.

"Can I ask you a question?" Eliza leaned in, holding her cup.

Okay, so maybe the small talk was over. "Of course. Remember, total honesty, right?" Claire lifted her paper cup in a mock toast. "I can take the toughest of questions."

"It isn't tough. When are you going back to New York?"

Claire laughed. "It *is* a tough question, because I don't know."

"I'm not pushing you, believe me, but don't you have to work?"

"I actually have been reviewing documents, writing briefs, and even doing some billable client meetings over video conference while I'm here. So I thought I'd stay at least until we hear from the probate court. I'd hate to get back and have to turn around the next day and zip down here for testimonies."

"Well, I'm not complaining," Eliza said. "I love having you here. Stay as long as you want. God knows I'm in no rush to leave."

Claire lifted a brow. "I noticed."

Across the table, she rested her elbows and locked her gray-blue eyes on Claire. "I may never leave."

"Really?"

She shrugged. "I'm so over Los Angeles, and without my kids or Ben, I can't even bear to walk into that giant house again."

"You should definitely sell it," Claire said. "I mean, I imagine your home is jam-packed with memories of Ben and better years—different years—" she added quickly. "But what's stopping you?"

Eliza gave her an "are you kidding" kind of look. "If this place ends up belonging to either your mother or Birdie, then obviously I'd leave. Probably take Teddy with me," she added on a laugh. Not that Claire suspected that was a joke. The two women were close, like mother and daughter.

"I don't think Birdie's going to win," Claire said. "And I have no reason to believe my mother won't keep her promise, so..." She lifted both brows. "You could stay. In fact, I think you should."

"Why?"

"You belong here."

"That's only because this is the only place you've ever known me," Eliza said. "Although, I have to say I've never felt so at home anywhere, not even, well, my own home. Weird, huh?"

"Not really. Shellseeker Beach is special."

Eliza nodded, thinking. "Sure would be a different life."

"From Los Angeles? I imagine it would."

Then she inched forward. "And from New York."

Claire searched her sister's face, catching her drift. "Eliza. What would I... No. Don't go there. I can't even think about it. I'm up to my elbows in—"

"In what?" Eliza pressed. "What really is keeping you in New York?"

"My life," she said, hearing the defensive edge in her voice.

"I know, I know. You do have a stunner of a job and it

sounds like your apartment is gorgeous and I'm sure you have a ton of friends."

Claire looked down at her drink, thinking how all that was true. But was it *enough*? She felt a smile pull as she looked up. "You're really good at making me do the whole self-examination thing, aren't you?"

She shrugged. "Just doing my sisterly duty."

"You're doing that by going with me today."

"Of course. I'm happy to. But brace yourself, Claire. Miles is very good at his job and if you ask him to find someone, he probably will."

She blinked and stared at Eliza, taking a ragged breath at the thought, pushing back from the table. "Then let's go get him on the job."

"Are you nervous?"

"A total wreck," Claire admitted with a laugh.

"I figured."

"Which is why you've talked about everything but why we're here."

"Exactly," Eliza acknowledged.

"And that's why I love you," Claire whispered, the words surprising her a little.

But Eliza wore a smile all the way to Miles's house, and it didn't go away when they arrived. Of course, she was loved and licked by Tinkerbell, and Miles made them both feel so comfortable.

"Why don't you two talk alone in the office?" Eliza suggested. "I see a leash and I'd like to take my girl for a walk."

Claire nodded and thanked her for the privacy,

following Miles and the scent of his coffee back to his office.

"That dog may never love me again now that she's been walked by Eliza," he joked as they settled in a brightly lit office with a huge desk that held several large monitors and keyboards.

"I think it's mutual," Claire said, settling onto a comfy sofa while he took the guest chair and faced her.

"So, Eliza says you have a special request. That's all she told me."

Claire took a deep breath and let it out slowly, trying to center herself for this. "I gave a baby boy up for adoption when I was nineteen, which would make him twenty-six now. I did it in New York, and it was a closed adoption, which means no contact with the child or parents after birth, but the baby was born in New York State."

He nodded, obviously understanding the impact of that. "New York passed a law a few years ago allowing parties from a closed adoption to seek each other out," he said. "But the seeker cannot force themselves on the seekee."

She nodded, immediately reassured by his knowledge of a fairly arcane law. "I know that, and I would never try to meet him if he didn't want to. In fact, I've waited since the law passed, hoping he'd reach out to me, but he hasn't. So now...I'm ready to try."

"If I can find him, I will inform him that his birth mother wants to meet him. But if he says no?"

She held up her hand. "End of story, I promise."

Maybe not in her heart, but in her head. She understood that. "But I am worried about something. What if he doesn't know he's adopted?"

Miles tipped his head and scowled. "It's rare, but not unheard of. There really is no good reason *not* to inform a child he's been adopted, and it isn't a safe decision. Your medical records are available to him, if not your identity. Adoptive parents are urged to tell the child, at the right time and in the right way, that they are adopted. There can be more damage done by not telling them."

She flinched, hoping his parents didn't damage him. Not her baby. Not that little, tiny nugget with a shock of dark hair and a face that somehow looked like a newborn version of his father's. She saw him for a few precious, achy minutes before giving him up.

"Okay. Where do we start?" she asked.

"Tell me everything you know. The hospital, the date, the adoption agency, any names you have, anything that I can use to search records."

She closed her eyes and let herself drift back to that dreary day in 1996, to a rosy, warm maternity ward at the hospital in the Bronx, and the utter desolation she felt making her decision.

It was then that the feeling of loneliness started to plague her. Before that, she'd been a somewhat introverted only child of a strange set of parents. But the moment she handed that baby to a nurse, she knew true and bone-deep...isolation.

She tamped down the feelings and gave Miles as many details as she could remember, including the exact date and time, the name of the doctor, the nurse on duty, and the non-profit organization through Fordham University that helped her.

Miles took copious notes, asked a few pertinent questions, then finished up the interview when they heard Tinkerbell's bark and Eliza's happy laugh.

"Come and join us, Eliza," Claire called, only realizing then that her whole body was tense from the exchange and she needed Eliza's calming presence.

"Sure. Let me get Tinkerbell's leash off. Does she get a treat for doing what she was supposed to do?"

Miles chuckled softly, his whole expression changing as he pushed up. "I'll show you where they are, Eliza." As he walked by Claire, he put a strong but gentle hand on her shoulder. "You did well," he said softly. "Don't worry."

As he walked out, she realized she had blinked a tear down her cheek. She sat very still for a moment, trying to steady herself, listening to Miles and Eliza talk and laugh down the hall.

Just hearing her sister's voice pressed some peace on Claire's heart. Then Tinkerbell came bounding in, followed by Eliza.

"Claire!" She reached for her hands, pulling Claire up. "Are you okay?"

She wrapped her sister close and let Eliza's presence magically erase the loneliness. "I am now," she whispered. And, truly, for the first time since that day in the Bronx, she believed it.

# Chapter Fourteen

## Olivia

W hen she locked the front door of Sanibel Treasures and flipped the sign to Closed, Olivia peered into the street, looking left and right. She told herself she was looking for Scott, who said he'd be here to pick her up for dinner at five sharp, when the store closed. Maybe he'd be late, and she could finish the weekly sales report for Teddy.

She suspected this guy wouldn't be late for a dentist appointment, let alone a date with her. Still, he wasn't there, which surprised her. So she looked a little harder, toward the beach, then the street.

"Who are you kidding, Olivia Whitney?" she muttered to herself. "You're not looking for Scott." Of course she wasn't. Because didn't Deeley often find some reason to pass the store or stop in or eat his lunch on that bench and count the minutes that she spent with a particular customer he was jealous of?

Or had she imagined all of that, she wondered as she headed to the back office. Like she'd imagined the chemistry between them and the spark when they accidentally touched and...

"Stop it, Livvie!" she whispered angrily.

"Stop what?"

She gasped noisily at the sound of the man's voice, freezing in her tracks at the sight of Scott. "Holy cow, you scared me! What are you doing back here?"

He pointed to the back door. "Unlocked." He lifted a brow. "Probably not so safe, Livvie."

"Oh, I forgot." The fact was, the door had to be unlocked with a key from Roz's massive ring to go out or in, so when she unloaded inventory, like she had today, she just kept it ajar. Of course he'd walked right in.

"Well, you should have hollered," she said, the adrenaline rush putting an edge in her voice. "I wasn't expecting anyone."

"I told you I'd be here at five."

"Not expecting you in my back office," she clarified, still battling the irritation.

Was that because he'd startled her...or because he just wasn't the date she wanted to have tonight?

"So what were you chiding yourself about?"

She frowned, not following, trying so hard to see him as a tall, halfway decent-looking man—actually, he was three-quarters of the way decent. In fact, if she hadn't spent half her waking hours and a few of her sleeping ones thinking about Connor Deeley, he'd be a really fine-looking man. Fine as in okay, not fine as in *so fine*.

But, anyway, he paled in comparison to Deeley, as any mere mortal would.

"Just now," he urged when she didn't answer. "You said, 'Stop it, Livvie.' Stop what?"

*Stop thinking about Connor Deeley.*

"Stop obsessing about...work." She gave a weak smile. "I told you, I'm a workaholic."

"I think you're fine," he said, weirdly echoing her thoughts. "You're leaving now. You come in at, what? Nine most days? That's not a workaholic. You're very balanced. Are you ready to go?"

She sighed and nodded. "Pretty much."

"Unless I showed up too early and you do want to do some more work? I'm happy to help. Move some inventory? Work on the books? Order some fresh purchases for the store? I'll help you any way you want, Livvie."

She smiled at him and glanced at the roses on her desk, a constant reminder that he genuinely liked her. So, her heart softened a little, or maybe just got mushy with guilt. He was a good guy, and he wanted to help. And he wasn't Deeley, but was that his fault?

"Well, I could use maybe half an hour to run some quick numbers, and then I'd probably be more relaxed."

He gestured toward her desk, which was much neater than Roz had ever kept it. "Run away. Not literally, of course."

She laughed and pulled out the chair. "It won't take long to do the day's receipts. You want to go get a cup of coffee or take a walk to the beach or..." No, she could see by the look on his face he didn't want to.

"I'm an investor, Olivia. I'm kind of turned on by numbers, if that's not too bold to say. Can you share?"

"Sure." She laughed softly and gestured toward the only other chair. "Don't get too turned on now," she teased, "but I'm bringing up a spreadsheet."

He pretended to fan his face, making her laugh.

She *had* to give this guy a chance. He wasn't swoony, but he was here and interested in business. Wasn't that the kind of guy she always thought she wanted? One she could come home to, and talk about work over dinner?

With a guy like Deeley, they'd...kayak in the moonlight.

She stabbed a keyboard key with a little too much force. "Let me just grab the numbers."

He sat back, taking out his phone and at least pretending to be doing something remotely interesting while she tapped the keys and found the right files.

"I really can't believe how well that Christmas stuff sells," she mused, glancing at the numbers. "Ornaments are gold in this place. I just put in another order."

"People like to remember their vacations, I guess."

"But we definitely have a deficit in the message-in-a-bottle area. I guess I could reopen that part of the business and take a stab at selling George's concept."

He nodded and looked like he truly cared about that. "The one where people buy a bottle and note paper and leave a message in the water, then whoever finds it comes in and there's a donation to the Historical Society? Am I remembering that correctly?"

"Good memory," she said. "You really were listening."

"I listen to everything you say," he told her. "Even things you don't want me to hear."

She looked up from the keyboard. "Like, 'Stop it, Livvie'?" she guessed.

"And other things."

Her fingers slowed as she eyed him. "Like what?"

"Like throwaway things you say about what's going on with your mother and the lady who owns this place, Teddy."

She had told him bits and pieces along the way. "It's not that interesting," she said, returning to the keyboard.

"I think it's fascinating. You mentioned they were going to court. How did that turn out?"

Her fingers stilled again as she searched his face. He truly cared, and that was just a massive reminder that she was dismissing him too easily. He cared about her life, this business, her family, their future. It was sweet and, well, caring.

"It turned out...messy," she told him. "Teddy doesn't actually own the property."

He lifted his brows. "Who does?"

"My grandfather, as I mentioned, was the last owner. Teddy wasn't legally married to him, but another woman was."

"And she's contesting the will Teddy has?"

She laughed. "If only it were that simple. Teddy doesn't have a will, Camille does."

"Camille?"

"Camille Durant, who was married to my grandfather and has the will. You might have seen her around here now and again. French lady with sleek black hair, usually wearing something Chanel?"

He frowned. "Maybe. So she's in court against Teddy?"

"Noooo." She dragged out the word and laughed at how to describe the absolute mess. "She's in court against another lady named Birdie."

"Birdie? Like tweet-tweet birdie?"

"Short for Roberta."

His eyes grew wide as he inched closer. "What's *her* claim on the place?"

"A will, also legit, and older than Camille's. She was married to Dutch, too." The bigamy was just too much and too embarrassing, so she left it at that. "Those two are fighting about it in court."

"Oh." Slowly, he dropped back into his chair. "So either one of them could win." He actually sounded like it mattered, and that loosened a little bit of ice around her heart.

"We're rooting for Camille," she added.

"Why? Because you know and like her?"

"Because if Camille wins, then she's going to sell the property to Teddy for a dollar."

"What?" He sat straight up. "Sorry, I just...a *dollar*? This whole waterfront place with multiple cottages and this store and...*why*?"

"Because..." She shook her head. "Teddy's family built it and Dutch—that's my grandfather—wanted her to have it."

"Then why didn't he put her in his will?"

"Because..." *Because he didn't want to get busted as a bigamist and he was weird and complicated*, but neither of those truths seemed like the right thing to say. "He didn't, and we really don't know why. Anyway, it's not really my story to tell. All I can say is, my mother's invested in the outcome."

"She's put money into the place, too?"

"Emotionally invested. I guess we all are. Teddy's awesome and she and her family are basically Sanibel Island legends, so..." She'd already said too much.

"So when will it all be decided?"

"Soon, we hope. They've had a hearing."" She glanced at the computer, wanting to let the topic go and return to her numbers, but he was utterly rapt.

"What happened at the hearing?"

She shrugged. "Not much. He wants testimony, and we don't know when that's going to happen."

"She'd really sell this place for a dollar? That's really unbelievable."

"She wouldn't sell it to just anyone," Olivia corrected. "Only Teddy, because her family is so deeply connected to the land." She searched his face, still seeing a mix of utter fascination and disbelief. "I guess as an investor that throws you, but it's a symbolic thing. Camille wants to honor Dutch's final wishes, and my grandfather said he wanted to give it to her."

Now, he smiled at her. "So you come from a long line of romantics, huh? Would never have guessed it."

"I know, a hardened cynic like me."

His eyes danced a little, more flirtatious than she'd ever seen him. "Do the numbers, Olivia. I'm getting hungry."

"I'll try," she said, forcing herself to focus on the screen.

"I'll let you get to it." He pushed up. "I actually have one more call with someone on the West Coast, so let me make that while you work, and we'll be out of here in a jiffy."

"Perfect. Thanks."

With a nod, he stepped outside, using the back door and leaving her alone. She sat for a minute, thinking about the exchange, his interest and very low-key sense of humor.

He really wasn't a bad guy at all.

And she'd made no effort to even look great for this date. On impulse, she closed the document and grabbed her bag, heading to the small powder room tucked behind the shelves overflowing with shell-covered coffee mugs and candles that came in on a vendor's truck not two hours ago. Deeley still hadn't moved the shelves or secured them to the wall, so boxes were piled on the floor.

What did she like so much about Deeley? If she so much as uttered the word "shelves" to Scott, he'd have it done. No, he probably wasn't strong enough to move the unit, which Deeley could do with one hand.

Deeley again. She made a face and pulled open the bathroom door.

There was a frosted window that didn't close completely—another thing on Deeley's to-do list—but because of that, she could hear the soft tones of Scott's voice coming through from the parking lot, though she was unable to make out the words. She leaned closer to the glass panel, curious about his business and how Mr. Tall Dark and Not Deeley conducted it.

Maybe if she saw him in his element, she'd stop comparing them. Because until she did, poor Scott didn't stand a chance.

She peeked through the crack, catching a glimpse of Scott in the middle of the small lot, phone to his ear, face up to the sky, listening at first. Then, he threaded his fingers through his hair—see, it wasn't receding that badly!—and sighed.

"Do not agree at all. Sorry. The way I see it? Full-blown opportunity and another way to close this deal, which we will do. And you can guarantee our client that this is happening, because I am going to make it happen."

*Oh, now we're talking.* That was the world-beater, deal-maker, get-stuff-done kind of guy she wanted.

She turned to the mirror—and grimaced at a woman who did not look like she dated a world beater. Hustling back to her desk, she fished through her purse for a makeup bag, then headed back to the bathroom to *zhuzh* up a bit.

She touched up her makeup, ran a comb through her hair, and brushed her teeth. Smoothing her T-shirt, she grimaced, thinking of how he'd worn a dress shirt and khakis. She closed her eyes and pictured what she had in the store.

"Sold." In a flash, she went to the floor and snagged a white tank-top dress that was meant to be a beach coverup, but with a few puka shells, some sparkly flipflops, and a turquoise scarf around her waist, she fashioned a perfect summer date night outfit.

Dressed and satisfied, she grabbed her bag and

hurried to the door, a little excited about the evening for the first time all day. She strode with confidence to the back door, opening it just as he finished the call and turned to her.

"Are you... *wow*." He blew out a noisy and appreciative breath as his gaze lingered on her face and made its way over the dress. "Spreadsheets make you even prettier."

She smiled, getting a kick out of his reaction. "That's the magic of lipstick and mascara. Oh, and"—she brushed her hands down the dress—"our new summer line from Sanibel Treasures."

"You look amazing, Livvie."

"Thank you. How was your call? Big investment deal?"

"Honestly?" He laughed softly. "This one is huge and could be a game-changer for me."

"Really?" She slid her arm into his and guided him down the one step to the gravel parking area. "Tell me about it over dinner. Let's go."

For a few long heartbeats, he looked down at her and for one second, she was sure he was going to kiss her. He hadn't yet, and that was...fine. But something flickered in his eyes—doubt or just a change of heart—and he inched back and held the keys out again.

"Did you lock the door, Liv?"

"Good call, Scott." As she did, she couldn't help smiling. It was the little things, the acts of thoughtfulness that she should try to focus on, not who he *wasn't*. She had to remember that.

"Now, dinner and spreadsheet talk?" he asked.

"Oh, come on, now. You're making me swoon," she joked.

He put his arm around her and led her to his car. "That, Olivia Whitney, is exactly what I'm here to do."

# Chapter Fifteen

## *Eliza*

"Well, this is a surprise, Eliza." Miles placed his napkin on his lap and smiled across the corner booth she'd snagged at Doc Ford's, a popular restaurant that was hopping with the lunch crowd. "A pleasant one," he added.

"Thanks for agreeing to meet me, Miles. I needed a little break from the tension mounting at Shellseeker Beach and you've taken me on so many lovely boat rides, I thought it was time you be my guest for a change."

His eyes, dark bottle green in this light, warmed as his smile deepened. "You don't owe me lunch, Eliza, and I like spending time with you."

She waited for the internal reaction to his words and, yep, sure enough, there it was. That little bit of a heart jump that she shouldn't feel, didn't want to feel, and really would like to deny...but there it was.

She covered her reaction by looking down for one quick second at the napkin she smoothed on her lap. "Same," she said, striving for the casual note she'd often heard Olivia fling at Deeley.

Oh, God. If she felt about Miles the way Livvie felt about Deeley? She was doomed. She'd had a date with

Scott last night, and this morning? She must have casually mentioned Deeley ten times.

And that wasn't why Eliza was here at all, anyway. This had nothing to do with the bit of tautness in her chest that seemed to grow every time she was with him.

"So how tense is it over at Shellseeker?"

"Pretty darn tense with each day we wait to hear about the testimony, so I usually escape by going sight-seeing or shopping with Claire, but a big case exploded at her law firm this morning, so she's behind closed doors being a lawyer."

"And Teddy?" he asked. "How's she holding up?"

"She's Teddy, mostly calm. No crystals have been thrown, no one's drowned in too much tea, and you won't find any dead bodies buried under the gazebo."

"Yikes," he said with a laugh. "If that's the bar, then things must bad."

She thought about how to describe the mood when Teddy and Camille were together. "It's an undercurrent of..." Doubt? Distrust? No, that wasn't it. "Teddy and Camille just don't seem to really communicate well."

"I haven't met Camille, but if she's anything like Claire, I can't imagine she's hard to get along with."

"She's nothing like Claire," Eliza assured him. "And she's the polar opposite of low-key, empathetic Teddy. She's...high key. Is there such a thing?"

He laughed. "Sounds like there should be."

"And she doesn't know the meaning of empathy, which is what makes Teddy tick. No one else really exists when Camille's in a room. The light, air, and attention must be on her, which can be exhausting. Truth is? I'm amazed my father loved both women, they're so different."

He nodded, considering that. "Do you think she's going to back out of the deal she made to give the property to Teddy? I mean," he added, taking a sip of his own iced tea, "assuming she wins."

"I don't know, but we're all thinking about it all the time. She says she won't. There's no reason, other than pure profit, she would. But she's hard to read sometimes. And speaking of winning that case, that's kind of why I asked you to lunch, if I'm being wholly honest."

She could have sworn she saw a flicker of disappointment in his eyes. "Some Birdie intelligence?"

"Yes, if that's not pushing you outside of your professional comfort zone. I don't think Claire would ask you, not even wearing her lawyer's hat, or in her role as the executor of the will, but..." She made a face. "I'm not a lawyer and you're a..."

"Friend," he supplied. "I certainly am."

"Thanks, Miles. And you've met Birdie. You are our only connection to her. Can you give me any idea what they are going to face in that courtroom?"

He considered that for a long moment, taking a deeper drink of tea. "She's probably more like Camille than what you're expecting."

"Oh? A big personality?"

"A strong one," he said. "I didn't spend enough time with her to determine how that would manifest, but I got the distinct impression she's looking out for number one.

She may claim her religion has kept her from getting a divorce, but my gut says that woman has been waiting for Dutch to die so she could collect the inheritance."

"Well, she's waited a long time. And she couldn't get married, either."

"She might just be unbelievably patient."

Eliza grunted softly as the server returned with a fresh seafood salad for Eliza, and soft tacos overflowing with seafood for Miles. They thanked him, had their tea refilled, and finally returned to the conversation, giving Miles a few minutes to think some more about Birdie.

"It really doesn't matter who Birdie is or what her personality is like," he said as he gathered up a taco. "She'll fake it for the judge. She'll have a whole angle ready about how she gave up her entire life for this man who married her under false pretenses and she's owed this inheritance."

"Then tell me about Judge Macgregor," Eliza said. "You know him well. What do you think will tip the scales with him? Birdie's unfair treatment or Camille's life-long relationship?"

"The law," he said simply, wiping the corners of his mouth after taking a bite. "Jon's driven by the letter of the law."

"Jon? You know him that well?"

"I not only know him well, we went fishing on my boat the other day."

She sat up a little straighter. "Way to bury the lead, Mr. Anderson."

He laughed, a hearty, real chuckle that came from his

chest and was decidedly attractive. "We did not discuss the case, which would be wildly unprofessional, since both you and Claire are now on my client roster."

"Fair enough."

"And I cannot tell you more about him than what I've already said. Jon makes fair decisions based on the letter of the law."

"Did our names even come up?"

A smile tipped up the corner of his lips and he held her gaze for one second longer than she'd expect. "I can't say."

"Would that be stretching the bounds of professionalism?"

"It would be stretching the bounds of the fishing code."

She drew back and laughed softly. "Excuse me? There's a fishing code?"

"It's like, uh, a bro code is what Deeley would call it. For the over-fifty set. Although," he angled his head. "Not sure Jon qualifies yet, but he's close."

Totally intrigued and kind of wishing she could see that half-smile again, Eliza leaned forward. "Like a code of...secrecy?"

"Something like that." Still looking at her, he polished off the last bite of one taco, making Eliza realize she'd barely touched her salad. "Drop it, Eliza," he said as he swallowed. "You're not going to get anywhere. But we can talk about the probate case and the witnesses all you like."

"Oh, okaaaay." She smiled. "You know you're only making me way more curious about your fishing code."

He lifted a shoulder. "Nope. Not talking about it."

*Why*, she wondered. "Well, I'm not sure what else I can ask you about the case, however nuanced the case is. And it is."

"Not really," Miles said, sipping his tea. "The answer to the case is quite simple: what did Dutch want when he died?"

"Not simple," she replied. "Because if it was, he would have made a third will and named Teddy the heir. Also not simple, because there are different laws about which will carries the most weight, the newest or the oldest."

"The one not written under duress."

"So if we could prove he wrote Birdie's under duress, then we'd have a case."

"Maybe. But it would be much better if you could prove he wanted Camille to have the place. Something, anything that would verify that."

She shook her head. "We've got nothing."

"Or," he added, "something that would explain why he didn't make that legal change for Teddy but wanted to. And Camille could testify that she plans to honor that." At her look, he nodded. "But once again, nothing in writing. I know."

"Well, we know why he didn't make it legal for Teddy," she said. "At least we could speak to his motivation about not wanting to out himself as a bigamist."

"He knew it would come out eventually," Miles

countered, shaking his head with a frown. "It is puzzling why he wouldn't face that."

"He was afraid," Eliza said softly, lowering her fork before biting the cold mussel on the end of it. "He didn't believe in the afterlife in any way, shape or form. He honestly figured he'd be dead and gone and it was our problem to work out."

Miles curled his lip. "Sorry, I know he's your father, but...not cool."

No, it wasn't. "Sometimes," she admitted, "I forget how much I couldn't stand him when I first got here. He's always been the enemy, you know? My mother hated him with the heat of a thousand suns, and I grew up thinking he was the worst human on Earth. But here?"

"People liked him a lot," he said. "He was a big personality, liked to liven up Teddy's parties, and he gave everyone a nickname. People really like that."

She lifted a shoulder. "He was dying, so I guess he lived every day like it was his last."

"How long did he know he was sick?" Miles asked.

"When he got here, he thought he had six or seven weeks left, so he decided to live at his investment property. Then Teddy did her Teddy thing and gave him two extra years. I guess he was a kinder and gentler Dutch because of that."

"Knew he was facing the end."

She shook her head. "From what I know about him, that truly didn't matter. He was a hard-core atheist. My mother told me that was why he was so fearless as a pilot. When he died, it was over. So he lived life to the fullest.

As many flights, women, wives, and wills as he could produce." She heard the edge in her voice. "Damn the torpedoes and the mess he left in his wake."

He put his hand on hers, the first time she could ever remember such a personal touch from him, more than just helping her on and off his boat. No surprise, his touch was warm and comforting and even a little rough, probably from handling lines and fishing rods.

"Eliza," he said. "Are you going to eat or get yourself in a froth over your late father?"

She smiled. "Froth."

"Not worth it. Eat that salad and let's talk about something else."

She searched his face for a moment, giving in to the urge to just drink in every feature, which she usually did surreptitiously, because...because she felt guilty staring at a man who wasn't her husband.

But now, in this one second of face-to-face contact, she let herself admire his strong nose, the shape of his lips under a soft silver moustache and above his simple goatee. That bit of facial hair showcased a strong jaw and rather than aging him in any way, it actually made him seem younger and very handsome.

And...oh *crap*. She *was* staring at him like Livvie looked at Deeley.

"Something else?" she managed, her voice as stretched as her nerves. "I guess we're all so consumed with this at Shellseeker Beach that we don't talk about much else."

"I can imagine," he said. "It's a huge deal. But..." This

time he looked at her pretty intently, like he might be using the excuse to stare, too. "Once it's resolved, what are you going to do?"

"Either celebrate or cry," she said, finally getting a bite of the fish, which was amazing.

As if he'd been waiting for her to eat, he picked up his other taco. "I meant long-term. Say Teddy wins the day and keeps the property for herself. What will you do?"

"Funny you should ask." She took another bite, only realizing then how ravenous she was and how delicious the food was.

"Why funny?"

"Because that was the other thing I wanted to talk to you about today."

He lifted his brows, curious.

"What's it like to live here on Sanibel Island?"

He blinked at her. "Really? You're thinking about staying?" There was the strangest note in his voice, almost indecipherable. A little shock, a little hope, a little...something else.

"You think that's a problem or a good thing?"

"It's good." He grinned. "Wait'll I tell Tinkerbell."

She cracked up. "Yeah, you can travel at will, Miles. You know that Tinkerbell will always have a dogsitter if I'm here."

It was his turn to forget the food, she noticed, as the taco rested in his hand and he stared at her. "Are you serious, though, Eliza?" he finally asked. "You'd leave L.A. forever?"

"And live in paradise with perfect weather, fantastic

people, and..." *You*. She swallowed that thought. "Tinker-bell," she said instead with a laugh.

But he didn't laugh. He was still scanning her face, taco frozen mid-bite in his hand, a storm of questions in his eyes.

"Is it that preposterous that I'd move here?" she asked.

"It's kind of..." He shook his head a little. "I wouldn't want to...to..." He chuckled self-consciously at the stammer. "Don't want anyone to get their hopes up," he finally finished.

"Wait." Her smile faded and her heart dropped as she thought of another, less flirtatious way she could interpret that. "You don't think Teddy's going to win, do you. You know something—something from that fishing code with the judge—and you don't want me to think about living here because it isn't going to happen. Birdie's going to win and sell the property and Shellseeker Beach will be ruined."

"Shhh." He rested his hand on hers again. "I swear I don't. I don't know anything about what Jon's thinking regarding the case."

"But you know what he's thinking regarding...something."

"It's nothing, Eliza. Really. Couldn't be less of anything at all."

She eased back on the wooden seat of the booth, her lovely appetite forgotten, the low-grade—and probably imaginary—flirtation history. Now, there was nothing but a black ball of worry in her heart.

"She's going to lose, isn't she?"

"I do not know that," he ground out the words.

"Then what did you mean about not getting my hopes up?"

"Nothing, it was...nothing." He huffed out a breath. "I give you my word I don't know a thing that would help you one way or the other. But I will tell you that if you can find something, anything at all, that would prove to the court that Dutch wanted Camille to have the property, or," he added, holding up a finger, "for Teddy to have it by way of a deal he made with Camille? That will sway him."

"So it's okay for him to know that Camille plans to give it to Teddy?"

"If—and only if—you can prove that is exactly what Dutch wanted when he died."

She practically moaned thinking of how many times she and Teddy and Olivia and even Claire had combed through his belongings looking for exactly that, but found nothing of the sort.

"Even if Teddy can testify to his last words, under oath," he added. "Does she remember? Do you know what his last words were?"

She swallowed and closed her eyes. "Word," she whispered. "His last word was...Birdie."

When she opened her eyes, he looked...not good. Like she'd just handed the case to the wrong side.

"I'd keep that out of the testimony," he said softly.

She nodded. "Any other tips? Besides, you know, 'Don't get your hopes up'?"

He searched her face, his deep green eyes locked on her, then he smiled. "If I gave it to you, I'd be shattering the fishing code."

Hope crawled up her chest. "Please, Miles. Please shatter it."

Only when he added some pressure on her hand did she realize that he was still touching her, still connected. "You have a secret weapon that you don't realize. It has to remain secret. It really can't and won't affect the case, not if Birdie's attorney blows the roof off the court—and that could happen."

"A secret weapon?" she asked, inching closer. "What is it?"

He smiled. "Jon thought Claire was gorgeous."

Her jaw dropped. What? "Um. He's a *judge*."

"And a man," he said.

She let out a soft laugh, suddenly imagining these two guys fishing and talking about clients and attorneys and...*women*. "What did you say?"

A slow smile pulled his lips and his eyes danced, but he didn't say a word.

"Come on, Miles, the fishing code has been destroyed with that tidbit. What did you say?"

"I said..." He leaned over the table to whisper, "'You think? Well, wait till you see Eliza.'"

She sucked in a breath, and he laughed. Just enough that she wasn't sure if he was teasing or not, but...it sure felt good.

At least she knew one thing—the flirtation was *not* imaginary.

# Chapter Sixteen

## *Teddy*

I t shouldn't have been fun. Not in the traditional sense of the word. The conversation was heavy, there was a lot at stake, and except for Harper showing up with sprinkle-covered sugar cookies all shaped more or less like the continent of Australia, the small group gathered in Teddy's living room really wasn't laughing much.

There was serious business on the table along with those oddly-shaped but quite delicious cookies.

But to Teddy? How could she be anything but happy? She looked at Eliza and Claire, who sat close on the sofa, leaning in to exchange comments, easily sharing laughs and inside jokes like they'd been raised as sisters. Across from them, Olivia was regaling Katie with stories about life in the corporate lane, maybe making the younger woman very pleased she didn't have to go to an office every day.

Harper was on the floor, feet in the air, coloring a page from a book she'd found in the back. Even at her young age, she knew it was more entertaining in this room than in the one filled with *Frozen* toys.

Only Camille was missing from this gathering. She'd begged off the impromptu pizza party—even declining a slice of Papa Luigi's world-class pepperoni—and stayed in her cottage for the evening.

"Teddy, Claire and I think there's only one thing to do," Eliza said as Teddy came in with a refill pot of tea in one hand and an open wine bottle in the other. This group, she had to admit, seemed a little more interested in the wine.

"I know what you're going to say." Teddy set the bottle and teapot on the coffee table and took a chair. "We have to go through every single belonging, pocket, book, journal, and the backs of pictures Dutch owned and see if we can find something, anything, to support our case."

"If what Miles told me today at lunch is correct?" Eliza shrugged. "Anything, anything at all could be a turning point for the judge."

"I think I've been through it all," Teddy said. "You did quite a bit, too, Eliza. And Olivia."

"Everything," Claire said. "Checking the pockets of his clothes, reading journals, or flipping through old calendars."

"Even the backs of those photos," Olivia chimed in. "Look what a jackpot that turned out to be."

Eliza smiled at Claire, no doubt remembering how she'd looked at a photo that Teddy had always thought was of a two-year-old Eliza, only to learn that Dutch had another daughter.

Claire held up her hand and Eliza met it with a high-five, sharing a silent smile.

"Is everything upstairs?" Eliza asked Teddy.

"Because if you give us permission, we could search and you don't have to go through everything one more time, Teddy. I know it's hard."

She lifted a shoulder. "Not that hard, not...with you." She smiled at the two sisters, then at Olivia and Katie, finally looking down at Harper. "I love this," she whispered.

"Going through his stuff?" Olivia asked with a frown.

"No, this." She swept her hand to include them all. "You. All of you."

"Girls' nights are fun," Katie agreed. "I sure enjoy them."

"It's more than girls," Teddy said. "It's...family. And don't tell me that only some of you are related. You're all here and you're all...mine." She blinked back some tears and gave a self-conscious laugh. "And I am obviously an emotional wreck."

Katie was the first one who shot up to wrap her arms around Teddy. "You are just completely full of love, Theodora Blessing. Not a wreck at all."

Harper looked up, concern in her childish expression. "Are you crying, Aunt Teddy? Don't cry." She abandoned her coloring to join her mother on the other side of Teddy, reaching for the tray on the table. "Have a cookie. Pink sprinkles make you feel better."

"Oh, sweetheart." Teddy hugged her, too, looking over her little blond ponytail at Claire and Eliza. "I'm just a little...overwhelmed, and not with the idea of opening up those bins and digging through Dutch's life again, no. That's not it."

"What is it?" Eliza asked gently.

"The stress of the hearing?" Claire guessed.

"Not knowing what's next?" Olivia added.

Teddy took a deep breath and hugged Harper a little tighter, blinking and not caring that a tear threatened to trickle down her cheek. "Losing this."

"Of course you're worried," Claire said gently. "You've lived in this house your entire life."

"Your father and grandfather built everything here." Katie sighed at the thought.

"We all understand how much this means to you, Teddy," Eliza said gently. "That's why we want to do anything, *anything* at all, to help Camille win this case so you can keep all of this."

She nodded, searching for the right words. "I appreciate that you all recognize the true sentimental value of this whole place. But that's not what I'm afraid of losing. It's you. All of you. *The You.* My family that I've created."

They all sort of moaned and reached for her, piling on promises that they would always be her family.

After a long group hug, Olivia, always pragmatic, motivated them with a few quick claps.

"All right, ladies," she said, rubbing her hands together as if she couldn't wait to dive into a task. "One more time through the Life of Dutch?"

Katie rose immediately. "Teddy, remember? I moved some of Dutch's boxes to the spare room closet. Have you been through those?"

"Once, not long after he died. I was in a fog."

"Oof, I know that feeling," Eliza whispered, getting a sympathetic look from Olivia.

"I know where those boxes in the back are, Aunt Teddy!" Harper bounced on her toes. "I use them as the teacher's desk when I play school. I can help!" Then she looked up at her mother. "What are we doing again?"

"You're loving me!" Teddy exclaimed, throwing both arms around the dear, sweet child and kissing her head. "You are all just loving me so much."

No one argued with that as they made a plan of attack for one more pass through everything Dutch left behind. With Olivia's motto of, "No paper, photo, or clue left behind," they trudged to the back and carted a few boxes back up to Teddy's room.

There, they pulled more bins out of the closet and divided everything into sections so each of them could take a box and cover the room in memories of Dutch.

Claire and Eliza took the photos down and out of frames, Teddy pulled out "Dutch's drawer" from the dresser, and Katie and Olivia started sorting through his old clothes and checking pockets, linings, and every other place he might have hidden a slip of paper or a photo. Something. Anything.

While they worked, they all chatted and laughed, some sipped more wine, a few shared memories of Dutch, and Teddy wondered how and why Camille wasn't here.

Maybe it was better that way, or maybe not. Teddy didn't know, but she was so grateful to the family that *was* here, and so hopeful that they'd find what they were looking for.

THEY DIDN'T. Not a shred of anything other than a lot of memories of a life...not so well lived. Lived to the edge, but was it a good life? The whole thing just exhausted Teddy.

*What did Dutch really want in the end*, she mused as she climbed onto her bed where Harper had fallen asleep over an hour earlier. She wrapped her fingers around the oversized quartz pendant on its thick silver chain, the first one Teddy had ever given Dutch. Eliza had found it in a box of clothes, folded in a silk pocket square covered with the Pan Am logo.

At first, Dutch had worn it simply to please Teddy. He had no faith in crystals. Or tea. Or her empathetic, healing touch.

But with each passing day, his doubts and cynicism waned. Once he passed the arbitrary date the doctors had given him as the point in time when an inoperable brain tumor would likely kill him, he no longer scoffed at the crystal. He wore it daily until she found him a smaller one, but he'd saved the big one, laughingly calling it "his fake magic diamond."

And now it hung around Teddy's neck, like the weight of his memory...and the frustration of the evening's project.

All around the room, the others repacked everything, but they talked Teddy out of helping. So, she stroked Harper's wheat-toned hair, listening to Olivia and Eliza laugh about something as they carted the boxes to their proper places, and Claire and Katie talking softly about the challenges of any woman's life, no matter the path she chose.

How amazing that this group had come together. For that, she was grateful to Dutch. Maybe that's all he wanted in the end. Maybe he just wanted his women—related, close, distant, ancillary—to find each other and fill Teddy's always open arms.

If so, then he succeeded.

But she didn't know if that was true, because she didn't know *him* at all. An ache in her chest, familiar now, pressed on her heart.

She placed the crystal over it, but that didn't help. Something was in there, trying to get out, a pain, real and deep, that came with knowing that she might have imagined her love for Dutch, and his for her.

As she sifted through pieces of his life today, it was obvious that for a man who told her he loved her every day and shared endless stories about fascinating places he'd been and remarkable people he'd met...he didn't share his soul.

So, despite the unification ceremony and the laughter and love and long walks on the beach, and even with her gift of seven hundred and four extra days to his life...if he didn't share his soul, then they certainly were not soulmates.

She let out a groan as the pain of that burned. A little shame, a bit of remorse, and a whole lot of fear. Was that why he never told her he was married to two other women? Why he verbally promised to give her the family's land, but never put it in writing?

"Oh." She pressed her hands on her chest. Everything hurt.

Her eyes fluttered closed and she heard more whispering, then Eliza suggested they all hang out quietly downstairs while Teddy rested.

Half asleep, she felt Olivia pull up the blanket from the foot of the bed, aware that the sun had long ago set and warm evening air blew in through the open sliders. Claire perched on the edge of the bed and took Teddy's hand.

Eliza closed the slider, but not completely, and Katie kissed Harper's head before they quietly left Teddy napping in the dark.

The process of searching for something that didn't exist had wiped her out, and she fell asleep to the sound of beloved women's voices and some gentle laughter floating up from downstairs.

But she awakened with a start when a new one pierced her awareness, high-pitched and definitely upset.

Was that Camille?

She threw her blanket off and blinked into the dark room, inhaling the lingering scent of Claire's Chanel perfume and the mustiness of old paper and boxes. She reached for Harper, who was curled into a ball, sound asleep.

"He accosted me, that's what! I was terrified." Camille's light French accent mixed with serious fear propelled Teddy from her bed and to the door, shaking off the surprisingly deep nap as the questions were volleyed downstairs.

"Who was he?"

"What did he look like?"

"Did he touch you? Hurt you?"

"What exactly happened, Camille?" The last one, from Claire, was asked in that even, lawyerly tone she had, and made Teddy reach to close the door so the conversation didn't wake Harper.

Then she stood on the landing perched over the living area and listened.

"I opened the cottage door to get some air and there he was. Sitting on the porch like he belonged there." She whimpered. "I was terrified."

"What did he say?" Eliza asked. "Was he lost? Looking for someone?"

Teddy clung to the railing and hung back in the shadows so that if any of them looked up, they wouldn't see her, but she stayed very still to listen.

"He said he was looking for me," Camille said. "He knew my full name, including my middle name, I might add. He said, 'Are you Camille Marie Durant Vanderveen?'"

Vanderveen? Camille had never changed her name. A few of the others' comments echoed that thought.

"That's what really got me," she said. "And then he told me he represented the Baldwin Hotel Group."

Oh, no. They'd found her. One of the very most aggressive and sneakiest of the big hotel chains that had been circling Shellseeker Beach for years, trying to buy it.

Dutch had flicked them all away like they were disgusting little bugs, but since he died? They'd been relentless. She'd ignored all their offers with one statement: the ownership of the property is in probate.

When the voices settled downstairs, Camille continued. "He said he'd seen the court papers, he knew exactly what was happening, and was aware that I could very well be the owner in a matter of days. Is that possible?"

"Absolutely," Claire said. "The court records are public. What else did he say?"

"He told me that Baldwin Hotels is willing to pay me an insane amount of money for the property. And I do mean *insane*."

Teddy gripped the railing to keep from swaying. She knew exactly how insane it was. They'd given her dollar figures in the past. And who knew? Maybe they'd increased the amount. At this point, it could be an eight-figure number. And who would turn down that kind of money?

"What did you tell him?" Eliza asked, her voice as thin as Teddy's would be if she were down there.

"I told him that he was trespassing and he should leave."

"Did he?" Olivia asked.

"After a few minutes of making sure I understood just how much money he was talking about. And it was..." Camille blew out a whistle. "Let's just say the House of Chanel could come to *me*."

Teddy had to bite her lip to keep from whimpering aloud. How could she forget what mattered to Camille?

Looks, clothes, material things. Camille...a woman Dutch married and stayed married to for more than three decades, through every season of his life, including times when he was "in love" with someone else.

Now that? *That* was a soulmate.

She squeezed her eyes shut to keep from making a sound as they threw more questions at her, asking what he looked like, how old he was, if he left a card.

As she stood there, her heart slammed into her chest and blood thrummed in her head. She felt hot, dizzy, scared, vulnerable, and lost.

Where would she live? What would she do? What about Katie and Deeley and even Roz and George? How could she keep all her people together like a precious collection of imperfect but beautiful shells? Her throat grew dry and she felt a weird heat simmer in her belly, a little like nausea, a little like...defeat.

Without thinking, she let go of the railing with one hand and gripped the heavy crystal still hanging around her neck. It was cool to the touch, and thick in her hand. And she could practically taste the remnants of Dutch's energy all over his fake magic diamond.

Blocking out the chatter below, she lifted the crystal to her lips and kissed it lightly.

*What did you want, Dutch? What did you really want? I'll abide by the decision, but I have to know.*

"Hang on, everyone. Hang on!" Claire's voice cut through the competing conversations downstairs, bringing everyone to silence. "I have a text from the attorney in Miami."

More silence, except for a soft groan from someone. Eliza or Olivia, she guessed. She kept the crystal pressed to her lips so she didn't groan, too, as Claire read aloud.

"Judge Jonathan Macgregor has called for witness testimony tomorrow at ten a.m., sharp. He wants direct and cross-examination of any witnesses pertinent to the case. My counsel is asking for Roberta Vanderveen and Camille Durant, with an option to call Claire Sutherland, Theodora Blessing and Eliza Whitney."

"Me? Teddy?" Eliza choked. "Why would we be witnesses?"

"Our attorney, Michael Ortega, thinks it's good to have you as optional backups, based on Birdie's attorney's line of questioning."

"And who is the other attorney calling in for testimony?" Eliza asked.

"Camille, Birdie, and Father Sean MacDougall, a character witness."

"But Camille doesn't have a character witness," Olivia said. "How is that fair?"

"Camille didn't actually commit bigamy and Birdie did, whether she knew it or not," Claire explained. "She's protecting herself."

For a moment, no one said a word as the news sank in.

"Are you still insisting that you can't go, *Maman*?" Claire asked.

Camille let out a sigh, not her usual dramatic one but from the soul. Even fifteen feet above, Teddy could feel the confusion, doubt, and resentment coming from

Camille. In fact, it seemed the only time Teddy could get a good sense of what Camille was feeling was when that emotion was jagged-edged and painful.

"I don't know what I'm going to do," Camille admitted.

Of course she didn't. They were asking a lot of her. And for that, Camille was suffering. She was torn on the inside, and that meant there was only one thing Theodora Blessing could do: heal.

"Well, I have an idea," Teddy said, coming down the stairs and getting all their attention. "You're going to come with me to the gazebo."

"Now?"

"No better time." Teddy reached for her, sliding an arm around Camille's slender waist. "I heard everything and we're going for a walk."

"That man might be out there."

"The one throwing money at you?" Teddy asked on a laugh. "I'm not afraid of him." Although, deep inside, she was terrified of him and his Baldwin Hotels money. She urged Camille toward the door. "Come on. I want to tell you something. It's very, very important."

THE MOON WAS RISING over Shellseeker Beach, almost full, and casting enough light that the two of them could easily find their way.

Camille was uncharacteristically quiet, and unchar-acteristically willing to go along with this side trip to the beach. The day's humidity still hung in the air, along with the salty scent of the Gulf, tinged with the hint of the fragrance mother and daughter both loved to wear.

"You smell so good, Camille," Teddy whispered.

"Credit to Chanel No. 5, what I've worn since the first time I dabbed a drop behind my ears."

"I can't remember the last time I wore perfume," Teddy said. "I'm not even sure I own any."

"I would feel naked without it."

"I get that," Teddy said, grazing her finger over the heavy crystal she wore. "Certain things are like that to me. And that fragrance is so pretty, like everything about you."

Camille slowed her steps and gave Teddy a sideways look. "Thank you, Teddy. So what do you have to tell me? Or do you want to wait until we're in your special... *belvédère*?"

"Gazebo," Teddy corrected. "Although *belvédère* is such a beautiful word. Most things are in French, though. Words, places." She smiled at Camille. "Women."

"Ah, you're trying to...what's that expression? Butter me up? Teddy, are you that worried I'm going to back out of my deal with Dutch?"

"Actually, I'm worried that you *aren't* going to back out."

Camille looked confused, a frown pulling her brows. "Not sure I understand that."

Teddy didn't answer for a while, waiting to speak until they'd reached the empty gazebo. There, she touched the small light switch, bringing on some twinkling vineyard lights Deeley had installed around the ceiling.

They both sat on one of the benches, a few feet apart to face the water and watch the yellow glimmers of moonlight dance over the Gulf of Mexico. Teddy's heart thumped with what she had to say, and she gave the crystal one more squeeze so she could say it...right.

Although there was no wrong way.

"Camille," she started, "I think you are struggling with this decision for a reason."

"Struggling with giving you the resort? We're not there yet," she said. "I have a bigger problem now. I have to face a woman who..." She shook her head, fighting emotion. "I hate her so much, Teddy, and I don't want to look at her, speak to her, or be in the same room with her."

"I know. But you have to remember something. Dutch married you and never divorced you. Ever."

"He never divorced her, either."

"He *couldn't*," Teddy countered. "He wanted to. He never didn't want to be married to you and..." She swallowed hard. "He never wanted to be married to me."

"I'm sure he did," Camille said. "He loved you. He just had this legal...entanglement. If he hadn't—"

"He would *never* have divorced you," Teddy interjected. "I know that. You know that. Everyone knows that he loved you right down to your last drop of Chanel No. 5."

Camille laughed softly, but then her smile faded. "What are you saying?"

"That there's a reason he refused to rewrite his will. And that reason is simple. He wanted to leave everything —including all of Shellseeker Beach—to you, the woman who stood by him for forty-some years no matter what he did."

Camille just stared at her, silent.

"Yes, I love this property, these cottages, my home, and Treasures and, oh my word, I love my garden. But it doesn't belong to me, and it never did. Just like Dutch." Her voice cracked as she fought a tear. "He belonged to you more than anyone else. And I think that might have been why he said he wanted me to have it all, but he never did anything to change his will."

Camille's pretty face began to crumple like the emotional dam was threatening to break and all Teddy had to do was say one more thing and she'd go over the edge.

Teddy slid over and put a hand on Camille's arm, shocked by the first real jolt of feeling she got, a shot of true chaos in her heart.

"I don't want to push you to tears or make things any worse, Camille," she said, stroking the smooth, smooth skin to start what could be a long healing process. "I promise you that. I only want you to know that whatever you decide, I will not only accept that decision, I will embrace it. If you win tomorrow and you decide to sell this property, I'll help you get top dollar. If you decide to stay here and run it, I'll teach you how. If you decide to—"

"Stop." The word came out as a strangled plea, caught in a sob as the first tears fell. "Just stop it, Teddy."

"I'm trying to—"

"You don't know the truth!" she shot back, her tear-dampened eyes wild. "You don't know...what I did. I don't deserve this gift. I didn't deserve the time I got with him. I don't deserve your firm belief that I was the great love of his life. I...I..."

Teddy just stared at her, finally feeling the vibrations she'd been waiting for from this woman. And, good heavens, they were dark with guilt and shame and regret.

"I don't deserve it, Teddy," she ground the words out. "He wanted to be a real family, a whole, normal family. He was willing to give up flying and teach lessons, just so we would all live together and raise Claire and be a perfectly happy, normal family."

Teddy inched back. "What happened?"

She folded in half and let a sob wrack her whole body. "I cheated on him. I slept with another pilot and I broke his heart into a thousand pieces."

Teddy pressed her hand to her lips, certainly not expecting this. "Why?"

"To sabotage everything. I never deserved Dutch. I don't deserve anything good. My father, who made Dutch look like a saint, told me every day of my life that I was ugly and worthless. I only became a stewardess to prove to him that I was pretty."

Teddy shuddered at the confession, her heart aching.

"But why would you cheat on your husband?"

"Because we were so close to that...that perfect life he

wanted, and I purposely ruined everything with one night in a hotel. Proving that my father was right: I don't deserve perfection because I am not perfect."

"Oh." Her whole body ached at the unfairness of what one bad parent can set into motion. "I hope you don't still believe that, Camille."

"I don't know what I believe, but I know that when I told Dutch—I had to, the guilt was killing me—he blew out of the house and headed to the airport to get a plane somewhere, anywhere I wasn't. He met her that afternoon, in the airport, and they were married in a matter of weeks."

What a horrible, horrible situation. And how different it was from what Camille had first presented to her when she showed up on Sanibel Island. She'd blamed Dutch and his larger-than-life appetites for risk and thrill and all the while, he'd had a broken heart.

That still didn't justify bigamy, not by a long shot.

"You see why I can't go to that courtroom and claim everything as mine?" Camille asked. "I do *not* deserve this." She swept her hand around the gazebo and toward the cottages. "None of this."

"If you don't go, then Birdie will get it all."

Her eyes shuttered. "Maybe of all of us, she deserves it the most. We went into our relationships with Dutch with our eyes wide open. Birdie was...conned. She was used as retaliation against me, and Dutch got in so deep that he literally married her when he was already married to someone else."

Teddy considered that, and tamped down the white-hot fear that Birdie would get it all.

"But he came back to you," Teddy said. "You reconciled."

"I told you that things were never the same, but not just because of Birdie. I was one hundred percent complicit in ruining what we had. We grew into distant friends who cared for each other, but..." She gave a sad smile. "He didn't come to me when he was dying. He came to you."

"He barely knew me," Teddy said. "He came to Shellseeker Beach."

For a long, long time, they sat in the golden light, next to each other, quiet. After the moon rose higher, Teddy turned to Camille.

"What are you going to do?" Teddy asked.

She pushed up. "I don't know. And that's the truth."

As she started to walk out, Teddy shot up and reached for her. "Wait."

"No, Teddy, I—"

"Please." She closed her fingers over the chain hanging around her neck, sliding it over her head. Without a word, she slipped it over Camille's shiny hair and let Dutch's beloved crystal hang to her chest. "He'd want you to have this."

Camille just closed her hand around it, staring at Teddy.

"He'd want you to forgive yourself," Teddy whispered. "He'd want you to heal, and have hope."

Still silent, Camille swallowed, then turned and walked away, slowly disappearing into the darkness.

It didn't matter, Teddy realized. It didn't matter what happened in that courtroom, who testified, or what the judge decided. Teddy had most likely already lost this place and this life and...everything. By this time next year, Shellseeker Beach would probably be owned by Baldwin Hotels and there really wasn't a thing she could do about it.

Except hold on to the family she'd created. And that thought was what gave her hope of her own.

# Chapter Seventeen

*Claire*

C laire came out of the second bedroom after brushing her teeth, searching for coffee that she'd surely need today, and stood stone still in Junonia's undersized living room as a cold chill crawled through her.

The cottage was much too quiet.

Would her mother take a walk when they had to leave for the courthouse in an hour? It took her that long simply to do hair and makeup, and another thirty minutes to pick an outfit. Why was her bedroom door open, and...

She stood in the doorway and looked at the unmade bed. She never left the room without making her bed. And laying out her clothes, shoes, and jewelry for the day.

"Camille?" She walked in and looked at the ensuite bathroom, which was empty but for the massive amount of beauty products lined up on the counter.

Back in the living room, she checked the sliders, which were closed, but not locked from the inside. *Camille Durant has left the building.*

"Oh, *Maman.* Why do you have to make life diffi-cult?" Claire headed outside, barefoot and still in sleep pants and a T-shirt, looking left and right, seeing no one. Camille had been known to walk the beach, so Claire headed down there and scanned the sand, seeing a few stragglers searching for shells, but no sign of her mother.

Back in the cottage, she texted Camille's number and grunted in frustration at the soft vibration on the kitchen counter, confirming she hadn't taken her phone.

When Claire followed the sound and picked it up, hoping for some clue—a text, maybe—she spied a piece of paper under the phone, with Camille's distinctive writing.

*Good luck today. I just can't do it. C*

What? She was bailing? Do what?

Tamping down mounting frustration, she tried to think of where her mother would go. To talk to Teddy again? Camille had been very quiet after she and Teddy walked last night, heading straight to her room when she came in.

Instead of walking to the house, Claire texted Eliza to find out if she'd seen Camille. While she waited for a reply, she headed back into her room to pick court clothes and start to get ready.

Eliza wrote right back to say neither she nor Teddy had seen Camille this morning.

Oh, *God*. Where could she have gone?

She showered quickly, dried her hair, put on some makeup, and chose a simple navy sheath and sandals, all the while waiting to hear something. Like a footstep in the living room and a call of, "Don't worry, I'm here!" from her mother.

But she was worried. Very, very worried. Not concerned that Camille was hurt or in trouble, but that this whole thing was a lost cause.

Grabbing Camille's note on her way out, Claire walked the path down to the gazebo, but that structure sat empty. No one was near Deeley's rental cabana, so she trekked up to Sanibel Treasures, and arrived there just as Olivia did, also on foot.

"Hey, Livvie," she called, getting a warm smile in response.

"Ooh, you look official and gorgeous," Olivia said, slowing her step to look at Claire. "That dress is so... Camille. Did she pick it?"

"No, but only because"—she made a face—"I can't find her."

Olivia sucked in a soft breath. "What? Don't you have to leave soon?"

"Yes, and my mother takes a full ninety minutes to look like she does on a normal day. On one when she's facing down her nemesis? I would have expected her to start battle preparations at dawn. But I'm afraid..."

"She's retreated?" Olivia guessed.

Claire nodded.

"Would she really do that?" Olivia asked.

"My mother? You never know what she'll do."

"Oh, Claire." Olivia's shoulders lowered. "We'll lose. Birdie will win if Camille doesn't show. Right?"

"I think we can consider it a forfeit. As it is, without physical evidence of what Dutch wanted to do, it could go either way. But without my mother?"

Olivia wrinkled her nose. "I'd love to offer words of encouragement, but the cynic in me says she might have been planning this all along. Although, after she heard what Baldwin Hotels would give her? Well, I'd have expected her to at least go for the win, regardless of what she does with the property."

With each word, Claire felt a little more deflated. "When we came down here, she was so certain of what she would do," she said. "She wanted to help Teddy, wanted to honor this verbal agreement she had with Dutch. Now I don't know what she wants."

"Maybe she's finalizing a deal with her mystery man and you, my friend, are about to be the daughter of a multi-millionairess."

Claire just made a face and gave her head a shake. She'd rather have a wonderful relationship with her sister.

"Sorry," Olivia added, no doubt reading Claire's sad expression. "Go back to the cottage, Claire. She may surprise you—isn't that what she does?"

"On a daily basis," Claire said, rolling her eyes. "You have my number. If you see her, text me. I'll continue looking until it's time to go, which is..." She checked the phone in her hand. "In ten minutes."

"Go." Olivia nudged her. "I'll keep an eye out, search the grounds more, and ask customers if they've seen her."

"Thanks." Claire started to step away, but Olivia reached for her again.

"And good luck, Claire," she said with a warm smile. "You? I trust completely."

The words folded Claire's heart as she put a hand on Olivia's smooth cheek. "My sweet niece."

Olivia smiled. "Not sure about sweet, but I like being your niece, Aunt Claire."

With one more quick hug, Claire took off for Junonia, the echo of the familial term in her head. She didn't want to lose this battle. She didn't want to part ways with *family*. She didn't even want to leave Shellseeker Beach!

But now her fate was in her mother's hands, too, she thought as she rounded the back of the cottages to check the resort parking lot. Her rental car sat where she'd left it, so Camille was on foot. And couldn't be that far.

Unless...she didn't leave on her own.

With that thought punching at her chest, she came to the front of the cottage, where she found Teddy and Eliza waiting outside on the Adirondack chairs. In gauzy pants and a loose but sparkly top, Teddy was more dressed up than Claire had ever seen her, with a touch of makeup and her gorgeous white curls pulled back in a colorful clip.

"Any luck?" Eliza asked as she stood, concern etched on her features.

Claire shook her head. "Nope. And we have to leave. The only thing worse than a no-show witness is being late for court." She showed them the paper she'd been carrying around. "She left a note."

With that, she could see any smidgeon of hope disappear from their faces.

"At least you know she's safe," Teddy said, putting a comforting hand on her back.

On a sigh, she stuffed the paper in her bag. "We gotta go."

"Let's take Eliza's car," Teddy said.

"I can drive us," Claire assured her.

"No. Camille will need a car to get to court." Teddy's smile was tight but genuine. "I mean, if she changes her mind. Heck, for all we know, she took an Uber and is already there, waiting for us."

Claire reached to give her a hug. "I love your optimism."

"That's not just optimism," Teddy said. "I know people. And I think Camille is going to do the right thing."

"We can hope," Claire said, fighting the urge to add a "get real" laugh. Instead, she put one arm around each of them and headed toward Eliza's car in the resort parking lot. Which was, ironically, really Dutch's car, so that was fitting.

She wasn't quite ready to give up yet, but she could already taste defeat.

No surprise, *Maman* wasn't waiting for them at the courthouse.

But as Claire, Eliza, and Teddy walked out of the public parking garage near the Lee County Justice Complex and crossed the street, she was surprised to see Miles Anderson waiting for them on the red brick path that led inside. He was chatting with Connor

Deeley and Katie, who turned and waved when she saw them.

Miles stepped forward, his gaze locked on Eliza. "I hope you don't mind," he said. "We just want to be here for you, no matter the outcome."

"Thank you, Miles." Eliza gave him a quick hug and they greeted Deeley and Katie.

"Where's Camille?" Deeley asked.

"MIA," Claire admitted. "You didn't see her on the beach today, did you?"

"I have a part-timer running the rentals today," he said. "But I can text him and ask."

"Please do," Claire said. "She left a note, but I'm still a little worried about her."

"I don't need to be here," Miles added quickly. "Would you like me to comb the island and look for her instead?"

"I can search, too," Katie said.

Claire looked from one to the other, a mix of relief, hope, and gratitude in her heart as she considered the offer. "She knows where she's supposed to be. And we all know why she doesn't want to be here."

"But that man who talked to her last night?" Teddy said. "Maybe he came back."

"What man?" Miles and Deeley asked in unison.

Eliza explained that one of the more aggressive reps from Baldwin Hotels must have gotten wind of the legal proceedings and approached Camille at the resort, waving big profits for the property sale.

"I don't like that," Miles said. "You all go into the

courtroom. I'm going to do a little hunt and talk to some of my buddies in law enforcement. Did anyone get a description of this guy?"

"Camille said he was not that old, and not that handsome." Claire lifted a brow. "Honestly, that's what she told me. And he didn't accost or harass her," she added. "To be perfectly honest, I think it was a far more casual encounter than how she first presented it, but my mother is given to dramatics."

"I'll go with you, Miles," Deeley said, stepping forward. "I have a few contacts of my own."

"I can help, too," Katie added. "I can go back to Shellseeker and search for her."

"Thank you." Claire pressed her hands to her lips. "Thank you all."

When they left, Eliza put a comforting arm around Claire's back and they walked with Teddy toward the complex.

Once through the metal detector in the main lobby, they followed the signs to the probate courtroom, where Michael Ortega sat on a bench outside the closed doors waiting for them, reading his phone. She'd already texted him a warning about Camille.

The attorney looked up and greeted Claire with a smile, then shook their hands as she introduced him to Teddy and Eliza.

"Why don't you two go in ahead of us," he suggested. "I want a quick word with Claire."

Teddy and Eliza agreed and slipped behind the

heavy wooden doors while Michael ushered Claire toward a private corner.

"She's not coming," she said before he asked again. "I know her, and this is her type of theatrics."

He grunted softly. "Not gonna lie, Claire. I don't think we have a real shot without her. I can put you up there, though." He grunted, at a loss for words. "Why wouldn't she be here?"

"Fear," she said without hesitation. "She's terrified of facing that woman sitting next to Lenny Buckells."

"She's not very fearsome, just a middle-aged lady with glasses and blond hair. She looks like she'd shrivel at the sight of a powerful competitor which, I assume from all you've said, your mother is."

"I don't know how powerful she is," Claire mused, "or she'd be here. I've seen your questions and practiced with my mother. I know what to expect in your line of questioning if you put me on the stand."

He nodded and checked the time on his phone. "All right, let's get this thing done. I'll do my best to explain why she's not here. She was requested, not subpoenaed, so it's an optics thing, not a legal one. I'll explain that she felt the will spoke for itself."

Claire took a deep breath as Michael held the door for her. At the sound of it opening, Lenny Buckells, sitting at the right-side counselor's table in front of the bench, turned and looked at her, then murmured something to the woman seated next to him.

Birdie Vanderveen looked over her shoulder, staring at Claire for a few long and terribly uncomfortable seconds, her features pinching as they held eye contact. She looked past Claire expectantly, and not seeing the person they were all expecting, she turned to face forward, no doubt savoring the sweet taste of victory.

Wordlessly, she slipped in to sit next to Teddy and Eliza a few rows behind the counsel tables.

"I'm rarely nervous in a courtroom," she admitted. "But today?"

Teddy reached into her bag and pulled something out, handing Claire a palm-sized crystal, which she gratefully accepted as they waited for the honorable Judge Macgregor to come and decide their fate.

# Chapter Eighteen

## *Olivia*

**O**livia looked up when the bell on the front door dinged, her heart dropping when she saw Scott lope in with a shy smile and a...toolbox? That was unexpected. So was the heart-drop of disappointment, but she told herself that was because she so hoped it would be Camille.

"I wasn't expecting you today," she said.

He raised the red plastic box, which was so shiny compared to the battered thing Deeley brought over here, she wondered if an hour ago it resided in the hardware store.

Oh, man. *Why* was the first thought with this guy always that he *wasn't* Deeley? She had to stop that. Now.

"Handyman, at your service." He reached the cash register and plopped the box down on the counter. Yep. She could still see a price tag on the side.

"You're here to..."

"Fix the things you complained about at dinner," he said. "That wonky back lock for starters, then your shelves."

"Scott." For a second, she forgot all about the morning's drama and let out an appreciative sigh. "That's so sweet of you."

"Hold the praise until I succeed." He tapped the box. "I'm just getting to know this guy."

"You're not a fixer, I take it."

He laughed. "I fix bank accounts, mostly, and pay for others to do the dirty work. But I have a brain and now I have tools, so wish me luck."

She reached out to touch his hand, feeling guilty that she didn't want to throw her arms around him, didn't want to plant a smackeroo on his lips.

Was chemistry *that* important? He was here, ready, willing, and maybe not so able. That's what mattered. Deeley had been scarce since the night on the tandem kayak, always with an excuse about why he didn't get to the things he said he was going to do.

It was almost like he'd been avoiding her.

And here she was thinking about Deeley again.

"You seem preoccupied," Scott said, searching her face. "Everything okay?"

She snagged the first response that landed in her head. "Big doings at Shellseeker today."

"Something with the whole ownership thing? Is there a hearing scheduled?"

The fact that he cared about the mundane details of her life—not that who owned this property was mundane, but it was to him—touched her. Shouldn't that be enough for her to want to pull him in, take a much-needed hug, maybe kiss him?

It should be, but it wasn't.

"Yes," she told him. "The hearing is this morning, which surprised us all."

"Why aren't you there?"

"I need to run the store and...hopefully find Camille."

He scowled. "Shouldn't she be at the hearing? I mean, based on all you told me, she's one of the people named in the will, right? The one you want to win? The one selling the place for a dollar?"

"Wow, you do listen."

He gave the slightest snort of disbelief. "Livvie. I *like* you. I listen to you. I care about what's going on in your life. Why does that surprise you so much?"

She smiled at him, reached for his hand again. This time, he snagged her fingers and grasped her hand first, bringing it to his heart.

"Tell me everything. The handyman stuff can wait."

Smiling, she came around the counter and did what she should have done when he walked in. She slid her arms around his waist and gave him a grateful hug.

"What's that for?" he asked on a laugh.

"For being who you are." And who you are *not*, she added silently.

Still holding her, he drew back and looked at her, his expression not quite as happy as she'd expect from a man who just told her he liked her. He looked almost...unsure. "So, where is Camille?"

It surprised her that he slid the conversation back to that subject after a hug, but by now she knew he was kind of shy about anything physical.

"If only we knew," she said, stepping away. "She found out about the hearing last night, had a long talk with Teddy, and this morning? MIA. We can't win the case without her. Or, at least, it will be very, very tough."

"So the other lady wins. Roberta?"

She nodded. "And she's going to sell this place to a hotel chain for sure."

His eyes flashed. "She is? How do you know that?"

"She said it to the private investigator who tracked her down."

"Really? So that's why—"

They both turned when the bell dinged and a man walked in, looking around like he was lost.

"Welcome to Sanibel Treasures," Olivia said.

Scott picked up the toolbox. "I better get to work."

She nodded to him as he went in the back, eyeing the new arrival, since he looked like he just stepped off the fishing pier and not at all like one of her customers.

"Can I help you find anything?" she asked, taking a few steps closer.

"A guy named George?" the man replied.

"George Turner," Olivia said. "He and his wife are out for a while, but I'm managing the store. Can I help you?"

"He's the message in a bottle guy, right?"

"He sells them for people to fill and toss in the water. And..." Her gaze dropped down to his hand and her eyes widened at what he held. "Did you find one?"

"Yeah." He lifted it slowly. "I've had it for a few days, and I was going to just, I don't know, keep it? I know the instructions on the back of the paper say to bring it here, but it was kind of a bother."

"I'm so glad you did," she said, reaching a hand out, anxious to see the message he'd found. "George will be ecstatic, because they don't come in that often."

"Yeah, George." He eased the bottle back possessively. "Um, I mentioned it to some of my fishing buddies and they said he's been known to slip in a nice reward if you found one."

She smiled, remembering George whispering that he sneaked a hundred-dollar "bonus" to anyone who found one of the bottles.

"I've heard he does," she said, thinking of how much cash she had in the drawer. "Are you sure this is one from Sanibel Treasures?"

He nodded, holding the bottle with two hands now. "Yeah, positive."

"Cool. Where did you find it?" she asked.

"I was fishing down by the lighthouse and I hauled it in. So..." He rocked the bottle from side to side like it was his negotiating tool, his brows lifting in a question. "What do I get?"

"A donation to the Historical Society and a free message in a bottle, for starters."

His expression dropped. "That's all? I want some cash."

"Who doesn't?" she joked. "Let me look at it and we'll figure something out."

"Something like..."

She laughed. "A free T-shirt and a shell-covered

frame where you can put a picture of you standing next to the bottle on our shelf. Teddy Roosevelt once wrote one, you know, and the grandfather of the lady who owns this place found it."

He rolled his eyes. "I knew those lug nuts lied to me. I don't want any of that. I'll keep the bottle and the message."

He would? She wasn't just going to shell out money until she was certain he wasn't conning her. "Can I read it?"

"It's pretty, uh, personal. Like some dude's journal and not that old. Less than a year. I might try and find the guy who wrote it and see if he has any cash for me."

Disappointment tugged. George would not be happy if she let this slip through his fingertips. "Is it signed?" she asked.

"Yeah. Someone named..." He screwed up his face. "I don't know how to pronounce it. Alo...Alloy...Alo-something."

A chill tiptoed up her spine. "Aloysius?"

"I guess."

"Aloysius Vanderveen?" she barely whispered the name.

"Yeah, that's the guy. Do you know him? Or is it some kind of hoax that you always put out the same..." His voice trailed off as he stared at her. "Are you okay, miss?"

"How does two hundred dollars sound?"

He jerked back. "Better than a picture frame."

"Please?" She reached for the bottle with trembling hands. "It's very important. Very, very important."

"Then you must know this Theo person."

"Excuse me?" Her heart hammered against her ribs.

"Theo...somebody who's a blessing? I dunno." He gave her the bottle. "I just skimmed it. Guy had crappy writing, but he wanted to leave everything he had to Theo, or so he says."

"*What?*" She choked on the word. "That's what it says? Really?"

"You can read it."

With trembling fingers, she reached into the opening and slid out the cylinder of paper, recognizing it immediately as the environmentally-friendly parchment that disintegrated, along with the glass bottle. The paper was bone dry—a testament to George's perfect corks—and covered with scrawling handwriting on one side.

The words were darn near illegible, the lines all traveling up the page unevenly, like whoever wrote this had a lot to say and maybe not such great vision.

Her gaze slipped down to the bottom, where it was signed Aloysius "Dutch" Vanderveen and dated October of last year. Her heart went way past hammering now. It was darn near popping out of her chest.

She squinted at the words, skimming the page, looking for...

*Everything I own belongs to Theo Blessing.*

Looking for *that*.

"Oh my God." She could barely speak as she truly started shaking. "This is it. This is..."

She finally looked up and met the man's gaze, who

tipped his head, impatiently. "So, two hundred?" he asked.

Her brain whirred through the possibilities, the need to get this to court, the timing and...could she even present it? Could Claire or the lawyer? This was *everything* Teddy—and Mom—deeply wanted. Everything everyone wanted. But it had to be real.

She looked at her watch. *Gah!* The trial started four minutes ago!

"Five hundred," she said to the man.

"Seriously?"

"If you meet me at the Lee County Courthouse in... however long it takes you to get there."

"But...five hundred?"

Was he going to negotiate? "Could be more. There's at least one woman there who'll double that."

He searched her face, obviously thinking it over. "What do I have to do?"

"Testify that you found this, when and where. Under oath. Can you do that?"

"For a grand?"

"Yes," she hissed. "But you have to be there. Do you know where it is?"

"Yeah, I do. But only 'cause I had to fight a speeding ticket a while back," he added quickly.

"Well, use those powers for good and I'll see you there ASAP." She elbowed him to the door, still clutching the bottle and paper. "But I'm keeping this."

"A grand? You swear?"

She held up the letter with her right hand. "I swear by my grandfather, Aloysius 'Dutch' Vanderveen."

"Are you for real?" he choked. "That's your grandfather?"

"It is."

He nodded, fully persuaded. "I can be there in half an hour. I'll meet you in the lobby. Can I testify dressed like this?" He plucked at a faded T-shirt that hadn't seen the inside of a washer in a long time.

"Absolutely."

As he left, she pivoted and darted into the office. "I'm leaving!" she announced to Scott, who was kneeling at the back door with an array of tools at his feet, tapping the screen of his cell phone like the poor thing had just Googled "How to fix a wonky lock."

"What? What's going on?"

"No time to explain! I have to go. Can you watch the store for me? And keep an eye out for a French lady who is seventy-going-on-forty-nine and probably overdressed? Call me if you see her!" She grabbed her bag and prayed her mother didn't drive so she could take Dutch's car with the spare keys she had.

Without waiting for his goodbye, she shot out to the floor and tore through the doors, still holding the letter in one hand and the bottle in another, her bag clunking against her hip.

As she took off for the path, she mentally composed a text to her mother that she'd dictate when she got in the car, telling her to instruct their attorney to *drag things out.*

She ran so fast down the path that led to the cottages that she could hear the air whistling around her ears, along with her own breaths and the slap of her sandals on the ground. She was so focused and determined, she almost didn't notice the sliding doors to Junonia were wide open.

She slammed to a stop and stared at them, certain Claire wouldn't have left them like that. Did that mean...

"Camille?" she called, stepping up to the wood porch. "Are you..." She stopped when she heard the sob. She stepped inside and found the older woman curled in a ball on the sofa, wailing.

"Camille!" She folded in front of her, hating to lose even a minute but she was too important to leave behind. The letter *and* Camille's testimony that Dutch wanted her to give the property to Teddy? They could win this. "What's wrong?"

"Go away!" She had both hands over her face, her shiny hair an uncharacteristic mess and...did she have shorts and sneakers on? This *was* a crisis.

"I'm not going anywhere except to the courthouse, and you are coming with me. Now."

"No! I don't want to win." Her voice was muffled through her hands. "Let her have it!"

"Are you out of your mind? Look! Somebody just found Dutch's message in a bottle. It's a will, kind of. A letter. He wants Teddy to have everything!"

She slowly lowered her hands, revealing a tear-ravaged face that finally looked somewhere close to her age. "What?"

"It's right here! He wrote a heartfelt message in a bottle. George told me he threw one out into the Gulf about eight months ago. This is the proof we've been looking for, Camille. Come to the courthouse with me. Your presence and testimony could absolutely seal the deal."

She stared at Olivia, easing herself up. "He left it to Teddy? Are you sure?"

"I just glanced at it, but yes. I mean, you could fight her if you want, but—"

"No. No. Teddy should have everything. She earned it. She kept him alive for two extra years and she loved him and she's so..." Another sob cracked. "She's everything I'm not."

Olivia couldn't argue with that. "Then you should help her. Now."

She dropped her gaze to her clothes, suddenly horrified. "I need time—"

"There is no time! Suck it up, buttercup. The world is going to see the true you. A generous, caring, real woman who helps her friends and keeps her promises."

For one long, suspended second, Camille didn't move. Then she sat all the way up, knocking something to the floor as she did. Olivia looked down and saw a heavy crystal pendant on a chain that she must have had on her lap.

She picked it up with one hand and stood, yanking Camille up with the other. "Wear it with pride," she said, surprised by how dang heavy it was. "You can pitch it at Birdie if we lose."

That made Camille smile. "Let me get my bag and keys. I saw that Claire left her car for me. I guess she hoped I'd make it after all."

"And you will." Olivia draped an arm over the woman's shoulder. "This is a good look for you, Camille. Kind of Bohemian bedhead with a dash of *je ne sais quoi.*"

"Shut up."

Olivia just laughed all the way to the car, but she cried when Camille read the letter out loud. And totally forgot she was going to text her mother until they were in the lobby with a fisherman about to be at least a thousand dollars richer.

That is, if they weren't too late and Birdie didn't have her own last-minute surprise.

# Chapter Nineteen

## *Teddy*

W hat in God's name had Dutch seen in Birdie?
Teddy stared at the bottle blonde on the stand, searching for some truly redeeming quality, but seeing none. She didn't have to touch the woman to feel her pitiful hatred for the world, or the jealousy and insecurity and bitterness that darkened every one of her answers.

What made her so miserable? Could it have been...Dutch?

The thought made Teddy's heart drop a little. If that was true, then maybe she deserved some recompense. But did she deserve all of Shellseeker Beach?

Birdie's attorney, Leonard Buckells, used his deep Southern drawl and low-key charm in his attempt to persuade the judge that, yes, she certainly did. And he did a good job as he asked questions that allowed her to paint the picture of a young woman of twenty-five swept off her feet by a dashing pilot who would do anything to consummate their relationship, including marry her. Which he did, but never mentioned that he was already married to Camille Durant.

Teddy shuddered, trying to imagine Dutch making

that decision, driven to lie to a woman just to sleep with her.

In point of truth, it didn't make sense. Of course, she only knew Dutch as an old man, but she was familiar enough with his life to know that if he'd wanted a woman in his bed, he invariably got her. Not to put too fine a point on it, but Dutch didn't need to marry someone to have sex. Women flocked to him.

So what *was* it about this one?

"Did you ever consider a civil divorce or an annulment, Mrs. Vanderveen?" the attorney asked as he seemed to come to the end of his questioning.

"I believe that God says what He's put together, let no man tear asunder." She took a slow breath and looked down at her lap for a moment, then up. "So, no. I did not."

He nodded. "I have no further questions."

Judge Macgregor shifted his attention to the table where Michael Ortega sat alone, the empty chair next to him the most damning thing in the small and modern courtroom.

What was wrong with Camille that she wouldn't even show today?

Teddy shifted again in her seat next to Eliza. The two of them, and Claire, filled one small row in the gallery, which could only have held about twenty-five people if it had been packed. But it wasn't. In fact, the three of them, and a priest who hadn't yet taken the stand, were the only people watching the proceedings.

"Ms. Vanderveen," Michael said as he stood,

buttoning his jacket to look more formal for his cross-examination. "Do you own a computer?"

"Yes."

"Do you have internet access?"

Her eyes shuttered with a put-upon sigh. "Yes."

"And do you know how to use Google?"

Now she rolled them. "Yes."

"And have you ever searched for information about the man you married and refused to divorce?"

Teddy glanced at Eliza, trying to swallow but her mouth was too dry from nerves. "Not sure where he's going with this."

Claire leaned in. "He's establishing that in the past twenty years, Birdie could probably have found out how long Dutch was married to Camille without too much trouble."

But Teddy hadn't Googled him, either.

At the sound of the courtroom door opening behind them, Eliza glanced over her shoulder and sucked in a noisy breath.

"What? Who is it?" Teddy turned, already praying. *Please, God, let it be Cam—*

Whoa. *Was* that Camille?

The woman walking into the courtroom looked like Camille's lost, maybe drunken, definitely unkempt older sister in a T-shirt that she'd gardened in and never washed, untucked over rumpled shorts. The crystal Teddy had given her hung around her neck, looking woefully out of place.

Still, Camille held her head high, as if she wore one

of her runway-worthy outfits and had a fully made-up face. She continued forward, her gaze locked on Michael, who stumbled over his next question as he stared at her.

"Livvie's here, too?" Eliza whispered as two more people entered the courtroom.

Olivia, who was literally beaming from ear to ear, and a stranger who looked like they'd found him fishing off the causeway.

"What is going on?" Claire murmured as Camille marched past her.

She ignored the question and headed to the front of the courtroom. Judge Macgregor looked surprised, and the other attorney looked a little ticked off. But Birdie?

She paled as every drop of blood in her face disappeared as Camille sat at the empty table and thunked a glass bottle in front of her. Was she drinking? No, wait. That was—

"We found a message in a bottle." Olivia, in the row behind them, leaned forward and whispered in their ears. "Written by Dutch."

Chills blossomed over Teddy's arms as that sunk in.

Olivia put her hands on Teddy's shoulders and squeezed. "Just listen."

They all turned back to the proceedings, which had come to a halt as Michael asked for a moment to confer with his client and the judge granted it.

At the front of the courtroom, Michael had pulled a paper out of the bottle, read it, whispered something to Camille, and then looked to the back of the courtroom where the stranger sat. He nodded, took a deep breath, and turned back to his witness.

"Ms. Vanderveen," he said with slow deliberation. "Is it your sworn testimony that you did not know Aloysius Vanderveen was married when you met him?"

"When I met him?" She shook her head. "I did not."

"And when you first slept with him. Did you know he was married then?"

She flinched. "We consummated our marriage, so yes, he was married. To me."

"Oh. So, let's get this timeline correct. You married Captain Vanderveen on...May 6, 1990, when you had just turned twenty-five years old."

"Correct."

"So you did not consummate your marriage to him until that date, correct?"

She looked a little put out by the implication. "That is correct."

Buckells stood. "Objection, Your Honor. Asked and answered. And the private details make no difference in this case."

"I'm establishing a timeline," Michael replied, "and I will show that they most certainly do make a difference."

The judge nodded, overruling the objection.

"Ms. Vanderveen," Michael continued. "Can you confirm that you were admitted to a hospital on September 14, of that same year?"

She stared at him, all color gone. "I don't recall a specific date."

"But you *were* in the hospital in September of that year, following a car accident?"

Teddy sat up straighter, glancing at Eliza and Claire, who were as confused by the question as she was.

"I think so," Birdie said softly.

"You think so? You don't remember a car accident as a passenger, with Captain Vanderveen driving?"

She shifted in her seat, shot a look at her lawyer, then nodded. "Yes, that happened."

"When?"

"That month, I guess. September."

"You guess? It was a rather monumental day in your life, wasn't it?" Michael took a few steps closer. "You lost the baby you were carrying."

Teddy hissed in a breath. *What?*

"Yes, I did."

"And that unborn child was how far along?" he pressed.

"A few months." She gave a tight smile. "A honeymoon baby."

"Oh. I think the records of that hospital will show otherwise. The baby that was killed in the accident, in utero, was, in fact, eight months." He let that sink in. "So can we dispense with your perjury about when you and Captain Vanderveen consummated your relationship?"

Buckells stood. "Objection, Your Honor. This historic detail is doing nothing but upsetting my client and showing that she engaged in pre-marital sex. She's not on trial here, and it has absolutely no bearing on the issue of a contested will."

"I can prove that it has every bearing on the contested will," Michael said to the judge. "Just a few more questions."

Once again, the judge nodded and let Michael continue. Teddy held the hands of the women on either side of her and waited, breathless. Something big must be in that message in a bottle, something that would get Camille Durant to go out in public looking like she'd crawled out of bed.

Holding that thought, she leaned forward to listen.

"Ms. Vanderveen, can you tell us about the day you first met Dutch? When it happened? Where you were?"

One more shuddering breath. "I don't really remember the details. We met at, um, a park, near my house."

*No, that's not what Camille said*, Teddy thought. She said he met her at an airport after he learned Camille had been unfaithful.

"I see, a park. Now, can you tell us the truth about when and where you met him?"

She stared at him, silent.

"You've known Captain Vanderveen, who was twenty-one years your senior, since you were a child, am I correct?"

Birdie swallowed, and said nothing, but Teddy's head buzzed. A *child*? How was that possible?

"In fact, you met Captain Vanderveen for the first time when you were about five, after he came home from Vietnam. Am I correct?"

"I don't remember."

"Let me refresh your memory. Captain Vanderveen was a friend of your father's, and they served together in Vietnam, until your father was killed in combat. And Captain Vanderveen bore some responsibility for that, didn't he?"

She wet her lips and shifted her gaze to Camille, daggers in her eyes. "Yes," she hissed.

"And because of that responsibility, he paid for... everything. Including your college education. Is that true?"

Her lawyer said, "Objection, there's no—"

"Overruled. Answer, please, Ms. Vanderveen."

"Yes, he did," Birdie ground out. "But we were still married! We were married by a justice of the peace and—"

"Not in a church? A good Catholic like you?"

She squirmed. "That was...too much for me."

"Ah, I see. Was it too much because you knew he was married to Camille Durant and you didn't care?"

She breathed so hard her nostrils flared. "That man," she ground out. "That son of a.... He was reckless! His recklessness killed my father, a fact he covered up and blamed on the enemy in Vietnam. Then that recklessness killed my baby—"

"Was that baby his?" Michael demanded.

Her whole body seemed to buckle under the weight of the question. "No. But he didn't care! He wanted to help me! He owed me. He owed me then and he owes me now and he knew it, or he wouldn't have signed that will!"

"Did you coerce him to sign it?" he pressed.

"I...I..."

"You threatened to contact Pan American Airways and tell them he was drunk when he was driving the car, which he wasn't, and that he'd knowingly committed bigamy, which he did to protect you. He protected you for twenty years out of *guilt*. Guilt that you exploited for money and to save your reputation when you were a young, unmarried, pregnant woman who didn't know the name of her baby's father. Is that true, Ms. Vanderveen?"

He let the name ring through the courtroom, silencing everyone, including Birdie. Tears poured down her face as she stared straight ahead for five, six, seven interminable seconds.

Finally, she nodded and rasped the word, "Yes."

"I have no further questions, and no need to call any other witnesses, if it pleases the court." Judge Macgregor looked like nothing pleased the court right then. "You may step down Ms. Vanderveen."

She stood on shaky legs, stepping out of the enclosed area, eyes downcast as she returned to the table.

"We will adjourn, and I'll talk to counsel privately in my chambers." Judge Macgregor dropped the gavel and everyone stood while he left through a small door at the front of the courtroom.

Before following him, Michael grabbed the rolled-up piece of paper, but left the bottle.

For a moment, no one spoke. Then they all looked at each other, a million questions ready until Birdie shot up and whipped around to look at them.

"This is so wrong!"

Camille lifted the empty bottle on the table. "This says differently."

What did it say?

Birdie marched out from behind her chair, stopping in front of Camille. "He took everything from me," she spat the words. "He owed me everything he had."

"He didn't owe you a thing, *cherie*."

Closing her eyes, Birdie stormed down the aisle. "You haven't heard the last of me!" she hollered as she shoved the doors open and disappeared.

OLIVIA WOULDN'T SAY what was written in the bottled message, but as soon as the court recessed, she took the man she'd brought aside and talked to him privately. Claire went straight to her mother at the front and sat with her in quiet conversation.

And Teddy, still trembling, sat staring at Eliza, neither of them even able to articulate the hundreds of questions they had. A moment later, the back doors opened and Miles, Deeley, and Katie came in, having been alerted by Claire that Camille had been found.

They sat in the now empty row behind Teddy, while Eliza did her best to recap what they'd missed.

Their questions poured out as Olivia brought the man over and introduced him as the person who found the bottle, but before they could say too much more, the chamber doors opened and both attorneys walked out.

Teddy couldn't decipher either of their expressions, but she did notice that Buckells didn't seem too concerned or surprised that Birdie had left. And Michael greeted Camille with a smile.

A few moments later, they all stood for the judge, who took his place on the bench with a single piece of paper in front of him...the rolled-up scroll from the bottle. He rattled off some case numbers and instructions, then announced he had reached an opinion on the case.

"This court rules that the will filed by Roberta Vanderveen is hereby null and void, having been obtained under duress and through improper procedures and undue influence on the testator, Aloysius Vanderveen." He glanced at Roberta's empty chair. "Ms. Vanderveen will be held in contempt and charged with perjury for her testimony and signed affidavit."

Before they could react, he leaned closer to his microphone to continue.

"With that will rendered invalid, the second will, filed on behalf of Captain Vanderveen, is hereby recognized as the legitimate document for the appropriation of assets, which include but are not limited to the property at 143 Roosevelt Road, the rental property known as Shellseeker Cottages, and the retail storefront, Sanibel Treasures." With that, he dropped his gavel and Teddy finally let go of a breath she hadn't realized she'd been holding.

The next few minutes were a blur of hugs and congratulations and kisses and gratitude. Teddy may have promised that guy named Rick five hundred more dollars, or Eliza did. Teddy wasn't sure of anything, except she was one step closer to what she wanted.

More than that, all of her questions and doubts about Dutch were finally answered. He was motivated by guilt, not selfishness, and a desire to help someone who'd suffered because of him. Now that felt like the Dutch she thought she knew and definitely loved.

As that settled over her, Camille approached her, smiling through eyes as happy as any she'd seen since the woman arrived. She'd gotten answers, too, and that had to ease her personal misery.

"Can we talk?" Camille whispered, taking Teddy's hand. "Privately? Outside?"

"Of course." Still holding Camille's hand, the two of them left everyone behind and walked outside, down a flight of stairs, and out to the open air. Camille was silent —or at least she wasn't talking.

Her body, soul, and spirit, however? They were finally singing, and Teddy was loving the sound of it.

"Over here," Camille said, walking her to a park bench under a tree. "I want you to read his letter."

"Thank God," Teddy whispered. "I thought I'd lose my mind not knowing what was in that bottle."

"It...explains a lot."

"Birdie explained a lot," Teddy said. "Did you know any of that?"

She shook her head. "He never told me. But remember I told you about the man in Vietnam? The one he told me he left for dead, an enemy soldier?"

Teddy nodded.

"I think that wasn't an enemy soldier. I think it was Birdie's father, but he couldn't confess that." She handed her the letter. "Do you remember when he wrote this?"

Teddy nodded. "I think I do. It was a dark day and I'd stupidly brought up the subject of the will; that always sent him into a spiral, and he'd disappear. I looked for him for hours and George told me he'd taken a message in a bottle and headed to the gazebo." She shook her head. "He didn't come home until midnight that night."

"I spoke to him that day," Camille said. "He told me it was the beginning of the end."

"He died two months later," Teddy said, taking the paper with trembling hands. "Now?"

Camille nodded and leaned all the way back, closing her eyes, wrapping one hand around the crystal pendant. "Go ahead. I don't need to read it again."

Teddy situated herself in the shade, slowly unrolling the paper she recognized as the sheets that George sold with the bottles. And as she did, she instantly recognized Dutch's handwriting. But more than that, she could feel him. His power, his energy, his...Dutchness.

It was all over the page, which even smelled like him, briny like the sea and earthy like her garden and fresh like the sky he loved to fly into. She could see him in her mind's eye, bent over in the gazebo, writing. She could hear his booming baritone as the words poured from his heart to the page, smiling as she read the first words that were so, so Dutch.

*To Whatever Sucker Finds This:*

*I'm gonna die. Real soon. And I don't much care that*

*I am, but I want the truth out there, somewhere. If it gets found, then it was meant to be. If it doesn't, then that God I don't believe in will at least know that I tried. He can do with that what He wants.*

*On October 22, 1966, I killed a man. Not on purpose, not because he deserved it, but because I did a dumbass thing with my gun. His name was Corporal Jimmy Milton and he was twenty-eight years old. He had a wife and daughter back in Alabama, and his last words to me were, "Take care of Birdie."*

*I regret like hell killing that man, and live with the self-loathing every day. I covered up my mistake, left his body so he'd forever be MIA, but of course he was found, and started my life of living in fear. Fear I'd get caught. Fear I'd have to pay. Fear I'd have to look in the mirror every morning and see...Jimmy.*

*Anyway, I kept my promise and took care of his girl, Roberta "Birdie" Milton. From the day I got back until last week, I sent her money to help her. I put her through college, helped her get a job as a teacher, bought her a house, and paid for her mother's funeral. And when she asked me for money to get an abortion 'cause she got knocked up and never saw the guy again, I had a different idea. I told her I'd marry her so she wouldn't be shamed in her small town. Then after the baby was born, I'd set her and the kid up for life, and we could quietly get an annulment.*

*She knew I was married to Camille, but no one else did. Her church, her town, her students, they just thought she married some big-mouth older guy. We did the deed on*

*May 6, 1990, and the justice of the peace never even checked on me.*

*So then I was a bigamist and a killer.*

*But things with Birdie didn't work out so good. When she was eight months pregnant, on September 15, 1990, I was driving her to a doctor's appointment and we were real late. I ran a red light and we got creamed. I wanted to die. I wish I had, but the only one who died was...James.*

*That's what we named the baby boy they had to take from her that day. James, after her dad. Worst day of my life, bar none. Birdie was wrecked. Ruined. And in a moment of drunken, miserable weakness, I told her about her dad.*

*I shouldn't have. She swore if I didn't give her everything I had, she'd tell the military and not only would my career be finished, I could face a court-martial and prison. Plus the whole bigamy thing. Giving her money wasn't enough. She wanted everything I had or ever would own in the future, in a will. So I wrote one.*

*And kept living in fear.*

*I went back to Camille, told her a bunch of crap about a mid-life crisis and she blamed herself for a mistake she made, but I didn't. Camille wasn't the guilty one, I was. I made myself scarce after that, although my sweet wife remained a good friend. A really good friend. But I couldn't look at her, I couldn't really do much of anything except fly hard and fast and wish I could leave this Earth for the damage I caused.*

*I got my wish when all that guilt and self-hatred centered on my brain and created a tumor. That might not be how it works, but it felt that way. I came to Florida to die alone and hope that those two women would figure something out.*

*I never, ever counted on Theo. That woman gave me hope and life and love and so much stupid tea it came out of my ears. She did it selflessly, because it was the right thing to do. She did it for me, a man who wasn't even honest with her. She did it every single day, without fail. She healed me, forgave me, and showed me exactly what a person should be, and it was better than a full-power unrestricted takeoff.*

Teddy tried to swallow, but she couldn't. Tears rolled down her face, and she couldn't even move to wipe them away as she read, remembering Dutch describing the thrill of taking a plane five thousand feet into the air, straight up.

He felt that way about *her*? She sniffed, and read on.

*I know I said vows with other women. I know I made promises I didn't keep. And I know I wrote a few too many last will and testaments.*

*But this is what I really want but can never have: to give everything I own to Theodora Blessing. Not because her grandfather found the land or her father built it or her family worked it. I want her to have it because she earned it with her love and healing and beautiful heart.*

*I lived one hell of a messy life, and I'm not proud of a lot of things. But one thing I'm proud of? That Theo Blessing loved me. And I loved her back.*

*I swear before God (even though I don't believe in Him, I guess I kind of do) that this is me, the absolute truth, and was not written with a gun to my head. Just a crystal on my heart.*

*I love you so much, Theo. I hope someday you know it.*

*Aloysius "Dutch" Vanderveen*

She stared at his name, not surprised when one of her tears hit the page. She didn't move, even when Camille put the rare arm around her and pulled her close.

"Now, I have peace," Camille said. "Because I know he didn't choose her over me." She eased back. "He chose you."

Teddy stared at her, still letting Dutch's words comfort her.

"So how does one dollar sound?" Camille whispered.

Teddy blinked. "For...everything?" she was almost afraid to ask.

"Well, you know, I think I'd like a cottage for myself. A place to spend winters when it's cold in Canada. And holidays when I'm lonely. And maybe...more than that. I don't know. But just as a tenant. I don't want to do any work. And I really don't want to garden. Ever."

Teddy smiled through her tears. "Okay, you don't have to. But really?"

"I like it here, and I've been thinking about that purpose we discussed. You said personal shopper, but I'm thinking I might open a little boutique to save this poor island from all the fashion *faux pas* the residents insist on making." She plucked at her raggedy T-shirt. "Including me."

"Camille, are you serious? I would love that," she said, hugging her.

"Oh, and one more thing, Teddy."

"Yes?"

"Could I keep this?" She clutched Dutch's crystal. "It really makes me feel good."

"Dutch's fake magic diamond is yours, Camille."

For a long time, they just looked at each other, then they hugged, and the sun poked through the trees to bathe them in a golden glow, and for that moment in time, everything was perfect.

# Chapter Twenty

*Olivia*

"What do you mean, open a store?" Olivia glanced at her passenger, taking her eyes off the causeway traffic to make sure she'd heard exactly what Camille had said. "Like a clothing store? On Sanibel?"

"It's not like the place couldn't use something a little more upscale than Beachside Boutique. Sarah Beth is very sweet, but her offerings, like the name of her store, are all so *très ordinaire*."

Olivia blinked at her. Of all the wild, preposterous, mind-blowing things she'd heard today, for some reason, this one just didn't seem like it was possible.

She found out her grandfather accidentally killed a man and made a couple of other seriously bad choices in his life. Yep, totally plausible. And Birdie Vanderveen had been lying all along and using Dutch's guilt for her own monetary gain? Made complete sense. Even Camille's final decision to give the entire property she'd officially inherited to Teddy? Yeah, *la grande dame* had a heart beating in that chest after all.

But she'd stay on Sanibel and open a high-end clothing boutique? This was too much.

"I guess I can see that," Olivia said slowly. "But..."

"But what? You're jealous?"

So utterly and completely, but it was too hard to admit that out loud. However, with Camille's intense dark gaze burning a hole in her cheek, she couldn't exactly lie.

"It's been my lifelong dream," Olivia said softly. "I mean, I'm doing it on steroids now, but—"

"Running Sanibel Treasures?" Camille scoffed.

"No, I meant working for Promenade Department Stores."

Even without looking at her, Olivia could feel the "are you kidding me" stare Camille was giving her.

"It is," Olivia insisted. "I'm a top buyer for one of the best department stores in the country and well on my way to..." She let her voice fade out.

The fact was, she hadn't had a single phone call from her boss since she'd started her sabbatical. One other buyer sent her a text now and again to complain about the reorganization—the very restructuring that had knocked Olivia out of the running for the VP of Merchandising slot.

God only knew what she'd find when she went back to Seattle and tried to pick up the pieces of her career.

"I'd like to bring some lines in from Europe," Camille mused, looking at her nails as if checking for chips in the perfection. "And select some *haute couture*, some labels, some *pret à porter*. I wouldn't mind a trip to New York for Fashion Week. The money's here, you know. Especially if I find a place in the heart of Sanibel. I'd love to create something really noteworthy in retail."

Who wouldn't? Olivia managed not to moan. "That sounds so...good."

"You could run it for me. Be my buyer. Help me with merchandising and sales."

She laughed. "Don't tempt me, because I..."

"Live in Seattle?" One of those perfect nails prodded her arm. "So, move here. Your mother's going to, you know."

"Oh, we don't know that for sure, but—"

"Please, Olivia, don't be naïve. Eliza is happy here and if you ask me, Claire's going to be a regular, too. Why would you leave?"

Olivia considered the question as she reached the turn to Shellseeker Beach, narrowing her eyes at the crowded lot behind the tea hut, dragging her head back to the little overcrowded shell shop she actually did manage.

She'd leave because she had a job and a life, even if they weren't exactly what she wanted them to be. She'd leave because she didn't want to work as a shop girl for Camille, who was as crazy as she was amusing. She'd leave because she had a crush on a guy who never told her where he went when he disappeared.

And her grandfather had just reached out from the grave to remind her what a bad bet a man like that was.

"I really need to relieve poor Scott, who's been minding the store for hours," she said. "And your cottage is closer to Sanibel Treasures than this parking lot. Mind if I drive down there and park in the back?"

"Please do," Camille said, and then leaned over to put a hand on Olivia's arm. "And think about it, okay?"

As if she'd think about anything else. She turned onto Roosevelt Road to drive the half-mile to the store, questions bouncing around in her head as she neared the small lot behind her store.

No, not her store. Another person's store, just like the one Camille would—

"Oh my goodness!" Camille gasped, ducking down in her seat like she was hiding. "That's him!"

"That's...who?" Olivia blinked into the late afternoon sun, getting a glimpse of Scott walking to the back door of Sanibel Treasures, probably having just thrown something in the dumpster in the back. Of course he was being an angel and cleaning out the store, because he was a good man. "That's Scott Greene, the guy I've been—"

"That's the man from Baldwin Hotels!" Camille exclaimed. "I don't want to see him."

"No, it's not. That's the man I've been dating who's running my store today. Come on in, I'll introduce you."

"No." Still ducking even though he was back inside the store, Camille shook her head. "I don't want to talk to him again."

"He can't be..." Olivia made a face. *Could* Scott be working for Baldwin Hotels?

"He was outside my cottage and offered me a ridiculous amount of money for this property, Olivia," Camille insisted. "He made it quite clear that Baldwin Hotels was his client and he was a broker or investor or something, and he was here to arrange a deal to buy Shellseeker Cottages when I inherited it."

*What?* Scott worked for Baldwin Hotels?

Olivia slammed on the brakes without pulling into the lot. "Are you absolutely positive, Camille?"

"One hundred percent. I wouldn't forget someone that bland and unattractive."

"He never said who he worked for, just...investments." Everything inside Olivia went cold as she felt her whole body sink with the realization. And suddenly... everything fit. His fascination with the business, his questions about the ownership, his interest in the outcome of the wills...his interest in *her*.

Oh, God, how could she be so stupid?

The realization rammed her in the gut like the day she found out she didn't get the promotion, yanking that proverbial rug out from under her, making her dizzy and unstable and so, so furious.

"Are you *sure*, Camille?" But even as she asked, she knew.

He hadn't been trying to worm his way into her heart. He was trying to worm his way into the property. *Really?*

He was lying when her mother heard him saying things like, "She's the one" and, "She could change my life" and, "I won't give up."

No. She *was* the one—the one who could give him all the inside information. She *could* change his life—if he was the Baldwin buyer who closed a huge deal like that. He *didn't* give up—he was in there now, running her business while she was in court. Fixing the shelves, seeing her spreadsheets, infiltrating her world.

So the whole thing was fake. He was fake. Not shy at all, just not really interested in her for anything but access to a business deal.

She closed her eyes and saw white lights exploding behind her lids.

"Can you walk to your cottage from here?" she asked, throwing her seatbelt off and abandoning the car. "I need to get that SOB out of the store and off this property and all the way out of my life right this very minute."

"Of course, I'll—"

She never heard the rest, and didn't even grab her bag, but marched, fueled by fury, to the door. He'd left it ajar, probably because he still hadn't fixed the lock. Maybe he didn't want to, so he would have a way to get in and out of her business when she wasn't there.

"Hey!" she yelled as she yanked the door open and strode in.

He was over by the shelves, surrounded by a mess of tools. "Oh, you're back!" He started to stand, a hand on the shelves, then laughed as they wobbled from the weight of some heavy boxes on the top shelf.

"What are you doing here?" she demanded, making him blink in surprise at the question.

She dug for some kind of plan of attack but couldn't come up with anything except *claw his eyes out*.

"No one's in the store, so I thought I'd work on...are you okay, Livvie? Did something—"

"Don't call me that!" she fired back, passing her desk

as she slowly made her way across the back office to get closer for the eye clawing. "You have no right to call me that, Scott. Scott?" She spat the word. "Is that even your real name? Scott Greene? Or is *Greene* just a handle for all the money you'd make by closing the Shellseeker Beach deal for Baldwin Hotels?"

He winced and then had the decency to go a little pale. "Liv—er, Olivia. I...I..."

"You really should have had a lie planned. You had to know Camille might see you and identify you."

He let out a breath and his narrow shoulders sank. "I hope you'll listen to my side."

"You don't have a side. You are standing in this office under utterly false pretenses, using our...our..." She wouldn't dream of calling it a relationship. "Using *me* to get whatever you wanted. Information? Access? Some kind of assist in finagling your way into a deal with Camille?"

He stood silent, then swallowed. "It started that way, yes, but—"

"Please. If you try and tell me you care, I will smack you." She got a little closer, her chest tighter with each breath. "Not that I care. Can we just be clear about that? I wanted to, but..."

"Something held you back." He tipped his head. "I get that."

Was he giving her a pass for not swooning over him? This half-bald, skinny, humorless liar?

"You need to leave now," she ground out. "Camille won the suit, she's giving Teddy the property, and it will be in her family, and mine, *forever*." As she said the word, it surprised her how much it mattered. How much she cared about this land. And now it was personal. She'd die before she let Baldwin Hotels so much as step foot on Shellseeker Beach.

He held up both hands. "Fine. Relax. I'm out."

His cavalier attitude just made her madder, sending fire up her spine. "Why?" she demanded as he started walking to the door. "Why did you do it? Why would you think developing some fake relationship with me would help your cause and not hurt it?"

He actually laughed like the question surprised him. "If you don't understand, who would?"

"Me?"

"You bow to the corporate gods, Olivia. And you know exactly what it takes to get to that corner office in Mahogany Row. You have to be ruthless and reckless, and think outside the box. You spent hours telling me that, maybe not in so many words, but I figured when it came out, you'd..." He shrugged. "I don't know. I guess I thought you'd respect me for it."

She just stared at him, her heart falling closer to her feet with every word.

Is that who she was? Because if so, it made her sick.

"Get out," she said softly, feeling the fight fade from her heart. "Just, please. Leave."

He nodded and backed up, giving her a tight smile. "I did have fun with you, Liv. We have a lot in common."

"No," she whispered. "No, we don't." At least she hoped not.

He walked out the door she'd left open and closed it with a click of finality, a punctuation mark on one really, really bad sentence in her life. She fell into a chair covered in Sanibel Island T-shirts, using one to dry her eyes.

SHE WASN'T sure how long she sat there before she heard the bell ring as someone entered the store. Pressing her hands to a flushed face, she pushed up slowly, ready to call her standard greeting and promise to be right out.

But she couldn't even get the words out. Instead, she took a steadying breath and tried hard to shake off the self-pity. Walking toward the door, she darn near tripped on Scott's toolbox. Grabbing the shelf for balance, she gasped when the whole thing shook.

*Nice job on the shelves, you dumb—*

The crash from the store was so loud, she nearly jumped out of her skin. Without taking one second to wonder what it was, she shot through the door to the front, blinking in shock to see it was completely empty. Then what—

Another crash, this one from the very back, around the corner in the historical section. The bottles! The messages! Teddy Roosevelt!

She darted there and threw open the door to a dimly lit area she rarely entered, coming face to face with a woman holding two broken bottles.

Roberta Vanderveen had wild, crazy eyes as she

waved the sharp-edged glass like a set of murderous knives, one in each hand.

"Birdie!" Olivia took a step closer, but her sandal smashed into broken glass, nearly making her slide and lose her footing. "What are you doing?"

"This!" She waved a jagged bottle in the air. "This ruined everything! A message in a bottle! How stupid is that?" She flung one of the bottles onto the floor, the glass crackling into a million pieces.

"Birdie, stop!" Olivia yelled. "This isn't going to change anything."

"But maybe the place won't be worth as much!" She used the other bottle to gesture toward the shelves where half of George's beloved "returned" bottles were missing, no doubt under Olivia's feet. But one still stood. On the shelf of honor, with a picture of Teddy Roosevelt, a plaque, and a photo of the letter that was rolled up inside the bottle.

"You're out of your mind!" Olivia lunged closer, but Birdie hopped up onto the small stepstool George kept under the shelf for those rare and special occasions when he brought Teddy's bottle down. That gave her just enough height to reach into the display and snag it with her free hand.

She spun back to Olivia, at least a foot taller now, looming over her in the shadows with the precious, historic bottle in one hand, a broken and potentially deadly weapon in the other.

"Hey, hey. Birdie. That's not going to help your cause," Olivia said, trying to keep calm.

"What cause? My lost cause?" She snorted. "I wouldn't have lost if it wasn't for this miserable...thing!"

She waved both bottles maniacally, a little too close to Olivia for comfort.

"Yes, you would have lost," Olivia insisted, trying to figure out how to handle this situation. Would reason work with her? Force? Should she just call the cops?

Of course, but her phone was in her bag in the car outside.

"This is what brings people to this store, isn't it? These dumb bottles?" She hurled the broken one a foot past Olivia and then held Teddy Roosevelt's in two hands. "Especially this one!"

"You wouldn't."

But she just gave an insane laugh that said, oh, yes, she would. Then she popped the cork and Olivia gasped when she stuck one finger into the top of the bottle, putting her grimy paw on Teddy Roosevelt's letter!

"Stop it, Birdie."

"Oh, can it. Who are you anyway?"

"Dutch's granddaughter."

Her brows shot up. "Eliza's kid?"

She nodded, uncertain how the other woman would react to this news. Based on what she'd seen so far, not good. Olivia considered lunging at the woman and knocking her down, but that would surely break the bottle...and George's heart.

So she stared at Birdie, who managed to slide the rolled-up paper out of the bottle. And snap it open, using her mouth to open it all the way.

Olivia just groaned and imagined the old Rough Rider rolling over in his grave.

"Why would you want to help Camille?" Birdie suddenly demanded, the letter snapping back into a cylinder shape when she let it go. "She broke up your grandparents' marriage, that French whore." Her whole face crumpled with hatred. "I despise her! I want her to die!"

"Stop it," Olivia said, eyeing the bottle as she took one tentative step closer. "You don't mean that. You're angry. Disappointed. And—"

"*Camille* got a daughter. *Mary Ann* got a daughter. But poor Birdie got nothing." A sob caught in her throat. "All because of him. No father, no son, just nothing. I hate him! I hate Dutch Vanderveen, I tell you!"

Olivia nodded, not even considering arguing with that. Her only hope was that Birdie would be so overcome with emotion she'd give up the damn bottle.

Or she'd toss it. And rip the paper. Oh, this wasn't good. How could she get it from her?

"Come on, Birdie. Give me the letter. You don't want to do this. You're not hurting Dutch or even Camille. You're already facing perjury and contempt. You don't want to go to jail, do you?" She rooted for her best calm, talk-someone-off-the-ledge voice. "And we can just sit down and chat. Okay? You can tell me everything you didn't have a chance to say in court."

"Oh, shut your piehole!" Just as she said that, she smashed Teddy Roosevelt's bottle on the shelf, shearing off the bottom and making Olivia gasp in shock.

Okay, the bottle was history. But the real "history" was that letter, and Olivia had to get it.

"Come on, Birdie." She took a step closer and lifted her hand. "You don't want to do this. You don't want to bring the Historical Society of Sanibel and the wrath of George Turner down on your head, not to mention the cops. And I won't tell them. I won't tell a soul if you'll just give—"

"I don't care!" She waved the broken bottle in Olivia's face. "I don't care about anything, because I lived for revenge, and now I don't even have that. I don't care."

And that, Olivia knew, was what made her truly dangerous.

And, sorry George and all of Sanibel Island, Olivia wasn't going to risk having her face gashed by this lunatic to save a letter written by a dead president. She held up both hands protectively, backing away.

"Fine. Take the letter. Do whatever you have to do. Just go," she said. "Leave me alone."

Very slowly, Birdie came down from the riser step, still aiming the sharp bottle bottom at Olivia's face, fluttering the letter. She didn't say a word, but walked around the broken glass gingerly, never taking her eyes off Olivia's.

"You stay right here," Birdie ordered, walking out and rounding the corner so Olivia couldn't see where she'd gone.

She stood for a few minutes, waiting for the bell to signal Birdie had left, but heard...nothing. She hadn't gone out the front door. So where was she?

Olivia pressed her hand on her chest, collecting herself, and then carefully walked to the doorway to peek out into the store. She let out a ragged breath when she didn't see Birdie.

She must have managed to leave without ringing the bell, which could be done if you closed the door very gingerly. She darted to the front door, flipped the lock, and added the safety latch so that no one—not even someone who stole a key, like Scott—could get back in.

Still shaking, she walked back to the office, and stopped dead at the smell of smoke and the orange flash of flames on top of her desk. Beside it, she recognized one of the souvenir lighters from a bowl beside the cash register.

She'd set it on fire! She'd set the damn letter on fire and left!

She lunged toward the desk, only to trip on the toolbox left in her path. She flailed to keep from falling, grabbing the side of the shelf that instantly slid, wobbled, and toppled right on top of Olivia.

Heavy steel beams came crashing down, along with at least three unpacked boxes that each had to weigh twenty pounds.

It all happened in slow motion, jabbing and stabbing and slamming her into the floor as everything fell on top of her.

For a second, Olivia didn't move, waiting for one more thud of agony. Then she opened her eyes, thanking God she wasn't unconscious, pushing up to...

*No.* She couldn't move. She couldn't budge. The

weight on top of her—full boxes and toppled shelves—pressed like she was under a car.

"Oh!" she cried out, ignoring the pain, thinking only of one thing: there was a fire in Sanibel Treasures and she was trapped under six tons of inventory and steel.

"Help!" she called, hating how weak her voice was. Hating that woman who would now go to jail for murder...unless Olivia survived this.

And she *would* survive this.

With a burst of superhuman adrenaline, she pushed and pushed and...moved one box, but that wasn't going to free her from the steel shelves that bore down on her back and legs.

"Please, God, someone help me!" she screamed again.

Smoke started to billow, but she was too trapped to see how bad the fire was. Once it caught cardboard, it was all over. Or the walls. Or that chair covered in T-shirts that would light up like a Christmas tree.

With another moan of horror and agony, she called out, shutting up mid-plea when she heard banging on the front door. A customer? Would they hear her?

"Livvie! Open up, honey!" The banging resumed. "Why did you close early?"

Oh, thank you, God. Mom was here!

"Mom! *Moooommmm!*" She screamed until her throat felt like it had to be bleeding, but did her mother even hear? If she'd go around to the back, she'd hear Olivia through the sliver of an opening in the bathroom window. "Eliza Whitney! Help me! Call 911!"

She waited another few seconds, listening but only hearing the crackle of fire as it caught something else.

She moaned again, squeezing her eyes shut as the smoke started to burn the inside of her lids.

And then she heard footsteps and rattling. Someone was trying to get in the back!

"Mom! Call 911! There's a fire!"

"Livvie! Oh my God, Livvie!"

"Help me!"

"The door's locked!" her mother screamed.

And she was going to die. Panic rocked her as she realized with absolutely no doubt about it, she was going to die without ever having fallen in love, or having her own store, or realizing what really mattered in life.

She was going to—

A deafening crash made her scream as she imagined the fire had somehow broken more glass. She grunted and groaned, trying to move and—

"Livvie!" The voice cut through everything, loud and determined and strong and oh, God, *Deeley*. He must have broken the bathroom window.

"Olivia! Where the hell are you?"

"I'm here! Deeley, I'm—"

He was next to her in an instant, tossing boxes and hoisting shelves like they were toothpicks. His long hair tickled her face as he bent over, his warm breath on her cheek as he said her name over and over, and his arms were strong and safe and perfect as he scooped her up and carried her out the front.

"Teddy Roosevelt's letter!" she cried.

"Is in George's safe deposit box at the bank."

"Oh." Her feet didn't hit the ground until he had her outside. Already, she could hear the screaming sirens from the Sanibel fire station. Her mother came running. Camille was crying. Teddy was right behind them. And Deeley.

Deeley was clinging to her like she might blow away if he didn't.

"Deeley," she gasped. "Deeley. That woman started a fire. She almost—"

The word was lost in the kiss that he slammed on her mouth, pulling her whole body so tightly against him, she could feel every wild beat of his heart.

When he finally broke the kiss, he just held her while the firetrucks screamed to the store and people gathered and questions were asked and she told the police everything. Through it all, every single minute, Deeley held her and wouldn't let go.

# Chapter Twenty-one

## *Claire*

Six Weeks Later

While she waited for her mother and Teddy to return from the lawyer's office, Claire wandered down the long boardwalk to the beach, letting her gaze travel along the horizon, feeling the sun bounce off the sand to warm her, getting an inhale of that Sanibel scent that Eliza wanted to bottle and sell.

And maybe she could...in the boutique that Camille was going to open once she found the right space.

"There you are!" Eliza came down the boardwalk behind her, a yellow cotton sundress swinging around her knees, her reddish hair getting more gold with each passing day in the sunshine. "Are we having champagne in the gazebo when Teddy and Camille get back with the signed papers to celebrate the official sale of the property? That is, assuming all goes well with those two."

"Good idea." She reached for Eliza's hand and tugged her closer. "We have a lot to celebrate."

"More than you know," Eliza added. "I just heard from Livvie that George and Roz are at the store to check out all the repairs Deeley did and, get this—they brought

Asia and baby Zane! I was just going over to see them when I spotted you down here."

"Asia and the baby are here?" Claire gave a clap. "How fun!"

"It will be. They couldn't miss George getting his special recognition from the Historical Society for having the foresight to secure and save one of the island's greatest treasures."

"They should give one to Olivia for helping the police nail Birdie before she reached the causeway," Claire said.

"And Deeley for showing up when I screamed and charging through the bathroom window." Eliza shook her head. "I still wake up thinking about it sometimes, but not as frequently."

"And Livvie? Does she wake up thinking about it, or that steamy kiss you told me Deeley planted on her as the firetrucks were pulling up?"

Eliza smiled. "She calls it an adrenaline kiss, and claims it didn't mean anything. Did it have something to do with her decision to extend her sabbatical? Hard to say. She says that she wants to help Camille find the right retail space and open a store, but whatever is keeping her here, I'm happy." She gave Claire a squeeze. "Now if we can only get *you* to find a reason to stay in Shellseeker Beach."

"I know that's what you want, Eliza," Claire answered on a sigh. "As tempting as it is to linger a bit longer, I'm going to catch a flight to New York tomorrow and...get back to the fat salary and cushy law job."

Eliza curled her lip. "I understand, but isn't there a way to work remotely? Or practice law down here? Or just...hang with your sister?"

She smiled. "I love all those options, but I really feel like I should be there, where I belong."

Claire could see the disappointment on Eliza's face, and even the confusion. "You belong with family," Eliza whispered. "And Miles is still looking for—"

Claire held up a hand to stop her. "Miles has shaken the trees and nothing fell out," she said. "However, the address he's used is my New York residence. I don't want to be here if...if..."

"If your son decides to knock on your door."

"I knew you'd understand," Claire said softly. "Of course, he has my phone number, but research shows it's more common for an adoptive kid to show up rather than call. And I haven't given up hope."

"I get that, I really do. How long..."

"Will I wait?" Claire finished. "I guess forever, Eliza. He's the hole in my heart and I just want to fill it."

Eliza hugged her again. "I understand, but couldn't you just change your address with the agency? If your son wants to meet you, he could come here."

"Not yet," she said. "But I'll think about it. Any nibbles on your house in Los Angeles?"

"It's only been on the market a few days, but the real estate agent thinks it'll sell fast. Then I'll have to go out there and pack it up and..."

"And ship your life here."

Eliza smiled. "I'll sell most of my stuff and then see

what happens. Teddy's seventy-two and I don't want her running this place alone. I love it here and..."

"Quit your rationalizing, dear sister of mine. I might not be planting roots in Teddy's garden of glorious fun, but you are. And if I had to put money on it, you'll be as close to a romantic relationship as your daughter in about a year."

"What?" Eliza blinked at her, but couldn't hide the soft flush that rose in her cheeks. "I'm not ready."

"Miles is."

Eliza rolled her eyes, as she always did when Claire teased her about Miles. "Come on. Let's go see George and Roz and meet Asia and the baby."

They walked toward Sanibel Treasures but only made it halfway when they saw a little gathering that included Roz, George, Katie, Harper, Deeley, and Olivia —all of them in a circle around a woman holding a baby.

"Welcome home!" Eliza called, rushing to greet them in a flurry of hugs and hellos and peeks at the new baby boy.

In the center of it all was Asia Turner, a stunning woman about Olivia's age, with fire in her ebony eyes and attitude in her gorgeous bone structure. She laughed easily, flipping her waist-length braids over her shoulders, and seemed remarkably comfortable as a first-time mother, happy to show off her brand-new beautiful baby.

And he was beautiful. He might not look like the baby Claire had given up, but the tiny rosebud lips and closed eyes, the wee fists and little round head took her back twenty-six years and made her pray that boy hadn't been knocking at her door in New York while she was down here.

She had to get back, just in case.

"Not too much sun on him," Roz said, shielding her grandson's eyes.

"Mother, he's Black." Asia inched Roz's hand away. "A little sun is only going to make him darker and more handsome. Isn't that right, my sweet Zane?"

Roz shot her a look, then sent a sarcastic glance to Claire and Eliza. "It's like I know nothing about children despite having raised two."

"You're too overprotective," Asia said, then she slipped into a wide smile. "But I know you love him."

"Well, if this arrangement is going to work," Roz said, "I have to have some say in his upbringing."

"What arrangement?" Eliza asked.

"Asia and Zane are staying down here with us for a while," George said, beaming like the proud grandpa he was. "That is, if my two girls don't kill each other in the process."

"Pffft!" Roz waved off the comment. "I'm the most easygoing grandmother who ever lived."

Asia choked dramatically. "Yeah, if by easygoing you mean control freak."

"Oh!" Katie pointed to the path behind them. "They're back!"

Everyone turned and let out a cheer as Teddy and Camille walked down the path, raising their joined hands in victory.

"They did it!" Olivia cried out.

More cheers and an outburst of applause made the baby squirm and Roz hush them all.

"Mother, it's just noise," Asia said, easing her bundle away. "He needs to know the world is noisy."

Claire and Eliza shared a look and George just chuckled at what they all suspected was an ongoing struggle, but it was forgotten as Teddy and Camille came closer and all the hugs and laughter started up again.

They didn't give many details of the "exchange" of property and Dutch's will, especially because of the distraction of the new baby and more introductions, but they both seemed incredibly happy with the outcome.

They crowded around wee little Zane, cooing and cuddling and laughing at the constant push and pull between mother and grandmother. Teddy nearly cried when Roz told her Asia would be staying on Sanibel with them.

"Oh, my life is complete!" she exclaimed, making everyone laugh.

"Please tell us how it went with the lawyers," Eliza pleaded with Teddy.

"It was all very simple," Teddy said. "I'm a dollar poorer"—she smiled at Camille—"and we're taking Junonia out of the rental rotation for the cottages. Camille owns it now, and will be living there while she starts her boutique."

Camille threw her hands up. "Speaking of all that work I have to do, I'm exhausted. I'm heading right into my new cottage for some downtime."

"Same," Teddy agreed.

"And this little guy needs to get home," Roz announced. "It's naptime."

Asia just laughed. "He's not on your schedule, Mom. But I could use a rest."

"And I need another hour to finish the last of the repairs," Deeley said. "If you can close up the cabana for me, Liv."

"Sure thing," she said. "But I thought we'd have some kind of celebration tonight."

"I have an idea," Eliza said. "Claire and I will set up a party in the gazebo and once everyone is finished, napped, and ready for a glass of champagne at sunset, meet us there."

With that plan in mind, they hugged and separated, and Eliza and Claire walked down to the gazebo to make sure it was empty and figure out what they needed for an impromptu party.

Sitting next to each other, they made a shopping list on Claire's phone, then both leaned back to stare at the view.

"I can't believe you're leaving tomorrow," Eliza whispered. "I'm really going to miss you."

Claire nodded, feeling her eyes fill. "I know. I kind of don't want a party tonight so we can curl up with a bottle of wine and share more life stories from all the years we've missed."

"We can do that after the party."

"Oh, look—there's Miles," Claire said, looking past Eliza toward the boardwalk. "And, of course, he brought Tinkerbell." She elbowed Eliza playfully. "He never misses a chance to see..." She squinted at a person who walked a few steps behind Miles. "Who's that?"

Claire squinted at the tall young man with dark hair fluttering in the breeze.

"A friend of his?" Eliza suggested, following her gaze. "He's awfully young to hang with Miles."

"Maybe he's..." Claire's voice drifted off as the young man stuck his fingers in his hair, dragging it back.

The gesture was so weirdly familiar that it sent a little shiver through Claire as she sat up straighter, chills rippling down her arms despite the heat.

"Do you know him?" Eliza asked.

"I...I..." Her strangled voice caught in her throat and her head suddenly felt light.

"Claire?"

She just clasped Eliza's hand and tried to breathe, watching as Miles spotted them in the gazebo. Miles leaned in and said something to the young man, who instantly looked right at them and slowed his steps as he stared at her.

Very slowly, she stood, pressing her hand to her chest as if that would be enough to contain the heart that was about to beat out of it.

"That's him, Eliza. It has to be. That's my son."

She didn't wait for Eliza's response, taking a few tentative steps. As she got closer, she could see his face, dark eyes, and that thick mop of hair.

She swallowed, paralyzed with fear and hope and disbelief, unable to look away or meet him halfway.

Instead, she stood in the gazebo opening, her hand closing around one wooden post as if she needed support.

With each heartbeat, he got closer, and she could see more details of his chiseled features, his strong nose, broad shoulders, and tall frame. She rarely ever thought about the boy who'd created this one...but right now she couldn't think of anyone else.

He was the spitting image of his father.

With Miles behind him, the young man came to a dead stop about five feet from the gazebo and looked right up at her.

"Claire Sutherland?" he asked.

She took a step down to the sand, her legs wobbling like she might just fold in front of him.

"Yes," she managed to whisper.

"Lady." He crossed his arms and narrowed his eyes. "You better have a damn good reason for screwing up my life."

"Oh." She took a step back from the sheer power of his words.

Staring at him, memorizing him, all she could do was rub her arms, trying to get rid of the ache to reach out and hold her son once again.

But something told her it would be a long time until that happened. From the look in his dark, dark eyes? It might be forever.

*Don't miss the next adventure in Shellseeker Beach!
Sanibel Mornings continues the stories of this "found
family" that stays together through every crisis, supports
each other through every moment, and always has the
humor and heart to face what life throws at them.*

# The Shellseeker Beach Series

Come to Shellseeker Beach and fall in love with a cast of unforgettable characters who face life's challenges with humor, heart, and hope. For lovers of riveting and inspirational sagas about sisters, secrets, romance, mothers, and daughters...and the moments that make life worth living.

# The Coconut Key Series

If you're longing for an escape to paradise, step on to the gorgeous, sun-kissed sands of Coconut Key. With a cast of unforgettable characters and stories that touch every woman's heart, these delightful novels will make you laugh out loud, fall in love, and stand up and cheer... you'll want to read the entire series!

# About the Author

Hope Holloway is the author of charming, heartwarming women's fiction featuring unforgettable families and friends and the emotional challenges they conquer. After a long career in marketing, she gave up writing ad copy to launch a writing career with her first series, Coconut Key, set on the sun-washed beaches of the Florida Keys. A mother of two adult children, Hope and her husband of thirty years live in Florida. When not writing, she can be found walking the beach with her two rescue dogs, who beg her to include animals in every book. Visit her site at www.hopeholloway.com.

Made in the USA
Columbia, SC
22 April 2023